THE ANNALS OF PETRONIUS JABLONSKI

By

PETRONIUS JABLONSKI

FOR HIERONYMUS

Contents

THE ANNALS OF
PETRONIUS JABLONSKI

AN ODYSSEY OF HISTORIC
PROPORTIONS

AND

PRICELESS TREASURE OF
PHILOSOPHY

Happy are they, in my opinion, to whom it is given either to do something worth writing about, or to write something worth reading; most happy, of course, are those who do both.

Pliny the Younger

Preamble

I, Petronius Jablonski, here set forth a chronicle of a perilous and momentous journey. Though conclusive understanding of it eludes my grasp, by withholding all judgments I shall furnish my narrative with the goal of historians throughout the ages: a clear and spacious window overlooking great events, free from the blemishes deposited by careless scholars who forget their proper role is to describe, not decipher.

As a consequence, I vouchsafe the Reader no small responsibility. The purity of this vantage confers upon his shoulders a noble yoke: interpreting the meaning of this wondrous quest by his own lights. It is possible that one who has not witnessed the marvels that bedazzled me will be in a superior position to untangle and assess their significance, as my heart and mind remain too inflamed for temperate discernment.

In Defense of My Preamble

Eager to begin the fantastic voyage, the Reader finds himself restive, the hesitant vessel of dissenting inquiries. He is to be commended on his scrutinous nature. The surest gauge of a student's health is inquisitiveness; the first symptom of illness, apathy. Neither presumption nor the antennae of prudence attune me to his enviable perplexities, but an extrasensory third ear pressed against the wall separating present and future, permitting me to anticipate his questions and respond before he needs to raise them. Be not jealous, for this prescience, the gift of foreknowledge, is more often a curse than a blessing.

"Scholar," he says, "no doubt it was an intoxicating side-effect of your divine prose, but it is all one can do to desist the impression that you promise pure objectivity. While the symphonic splendor of your preamble is above all praise, it induces the vision of a mythic creature. Such declarations are as mislaid in serious scholarship as the story of a unicorn. Furthermore, given the authority you convey it is easy to ignore the implied denigration of past historians, but should you not at least explain yourself?"

I avow nothing short of Objectivity and with this question I am more than a little concerned with the caliber of the man bumbling through my annals. Dear Reader, I mean no offense. Each man is, to no small degree, raised by his culture. After suckling at the withered teats of folly and nihilism, a child's preconceptions are skewed, his worldview a jagged montage. Do not despair, for great is he who pulls himself from this sewer. In the melancholy dusk of civilization we forget that Truth is not a harlot whose favors can be purchased by every Johnny-come-lately waving a degree. Rather, she is a chaste maiden who must be wooed. Come, let us woo her together.

The Reader needs to differentiate metaphorical promises from actual ones. A "threesome with a chaste maiden" is not what I had in mind. And his comparison of Objectivity to unicorns cries out to the gods for reproof. What does it insinuate about my intentions? Does he suggest that my preamble is a sonorous formality, that since I could not clash cymbals when he opened the book I had to *settle* for one? Make no mistake: out of the 250,000 words in common usage, and the additional 50,000 I use, I painstakingly selected those. In the same key, out of the innumerable combinations I could have formed with my lovingly selected words, I chose the precise order presented, not even tempted by others.

Regarding the belittlement of my peers: despite their innumerable shortcomings, Herodotus, Plutarch, Tacitus, Gibbon, Spengler, Wells, and Ferguson represent stages in the perfection of a science. I had hoped to avoid the threadbare expression, "standing on the shoulders of giants," but it seems the Reader has forced my hand. (If it gratifies his vanity, he may highlight the following sentence.)

While composing my annals, I, Petronius Jablonski, stood atop the shoulders of giants.

Now, with these disagreeable accounts settled we can proceed. Ever solicitous of his welfare, I fear the Reader's approach lacks the requisite gravitas. His informality is scarcely appropriate for the task at hand. A suit and tie would attune his attention far better than a mustard-splattered undershirt. Likewise, a seated posture in a sturdy chair is preferable to sprawling across a soiled and dilapidated mattress. I beseech him to close the book now and not reopen it until he has enjoyed a full night of rest (the contents of Part I are rather heady). He may wish to read my preamble again, reverently, in a suit and tie, before proceeding.

I:
The Commencement of My Odyssey, a Commentary on the Point of Life, and the Attainment of Quietude

An authentic voodoo doll prowled the dashboard, glaring at me with bulbous eyes as I took the helm. Ferocious claws ensured his adhesion and an ear-to-ear grin revealed shark-like teeth. I summoned the engine, its silent presence conspicuous like a warm body in a dark room, and drove into the fog.

Out of necessity, the designers had positioned tiny lights on the far corners of the hood. Without them, most occupants would be powerless to determine where the car ended and the world began. Simple notes became a melody for the eyes. Between the twinkling stars on the horizon stood the surrogate hood ornament, Shiva, god with a thousand-and-four names, guardian of the threshold separating the great orange plane from the emptiness beyond.

In the parking lot at Sandy's dormitory my thoughts assailed me like wasps. I closed my eyes and embraced the certainty that my future would suffer from a dearth of precedents. After she threw her bags in back, the tons on my back felt a few ounces lighter and I entered the wet lint that had settled over everything. Our paths first crossed in an algebra class two semesters earlier. Thirsting only for Truth, not the chicanery of juggling abstractions, I abstained from the odious sessions and spent the time in the student union discussing eternal questions with like-minded men of intellect. During the final exam, a beguiling vixen permitted my eyes to meander across her paper. After class I offered to buy her dinner, quid pro quo. From this simple meal all manner of carnal delights soon blossomed.

The intersection we crept through before vanishing into the labyrinth of the highway, was it not a silver passage connecting the fabled kingdom of eternity past to the prophesied land of eternity yet to come? A sign for the on-ramp materialized out of the static. Having defied time's attrition, my car handled the severe curve with ease. Out of the turn I tapped the gas, burying us in the depths of Corinthian leather.

My view consisted of nothing save the little stars on the hood and Shiva charging through a curtain of gauze. Though initially troubled by this, I bested the urge to decelerate and the fear of a collision evolved into exhilaration. My spirits ascended, freeing me from the servitude of my apprehensions, exorcising the specters of what lay ahead. But soon the boarders in the rooming house of my mind returned. Second, third, and fourth guesses came and went, slamming doors and stomping their feet, their discourteous tumult the only motion in the misty stillness of the night.

After we stopped for gas, adversity beset our path. Crossing a bridge over the highway, I felt like a mountain climber gazing at a layer of clouds from a summit, or Dante before his descent. I followed the taillights of a semi down the ramp until they disappeared. When the location of the road became subject to interpretation I hit the brakes. The speedometer said zero. I knew better. In our cherished time together, my car and I had traveled tens of thousands of miles, down each and every highway, in good times and bad. The bond between us, forged in the crucible of danger, sealed by the stamp of luxury, was deep and strong and true.

I pumped the brakes and spun the steering wheel. Neither measure subdued my withdrawal symptoms from the opiate of normalcy. I buzzed the window down, plunged my head into the gray vortex, and saw only the uppermost portion of the tires. I sat back as though nothing were wrong and hypothesized a lack of contact with the road, tentatively conceding the validity of inferences to the best explanation. Feeling uncommonly visible, I prayed that Sandy had not noticed our difficulties. Her closed eyes and open mouth bespoke the oblivion of sleep.

Perhaps this idiosyncrasy will abate, I hoped, and spare her from jumping to any hasty conclusions. Although wistful, this reflection was not bereft of rational elements. With the exception of a mild rising sensation, no differences earmarked our surroundings. My car normally drove with remarkable surreption and the wool fog abided. The only thing that will disclose our quandary, I thought, is my vexations becoming manifest, the dissolution of my calm demeanor. There could be only one priority: the attainment of Quietude. To fill the car with an atmosphere of normalcy and congeniality, the way one would pump oxygen into a strange and uninhabitable environment to make it safe for living creatures, I placed a CD in the deck, lit an English Oval, and reflected on the greatness of my fellow Stoic, Epictetus.

"This is no tragedy," said the voice of Reason. "Leaning back in this heavenly seat and listening to Sinatra while my Cadillac glides through the fog: as with all things misconstrued as hardships, it is simply a matter of becoming inured to it."

The Rat Pack always served as a potent tonic, infused with the ability to bandage my exposed nerves from even the most corrosive stimuli. My sanguine bearing, due in no small part to their curative styling, enabled the impeccable analysis to proceed.

"In time this will seem no stranger than driving down the street in the fog. The only reason no one questions the latter is due to its attainment of the humdrum status of familiarity, which hardly renders it comprehensible. According to Zeno of Elea motion is not even possible. (To travel from X to Y, one must first arrive at a point halfway between them; to reach that point one must first reach a halfway point, *ad infinitum*.) Unless I am prepared to refute him and provide a full discourse explicating the nature of motion I have no reason to disparage our present state."

From the starry dome of Reason I gazed into the valley of Quietude, basking in my soothing meditations. I assessed the prudence of putting the car in park, but rejected the idea. If it returned to the ground while moving (assuming the existence, comprehensibility, and occurrence of "motion"), the transmission could be injured. Though my faithful mechanic had informed me that my Fleetwood contained the finest one ever made, risks without recompense are foolish.

I flicked my cigarette out the window, lit another, raised the volume a notch, and sat back so my eyes were level with the dash. Midway through the fourth song, Sandy awoke. I turned to her with the guileless conviction that my unperturbed state would prove contagious.

"How can you possibly drive in this?" she said, jerking her head like a rotary sprinkler. Quizzical furrows scarred her soft Asian features.

"After a while you become inured to it."

"How fast are we going?" After checking the speedometer, she disemboweled me with her eyes, rupturing my precious Quietude and initiating an investigation I had to terminate posthaste. It was crucial that she remain sequestered from the Gordian theory regarding my tires and their relationship to the road. A few trifling details about our journey were not shared with her. Preoccupied during the elaborate preparations, I awaited a more sedate period for briefing.

Before I could respond, she put on her seatbelt: a resounding vote of no confidence, a damning indictment. Something inside me died. I turned the music down and fortified myself against the indignities that might charge. "The sheer density of the fog poses unique challenges to even the greatest driver," I said. "Are you familiar with the teachings of Zeno?"

"What's happening?" she said, digging her fingers into the armrest and clutching the door.

"I am waiting for it to clear."

"Why does it feel like we're moving?" Her words tore into me like harpoons.

"As the fog whisks past it departs an unsettling illusion, and you should not forget that a real car feels different in repose. This is not a Honda."

I buzzed the window down and dipped my head in the mothball soup. Assuming a disengagement between my tires and the road, the extent of the rift foiled visual estimates. I conceived an experiment to resolve this question. By dropping Sandy's CDs out of the window I would not only escape the agony of listening to them, the clarity of their union with the road would allow me to gauge the distance. The possibility of hearing nothing, which would block all paths to Quietude, hindered my research.

The density of the fog seemed greater at this altitude. Only Shiva's outline could be discerned in the ethereal haze. While smoky tentacles floated over the windshield, I distracted myself by discerning shapes in them, the way one might amuse himself on a cloudy day. Soon it was no diversion. The Rorschach looked back. Faces formed, existed for an instant, and returned to a blur. Their expressions bespoke unbearable sorrow, as though grieving the oblivion stolen from them.

Centipedes of panic crawled up and down my back.

"This is serious," I said, my voice not rising above a marvelous duet between Sammy Davis Jr. and Dean Martin. I prayed that Sandy had not witnessed this dreadful procession and turned to her. She continued to brace herself, eyes closed. Seeking fortitude, I focused on the sublime crest of Antoine de la Mothe Cadillac (1658-1730) and imagined brandishing the steering wheel as a talisman, running out on the hood to smite the ghastly faces.

"Like all things, they will eventually be buried by the sands of time," said Reason, healing my wounded spirit with the inimitable balm of wisdom.

I studied the *merlettes* on the shield beneath the crown and Sinatra started "My Way," a Stoic hymn to the virtue of constancy in the face of adversity. When the brilliant star of Quietude shone its gracious face upon me, I renounced my cowering posture and looked up: nothing but fuzz, amorphous and inert. As I exhaled, a mammoth face appeared and emitted a moan that shook the car.

"What was that?"

"What was what?" I said, awaiting salvation from my steadfast muse. "Oh, that? The bass on this stereo reverberates. The woofers cannot handle the lower end of equivocal frequencies."

Another of the doomed beings groaned before returning to vapor. While a fleeting but ominous cloud separated me from the golden rays of Quietude, I reminded myself that it was not the faces that disturbed me but the opinions I formed of them.

"Can't you do something about that noise?" said Sandy, more irritated than scared. "It ruins the song."

I increased the volume and gave it some bass as well, hoping this would prove sufficient to muffle the next horrible wail. I disliked hiding things from her, but justified it through a quick series of calculations revealing how a greater good would be achieved. Lacking my forbearance and analytic detachment, she would have experienced considerable hardship while becoming accustomed to this novel aspect of our surroundings. If one of them infiltrates the car, I vowed, then I will brief her. Paternalism is not bad *per se*.

Just as another of the frightful apparitions appeared, the heavens discarded us. The dolesome ghost appeared to shoot up like a rocket as we fell.

"What the hell's going on?"

"We are merging. Having assessed the visibility, I think it is safe to join the traffic," I said, gripping the wheel. Our gradient lessened, but hypotheses other than our continued plunge were not forthcoming. It felt like the descent on a Ferris wheel. Relieved as I was to be away from the meteorological monsters and grateful Sandy had not seen them, the prospect of landing a car for the first time concerned me.

"A natural driver, one born -- nay, destined to drive -- can always triumph," Reason assured me. "The uncompromising union of instinct and courage trumps all misfortune. It is a matter of driving conformably to nature."

Despite the gallant assurance derived from doing what you were created to, I felt as though I were parallel parking before an audience. The discomfiture peaked with hideous thoughts of potential injuries to my car's magnificent suspension.

I closed my eyes and listened in awe to the perspective described in "September of My Years": a meditation on the ephemeral nature of life, a celebration of the moment, and a forthright recognition of the inevitability of death -- sans gloom or doom. Truly it is rare for a single piece of music to express such a laudable outlook, and unheard of today. The solipsistic haze of ignorance, rage, and lust inflicted on us by the purveyors of contemporary noise may constitute a common vision of life, but it is scarcely a commendable one. Can today's "music" do no more than howl and grunt about how its hapless victims misconstrue the world? Could it not set the bar a millimeter higher with some expectation of how they ought to?

Even in my deplorable state, the inherent Stoicism of the song could not fail to edify me. In life I seek contentment through an enlightened indifference to the vicissitudes of Fate. But not when driving. There my very soul rebels against all tyrants and I will not suffer shackles of any kind. From the harshest of teachers, Experience and Reason, I learned there are pitifully few things worth seeking.

Fame, a function of the opinions of other men, is obviously worth less than nothing. A skillful concubine can bring joy to a man, but they are as plentiful as the stars and essentially as different from each other as Tuesdays from Wednesdays. The best that can be said for the pursuit of riches is that it serves to distract a man from the grievous uncertainties of his existence, assuming, as you should, that most would crumble if confronted with the ultimate puzzle. Posthumous glory, dependent on the beliefs of those yet to be born, is the most senseless of all. If the imbecilic estimations of the herd currently wandering the earth are to be ignored, how much more so the ravings of the brutes who will follow? Indeed, a wise man will shun renown like death itself. In this world of flux and woe, does anything warrant pursuit? Is anything intrinsically good?

Quietude, of course: a state of mind tranquil and serene, yet confident and affirmative of life despite its precarious nature. The courtship of Truth is long and austere, but it spares one from countless delusional allurements. Despite a paucity of honorable men, the pursuit of honor may seem a fool's errand, but aren't ideals unattainable by definition? Are they not the stairway from the swamp of our beastly nature? Dignity and heroism certainly merit striving, but intertwined with them, inseparable from them, is a man's car. But not any car will suffice.

If a wise man were asked to demarcate the epoch when the automobiles were most magnificent, he would name the golden age between the decession of Johnson and the inauguration of Carter. The cars were colossal and solid, forged from the purest sheet metal. Powered by the blast furnaces of the gods -- the grandest V-8 engines -- they had no peers in strength. In homage to Euclid, all the great four-doored ones exemplified rectangularity: the Cadillac Fleetwood and Sedan DeVille, the Lincoln Continental, the Pontiac Bonneville and Catalina, the Buick Electra and Chrysler New Yorker. These glorious bricks blessed the concrete seas with their majestic bearing. And in 1977, darkness fell. The Great Ones were desecrated ("downsized" was the coarse euphemism) with puny bodies and feeble engines. What is there for a man to do but cover his eyes and weep as he beholds the degradation of what was once mighty and proud?

Few mourn their passage. Few know what has been lost. Perhaps the Truth swims too deep and fast to be caught in the flimsy nets of most men. What ennobled this period in history was neither our knowledge nor the opulence some enjoyed. When the next great historian writes of the decline and fall of our empire, I will have no difficulty in pinpointing the zenith. What bestowed upon this epoch its only grandeur and greatness were the sedans of the late sixties and early seventies. And when a man possesses one and something afflicts it he is scarcely unjustified in thinking the world is coming to an end, for it is.

***

"What the hell was going on?" said Sandy with a nasty tone of exasperation, perched on the edge of her seat with the frazzled comportment of someone awakened from a deep sleep by a fire alarm. "What *was* that?"

I adjusted to the obedient gas, brake, and steering, casually switching from the emergency grip to the natural stance with one hand dangling over the wheel and eyes level with the dash. "That you can drive at all is nothing short of miraculous, given your hypersensitive nerves. A little fog whisks you straight to bedlam. No doubt that malformed dwarf of a car you drive is equipped with cyanide capsules for such an event."

Her exasperation begot irritation, which begot pestiferous curiosity, which begot accusatory insolence, the first four generations of an affective lineage that would endure throughout our journey and could fill its own *Book of Chronicles*. Her vacant blue eyes probed me. "No Petronius, there was something weird about that."

"Any experienced driver will tell you how dense fog has a bewitching, pixie dust nature. Consign this to your little book of lessons. Title: Dense Fog. Entry: do not drive in. Filed next to entry titled: Second-guess the Driver. Entry: do not."

Although my car drove splendidly, our discussions could not break free from the gravity of the troubles experienced earlier. My dignity befouled, I would tolerate no further ignominies and banished the baneful topic from all conversation. When we needed gas, I departed from the highway and drove down a narrow road drowning in wild grass. A shining cloud appeared and I entered it cautiously, discovering a little station entombed by the fog. I filled the tank while Sandy stretched.

The light inside hurt my eyes and I had to squint. The floor, either freshly waxed or treated with a mysterious coating, gave off a disorienting glare. Behind the counter, adorned in an immaculate white uniform, stood a young man with dark curly hair and a neatly trimmed beard. His confident smile gave his face a gentle intensity. I felt the warmth from his eyes as I approached. Even in the brightness of the station they seemed to shine.

The Anticipation of Questions Pertaining to Part I with Answers and Analysis

A historical document can in one respect be likened to a building. A poor foundation bodes ill for its intended height. To embed my base so what follows may touch the stars, some clarification is essential. I adjure the student to go no further until he masters the material presented here, for it is his safety I have in mind whilst I secure the bedrock of this tower to the empyrean.

However enthralled by the mellifluous grandeur of the prose, the vigilant student must nonetheless be pleasantly agitated with questions. Dear Reader, do not consider yourself the prisoner of your inquisitive nature, but rather the house guest of a noble and restless spirit. As Detritus of Ileum observed, "Truth cannot be found in the shadows of silent acceptance, but only on the open plains of philosophic discourse."

"Scholar," the Reader whispers into my third ear, my link between his present and my own, "after hitting the ground running, one is unable to look away for the duration, but doesn't Objectivity command you to begin in the beginning, not the midst of things?"

This adroit query vouches for the Reader's potential, but he fails to recognize that a "beginning" in the temporal sense is but one of many. It is the philosopher's task to determine which type is most important. I stand by my decision just as Galileo stood by his discovery of the planets orbiting the sun.

***

"Scholar, given the breakneck pace and dizzying assemblage of events it is understandable that no more than a glimpse of Sandy is provided. But in the name of Objectivity, is your heroine not worthy of more than a one-dimensional sketch?"

Mired in the squalor of contemporary "literature," the Reader is possessed by the delusion that I am condemned to pace my annals with the discordant velocity of the latest thriller he has read. Infuriating as it is to have inferior standards inflicted on me, I empathize with his plight. By this point in most of the books he whores around with he is already cognizant of the precise shade of the heroine's pubic hair. Her height, eye color, "heart-shaped face," and a whole constellation of minutiae have been carelessly tossed into a paragraph early in the first chapter. Note well: an FBI profile is not character development. This is one of the least pardonable crimes of lazy and ignorant scribblers and full proof of their disregard for Objectivity. In life one learns about another a little at a time. He is not blasted in the face with extrinsic details concerning her "small hometown," her "characteristic spunk," her "petite but perky bosom," her "stern but doting father," and so on. Axiomatically, the introduction of characters in my text will not occur via literary gimcracks. The Reader will make their acquaintance as he would in actuality.

Besides, where did I write that Sandy is the heroine? If a female is mentioned in Part I she must, of absolute necessity, on pain of twenty years hard labor, be The Heroine? On what tablet is this carved? What lawgiver decrees this? To what obdurate judge will the Reader turn if I transgress this sacred maxim? As a matter of fact, Sandy's role is peripheral -- at best. I only mention her at all because she accompanied me and to omit her would be a crime against Objectivity. And I serve no higher master.

***

"Scholar, your descriptions of Quietude and the solace it brought you are fascinating. Is it an Eastern or Western conception?"

Just as Aristotle gave philosophy his Golden Mean, I hereby contribute my Blender, by means of which the profoundest ideas can be mixed and pureed to produce original and superior recipes. This watershed, which the steely eyes of history may very well deem superior to Aristotle's much-ballyhooed scale, will be elucidated in graspable increments. Regarding Quietude: while the precise recipe shall remain a secret, it contains ingredients from Buddhism, Stoicism, Epicureanism, and Monadology. The name is from the ancient Skeptics (who should have chosen a more accurate description of their uncertain comforts). Through the use of my ingenious, innovatory Blender, these constituents have been combined to create a bold new flavor. Quietude, as I am using the term, is both an original and significant contribution to philosophy.

***

"Scholar, is Quietude a trance-like state?"

My Cadillac is not an opium den. I was neither "nodding off," nor "grooving," nor "getting down," nor succumbing to whichever degenerate state is sought by beatniks, hippies, slackers, and generations X, Y, and Z. It is indicative of our age that any pursuit of an enlightened conditioned is associated with intoxication. The sublime nature of Quietude will be presented in a manner befitting an otherworldly phenomenon. Meanwhile, I caution the Reader not to form base preconceptions.

***

"Scholar, is the description of Quietude in Part I exhaustive?"

A messenger with joyous tidings, I unveiled a concept onion-like in its manifold layers, yet sweet in its succor. Quietude is not akin to a two-by-four. I cannot pummel the Reader into understanding it. A good philosopher relies on the time-tested methods of gradual exposure and the use of context clues. My approach shall be as halcyon as Quietude herself.

***

"Scholar, a question regarding the interior of your Cadillac as it relates to the essence of Objectivity: Was it essential that you described, in no small detail, the voodoo doll on your dashboard? How are such details more relevant than a detailed introduction to the human companion who will be accompanying you on your journey?"

The Reader is clearly smitten by Sandy, delivered from the divine captivity of my annals by the mercenary of lust. But how can he be infatuated by a woman whose existence is scarcely hinted at? Will his jealousy not blind him to the countless virtues of my scholarship? I deliberately refrained from providing an abundance of details to forfend this very possibility. Now he has left the gravity of my odyssey and drifts through space, an intellectual vagrant, a philosophic hobo. I ask him: Is she worth it? How does he know her shortcomings do not outweigh whatever charms have ensnared him? On my honor, the fleeting thrills of her company do not compare to the abiding joy he will find in my annals. Come to your senses, man. If not, I am left with no choice.

To ensure that the Reader remains spellbound throughout the following section, I must posit a hypothetical feature: Sandy suffers from an advanced stage of leprosy. Patches of jade moss cover her "soft Asian features" and a putrefying stench emanates from her. This condition shall remain in effect until the closing pages of Part II. (This temporary contravention of Objectivity is necessitated on pragmatic grounds.)

***

Is the Reader pleased with what his heedless appetence has wrought, with what he has scourged Sandy? In Stoic magnanimity, I harbor no enmity toward him. He is, after all, a man like myself, a hapless rider on the wild horse of passion. But we must continue. I insist he cosset himself with a good night of sleep before proceeding. Then, during an ice-cold bath he should contemplate the gruesome condition of poor, wretched Sandy: mossy and fetid. This should etiolate his childish infatuation. He should then fortify himself with a substantial breakfast consisting of scrambled eggs, bacon, sausages, pancakes, hash browns, toast, milk, and orange juice. Requisite then is a brisk walk. Finally, he is advised to sip a caffeinated drink while he braces himself for a rapid ascent into the supernal regions of Part II.

II:
My Bonneville is Cherished, I Discover a Box, Compose a Letter of Critique to a Hack, Introduce Petronius' First Sensation and Petronius' Shovel, Encounter an Enormous Bird after My Bonneville is Abducted, Dream the First of Eleven Dreams, Strike a Dubious Bargain with a Sea God, and Select the Chosen Chariot

In the days before the Cadillac there was a massive and exquisite Pontiac, a Bonneville as old as the mountains, metallic blue, and equipped with rear wheel-skirts. Whereas its theft set everything in motion, this segment of my annals commands rigorous study.

The days of the Bonneville found me posted as a watchman at an abandoned factory on the edge of Lake Michigan. An empty warehouse, the skeleton of a foundry, a shanty of an office, and an old laboratory sprawled across a dense forest, connected via a network of gravel roads. Only the most gifted driver could navigate the stretch of potholes intersecting with the entrance. The sign, perhaps a proud beacon in ages past, had long since fallen prey to the insatiable appetite of rust. A waterfall of vines submerged the fence so that even the inquisitive sun could uncover few flecks of metal amidst the leaves. Though the office stood less than a quarter mile behind the gate, a serpentine road conspired with redwood-sized weeds to convey the isolation of an Alpine village.

After completing a tour of the complex I often walked to the edge of a cliff to reflect on the nature of things. It proved more propitious to this quest than any other place, as though the questions feared to follow, frightened by the spheroid ghost above and the tempestuous waters below.

Prior to my initial inspection, I would push an ancient leather chair onto the patio outside the office. There I could elevate my feet atop a planter and behold the splendor of my five-ton sapphire, the contemplation of which bleached the landscape, leaving a Vargas print of a bewitching harlot reclining across the hood (to minimize the possibility of dents, a petite harlot with the elfin proportions of a gymnast). Such meditations revealed Plato's Form of Beauty, diminishing the workload from my summer class and sending a cool breeze across the scorched terrain of my spirit, taming the fires within.

Obliged to survey the premises six times per shift, I began with the warehouse. From a distance the entrance looked like a mousehole but grew to a drawbridge as I approached. Opening it strained every muscle in my back, as though the occupants resisted until finally ceding territory to lay in wait. The air inside, dank and foul, was it not the necrotic tissue of a once mighty creature? Sparsely distributed over the center aisle, dangling bulbs cast little light on the dusty concrete. A few feet to either side, darkness reigned. Less valorous sentries lamented their gloomy plight. Two had ignominiously abandoned their posts. Their piteous supplications did not tempt the insolvent gods, whose impotent hands could not procure any items not "absolutely necessary."

One terrible night, so that I might gratify a swelling curiosity, I brought a flashlight to inspect the dark recesses, hoping something lay hidden, something not meant for my eyes, something forbidden. I could scarcely have foreseen how this innocuous inspection would uncover a fiendish plot, one that would rend the very texture of my being.

That night I walked slowly down the center aisle, uncertain where to begin my excursion. When I finally set off, abandoning the token security of the firefly bulbs, I flashed my light across a desert of dust and piles of rotting lumber. Like toys scattered by the offspring of a monstrous alien or the exoskeletons of insects destined to rule the earth, huge casting molds littered the area. Similar to a spelunker exploring an abominable chasm, a balance of powers guided my steps: apprehension and prudence stalemated curiosity.

As I prepared to head to the opposite side, my light conjured something from the darkness. I jumped back and bested the urge to flee. Almost hidden between a haphazardly stacked pile of boards and an enormous polyhedral mold sat a wooden crate wrapped in a dense veil of cobwebs. Its carvings, too elaborate for a piano box, bespoke a treasure chest from the orient. After slashing through the silken wrap, I pushed the top an eighth of the way off. It had the warmth, the unmistakable tactility of a living being. I brandished my light, prepared for whatever secrets it contained.

Before I could investigate, a remembrance struck my head like an arrow. In the bottom drawer of the guards' desk was a book titled *The Year's Best Horror Stories.* One featured a watchman in an analogous predicament. Per the traditional disparagement, he spent his working hours in a schnapps-induced stupor. After becoming lost on one of his rounds he found a mysterious box and opened it. Human heads with "kiwi-green skin" opened their eyes when he screamed. In a breathtaking twist, he dropped his flashlight. Their eyes, however, "glowed like creatures from the deep." The heads floated out of the box "wailing and snarling." Per another wicked stereotype vilifying his brave calling, the watchman "waddled" down a long corridor with dozens of little lights in fast pursuit. "They cast a shadow of his head on the door while he sought the right key." The story ended with "blunt bites from cold mouths."

An original thesis of mine is that the storage space of the mind is finite. A man should always be on guard not to clutter his head with nonsense, or, if he cannot abstain, he should force himself to forget it soon afterwards. The theoretical framework of this wretched story offended me on so many levels I tried to banish it before an entire floor of my brain became cluttered with objections and criticisms. As it clung to my mental dumpster like a mound of dog excrement, a tremendous urge swelled up within me to return to the office and lash off a letter to the author posthaste, as though this could purge my fury and nullify the malign spell of the book. Perhaps all critiques are thus. Glaring at the dark opening, I composed a draft in seconds.

***

Sir,

If you were banking on your readers being too horrified by "Rent-a-Cop and the Mystery Box" to notice its incoherencies and defamation, your judgment was grievously flawed. I noticed. The following objections were written in the order in which they provoked a rational mind. They could perhaps be written in a different order. Re-arrange them if you like.

Your story ended with the implication that the floating heads devoured the watchman. Question: How on earth does a disembodied head digest its food? The secondary disadvantage to being a disembodied head (the primary being death) is the lack of a body and the deprivations this absence entails. Before you commit any further scribbling I suggest you observe an autopsy. Ask the coroner for a quick tour of the digestive system and make a note of its proximity to the head. In the same key, your story had the heads making all sorts of noises -- in the absence of a respiratory system. Again, have the coroner explain the relationship between lungs and wailing.

Your rebuttal fails -- miserably. You maintain that these disembodied heads can transgress the laws of biology (apparently physics too, given that they were floating). They are obviously endowed with evil supernatural powers. Very well, how could "supernaturally endowed" heads be constrained by a mere box? Could they not have conspired to hover together and lift the lid? Your story says nothing about any locks. Could they not have gnawed their way out? What were they doing for food prior to the watchman? Did they come out at night to hunt for insects? Was someone feeding them? Was someone keeping them as pets? Who would want such pets?

Your portrayal of the watchman as a bumbling, overweight dipsomaniac is unforgivable. As a practitioner of this noble calling I take personal offense. (Should you ever suffer from the suicidal melancholy so common to writers of fiction, I recommend you attempt to trespass on the property I defend.) In case you were not aware, this portrayal is known as a cliché: writers are supposed to avoid them. Likewise, having the watchman fumble with his keys was simply masterful. I suggest, for a future story, a nubile girl whose car will not start.

In conclusion, "Rent-a-Cop and the Mystery Box" is, beyond certainty, the most incongruous and preposterous horror story since Bram Stoker's Dracula. Stylistically it is atrocious. Do not listen to the inbred parrots in your creative writing program. If I want "gritty realism" I will *defecate or watch my brother feed goldfish to his Piranha. Readers turn to books for Beauty. In the tragic event that you paid $250,000 for a degree that taught you otherwise you should retain the services of an attorney who specializes in fraud.*

Wrathfully,
Petronius Jablonski

***

This summed things up rather well, but in an instant I conceived of two new and even more damning objections. I decided against returning to the office. A proper refutation and healthful disposal would require nothing short of a Kantian critique and would have to wait. With a vow to abstain from all horror fiction, I returned to the edge of the cobweb-veiled crate, prepared to plunge my light into the darkness of the baroque chest like a saber.

The light flickered and died. It was second shift's responsibility to check the batteries. Judging from the lascivious periodicals polluting the desk, he had become enslaved by the merciless tyrant of onanism. (Does the suicide of our culture not vindicate Plato? Sanctifying freedom of speech is akin to extolling small pox: "I do not approve of the pestilence you spread, but I shall defend to the death your right to spread it.")

Upon my return to the warehouse I must have chosen a different spot to digress from the center aisle. My light revealed a staircase against the wall. Amber with rust like some remnant of the Titanic, it wound its way into the darkness above. Without making any conscious decision, I found myself on the steps, the metal groaning beneath my feet. I climbed and climbed but progress eluded me as though I were pulling some great chain out of a void. When I made the dubious choice of assessing my progress by shining the light at the ground, I found myself above an abyss whose evil gravity clawed at me, in the middle of outer space with no constellations for guidance or comfort. I clutched the railings and the flashlight hurtled away like a comet, making a crunching sound as it disappeared.

With an application of my excellent lessons in Quietude, I exiled all fears of my predicament. "It is not being trapped high upon a jagged staircase in the dark that disturbs me, but the opinions I form about it." I then exchanged the toxic opinion for a salubrious one. "Indeed, this is a marvelous turn of events."

Tiny lights twinkled in the distance, their parallelism demonstrating the propinquity of the ceiling. Reasoning from the inevitability of my return to earth, I approached the summit. My primary concern was striking the door and tumbling backward. Spurious concerns of sticking my hand into a silky web and struggling helplessly as a giant spider scurried down from the ceiling did not plague me. Nor was this scenario frightening when I read it in that execrable book.

A cool breeze whispered promises of liberation and my hand quickened its probe. The door had no handle and flapped open to another world. Anthills of rock rose and fell up to the edge of the cliff, beyond which the velvet blanket of the lake rustled beneath the nightlight in the sky. "No one is seeing this but me," I said in awe, succumbing to a philosophic spasm, overwhelmed by the inexpressibility of things. Even if I exhaustively described what I saw, smelled, heard, and thought, something frustratingly integral would remain untouched. Standing on the edge of a warehouse looking out at the lake, I experienced something I could never communicate to another. Maddeningly more than the sum of my senses, it yearned to escape but could not be freed.

I chided myself. To some degree all experiences are like this; one simply does not notice or care most of the time. Yet the provocative contemplation persisted. I suspect a few of the major philosophers may have experienced something not unlike it. Whereas I have not encountered a proper label for it in the course of my prodigious studies, I hereby name it the Petronius Sensation ("Jablonski," regrettably, does not have the ring or singularity of my first name). When a great philosopher (or a phenomenally gifted common man) experiences the Petronius Sensation, the natural inclination is to preserve and validate the intangible feature by sharing it, the way a scientist independently confirms his findings. And when its essence slips through all verbal nets, he begins to question its reality, to wonder if it ever happened at all.

With the regularity of the tide, another profound reflection supplanted the first. "Is my Bonneville the sum of its individual features or the base upon which they stand, the canvass where their beauty is displayed?"

By investing the time and cogitation proportionate to the prominence of this question, I expected a definite conclusion before the end of the summer, in time for my term paper. Realizing an analysis of the subject from a height could clinch things, I walked to the other side of the roof. Joyously prominent were my car's length and rectangularity, displayed by the selective glare of the moon beaming down like the spotlight from a watchtower.

"I should have parked in front of the office in total darkness," I whispered.

"Nonsense," scolded Reason. "Who is going to see your car out here?"

My return to earth was time consuming but not as disagreeable as I had feared. My meditations elutriated my mind and I attained secure possession of the poise required when climbing down a long staircase in the dark, wholly exempt from vacuous fears of big claws grasping me by the ankles and ripping me away from my tenuous moorings.

Exhausted and looking forward to some edifying diversions, I returned to the office. Flanking the remains of a desk and an iron coat tree, two windows covered with plastic insulation served as an interminable reminder of the nightmarish landscapes that must have haunted Monet. On summer, fall, and spring nights I spent my free time outside in the company of a beloved friend.

When I stepped onto the patio my heart lodged in the back of my throat. On the windshield glared an eerie orb like the headlight of a locomotive or the cataractal eye of some superannuated deity or a pearl the size of a beach-ball. The moon's reflection, rendered convex by the curvature of the glass, shone as though it were the cause and not the effect, as though it were a light casting an illusion in the heavens. (A serious author of fiction could deftly convert this into a fine story, wherein a protagonist in ancient times stumbles upon a wizard's garden and discovers how the moon and stars are projections. His conflict: Should he destroy the bewitching devices in the name of Truth or tolerate their deceit out of empathy for his deluded fellow man?)

An expatriate of Time, I could have watched the birth and death of galaxies or placed winning bets at glacier races. Had the windshield been a millimeter less in width, had my car been parked at an angle one ten-thousandth of a degree differently, the giant celestial snail would have deviated from its trajectory. But with the determinism of a planetary alignment or like cross-thatched strands in the weave of Fate, the fit and crossing were perfect, as though they belonged together.

When it left the windshield I staggered inside, catatonic from my curious encounter. "What an astounding series of coincidences," I said, reeling from the incredulity of a man who wins fifty coin tosses in a row. I gained repose by means of Lucretius' sobering teaching regarding the far stranger feats performed by atoms swirling aimlessly in the void (the creation of the world, among others), compared to which the synchronisms I just experienced seemed modest indeed.

My return to the patio discharged all notions of coincidences like bullets from a gun. I ran to my car but stopped several feet away to maintain a safe distance. A rectangle of white light perfectly circumscribed its shape, suspended about two feet above the roof.

"The moon did this," I said in awe and trembling. "But why?"

Engrossed by the halo, I skipped the rest of my rounds. Its light made the blue of my car come alive like the raging waters of an Amazon stream. Imposing and mystifying, it shone brighter than the fiery clouds billowing up from the aluminum recycling plant beyond the trees, and it attracted no bugs.

Toward the end of my shift I went to the edge of the cliff. The night's proceedings afflicted me with uncertainties and trepidation, diminishing the likelihood of Quietude. The water splashed against the shore far below, bruising itself black and blue. For a blissful moment the cool breeze and the gentle applause from the waves overthrew the tyranny of my thoughts and I faded away, glimpsing the Eden from whence man was banished, the nullity to which he is destined to return.

On the way back I rehearsed a response to the next sentry. "The halo is an experimental accessory that will not be commercially available until my brother, Hieronymus, perfects and patents it." Given that other guards had expressed rube-like awe at my stereo's ability to shake the office long before my car appeared on the gravel road, an appeal to the inscrutable nature of technology could scarcely fail.

To my relief and surprise, the halo had vanished. As crimson guts spilled from the belly of the night, I watched first shift approach, his 1974 Buick Electra stirring up clouds of dust like some chariot riding out of a whirlwind. Watchmen, sentinels of the remorseless hinterland between dusk and morn, priests of the rosary beading all the days, keepers of the promise that renewal comes with dawn, are we not warriors?

In subsequent weeks I discovered the halo only returned during a full moon when I was on duty. On those nights as I watched it bathe my car in its sparkling mist, a baritone of foreboding vanquished the lilting soprano of Reason. Fascinated yet apprehensive, I could not desist the impression that some predaceous force had designs on my car, designs I was powerless to foil.

Throughout the summer I spent all the time vouchsafed to me by Fate at the helm of my stately yacht. Our rudderless voyages, free from the dictates of a compass and map, where the sails were fanned by whims and the destinations existed only in retrospect, were in perfect conformity with Nature, whose pointless journey ought to be celebrated, not denied with vulgar myths.

Disquieting moments arose after the parade of a cruise. I parked in front of my house and emerged triumphant. Before leaving for work I went on the porch to fortify myself with a cigarette. After all the fantastic adventures on the concrete seas, the magnificent thunder of Beethoven, and the paralysis suffered by other drivers from sheer humility, there remained a big blue car parked on a quiet street and a man sitting in the dark. If there be gods, will they not feel the same haunting contrast when our world becomes vapor? Should they not be pitied?

Summer dissolved, leaving the skeletal remains of fall. At work I remained in the office between rounds, eschewing the lascivious periodicals hidden in the desk and listening to a transistor radio tuned to easy listening (opposed to the "agonizing listening" of most stations). It is a rancid scrap of conventional wisdom that no man is an island. Such nonsense stems from modernity's ignorance of the path to wisdom, for which solitude is essential. In the dwindling twilight of civilization we forget that philosophy is a way of life, not an idle game to be performed over cappuccino. The muscles of the mind, far more important than those this vain age is obsessed with, require steady and progressive exercise to adapt and survive in their inhospitable environment.

In the days of the Stoics men of wisdom and decency graced our foolish planet with indefectible teachings and superlative examples. When their noble breed perished, when their doctrines were kidnapped and prostituted by a noxious cult, a dreadful night consumed the earth. Rather than using the lantern of solitude to tread the narrow switchback of wisdom, to explore the humbling vastness above and the void within, modern man lobotomizes himself with an odious bric-a-brac of gadgets. As his mind atrophies, the ever-intrusive enemy, thought, is conquered. Darkness prevails.

Alone on third shift I was an island, hidden in an ocean of deep thoughts and surrounded by a steady rotation of sharks. From this I did not recoil. Quietude was not merely an acquaintance, but a mistress (with the exception of Tuesdays, Wednesdays, and occasionally Fridays when Sandy snuck in to visit). My spirit soared as I sought the Truth, a fearless explorer armed only with a map whose legend read HERE THERE BE MONSTERS.

And the halo? Though unable to study it with the detachment of a scientist, I gradually became inured to it. How? How could a man become *inured* to so extraordinary a phenomenon, to something so breathtakingly strange? With the shield of philosophy, of course. But this is too general an answer. For the particulars I must now unveil my *pièce de résistance*, the crown jewel of my contributions to philosophy: Petronius' Shovel.

(The Reader is advised to bookmark this section, if not for purposes of edification then simply for monetary ones. This concept alone is worth his $10. He will soon recall the use of my Shovel in Part I. He should then return and study that section. Given our expeditious pace, I could not make a formal introduction.)

Just as William of Occam gave philosophy his Razor (undeniably useful but somewhat overrated), I hereby contribute my Shovel. This tool will prove to be as easy to use as its namesake. An example of it in action will serve as a good first approach to understanding it.

Now, by what criterion are things considered strange or normal? According to the regularity by which they occur, one might respond. Unfortunately, by this standard a halo above a car is quite peculiar and the strangeness vs. normalcy of a great many things becomes a relativistic mishmash. But this is the mere surface of this issue. A true philosopher feels instinctively that the line separating them is, to an enormous extent (if not altogether), arbitrary or illusory. But how can he dig straight to the root of this quandary, to penetrate the imaginary surface and demonstrate the chimerical nature of the distinction for the common man to see?

"Is the halo stranger than the existence of life itself?" the philosopher asks.

"Certainly not. What can be stranger than that?" comes the reply from any man with the barest semblance of cognition. "Explanations of life, its origin and purpose, always seem inadequate, as though nothing could feasibly constitute an answer, as though the question is a gasp of dismay, not a serious inquiry. I'd rather not think about it. Isn't there a ballgame on?"

"Is the halo stranger than the fact that Something exists instead of Nothing?" the philosopher asks.

"Absolutely not," comes the reply from even a business student. "That's the most peculiar and disturbing fact there is." Rubbing his temples he cries, "My mind is awhirl. Bring me a video game. I beg you."

"And so," the philosopher concludes, washing off my faithful Shovel, his labor at an end, "the halo is not really strange. Compared to the existence of life, which we see every day, it is perfectly banal. Compared to the existence of everything, it is more akin to a sleeping pill than a mystery. Rather than giving it a pejorative label and running about in a tizzy, it is simply a matter of getting used to it."

"Agreed," chime the man with the barest semblance of cognition and his comrade, the business student. "Let's all compare cell phones."

Now, far from being a mere principle or abstract utility (like Occam's much-ballyhooed Razor), my Shovel has the unlimited potential for practical, everyday applications. In fact, as the Reader is about to behold, it saved my life, holding my wits together in the face of what a non-philosophic mind would have deemed unbearably strange.

***

At the abandoned factory the melting snow blended with the earth to create quicksand. On the last night of my former life I slopped through my first round, returned to the office, and decided that taking the chair outside would be a grand way to ritualistically mark the dawn of spring and defy the failing bulwark of winter.

A moonbeam illuminated my car like the searchlight from a distant helicopter and the halo throbbed with an unprecedented glare. As it flickered with greater rapidity, the flashes became painful and I averted my eyes. "Perhaps it is being recharged," I said. I should have known better, but naiveté, not cynicism, is the good man's weakness.

Before my next round, a frost of apprehension covered me. My heart drove down a flexuous road of all the wonderful times we had shared. I could scarcely pry myself away and walk back inside. I set out, not stopping at the side door for one last look, as I often did. Even now this stings. Regret, is it not a species of mourning, grieving the loss of what could have been?

Throughout the round my trepidation mounted. Though inured to the garden-variety "strangeness," I was daunted by the prospect of teaching a tow-truck driver how to use my Shovel in the event of halo-related mechanical difficulties. I returned and approached the side door, a condemned man on his last walk.

It was gone as though erased from the guestbook of Existence. There were not even tracks in the mud. The predacious moonbeam persisted, little more than a ghostly Roman column, as if sated. I fell to my knees and shook my fists at the sky while lightning bolts of anguish struck me. To escape their furious energy I pounded the soupy earth, battering a hollow in the mud. But nothing could hide from me what I had lost. Verily, the value of what we love is best estimated by the agony its absence instills.

Heading to the cliff, my only hope for the clarity of Quietude, I ran beside the warehouse. At the edge, swords slashed my sides. (My robust health was a function of manly anaerobic vigor, not the effete aerobic conditioning common to rabbits and roadrunners. Clearly, when the choice of fight or flight confronted my ancestors, the latter was nary a consideration.)

I bent over with my hands on my hips, gasping for air, my mind astir with fury. A cold rain shimmered the sheets of the lake. The nightlight above fetched my eyes. I rubbed them, not trusting their wild testimony. In the center of the moon sparkled a rectangular sapphire, brighter than any star. I swooned, inhaled for a minute, and from the depths of my being roared, "Return it at once!"

I did not think my voice could carry that far, but when a man is bereft of reasonable options he defers to the guide of instinct. The twinkling sapphire rent my heart, sending me into convulsions of longing and rage. However, through the use of my Shovel I preserved my wits. Whereas the common man (assuming he maintained consciousness) would have phoned the police or an astronomer, I, realizing the proceedings were no stranger than life itself, took matters into my own firm and capable hands.

"Damn you," I howled into a waterfall of rain. "Insolent satellite. The torrent of my wrath shall flood the valleys of --"

Reason interrupted me with the reminder that the distance separating us rendered threats idle. "When action is not possible, the groveling cowardice of diplomacy becomes necessary."

"What is it you want from me? I will give you anything."

The rain lessened. The lake became smooth and taught. An unseasonably warm breeze wafted up the cliff.

"Fool," said Reason. "Always begin the bidding with a lowball."

The breeze abated. I prepared to repeat my offer, with fingers crossed behind my back, when a voice whispered from below, "Petronius Jablonski, Child of the Four Winds, return on the morrow when the sun is highest and your grievance will be addressed."

I knelt down and grasped the edge of the cliff. On the beach, in the light of the moon and the sparkle of my Bonneville, stood a dark figure, a tremendous hulking mass. I could not make out its features, only its vast outline. It spread great wings and with a single flap took off, hoisting its colossal bulk into the air and up the cliff. I pulled my head back and lay prostrate, terrified the creature was coming to carry me away. It flew past like a jet while I probed the mud for a rock to brain it.

"No. This is the only link to your car," said Reason.

The bird's body was the length of a man's, only broader and red like a cardinal. Padded with dark and mangy feathers, its wings gave it the forbidding aura of enormity.

"Return here on the morrow when the sun is highest and the terms of your compensation will be explained," came a voice from above.

That voice is coming from the bird, I realized. Though my car had been abducted and taken to the moon, the existence of a giant talking bird struck me as far more incredible. (I had, of course, temporarily dropped my Shovel before making this callow judgment. Given the separation from my beloved, surely this lapse is pardonable. In actuality, as Petronius' Shovel will reveal, neither the bird nor the abduction are any "stranger" than the fact that dirt + water = mud. The ambitious student is encouraged to check the calculations for himself.) The creature circled me thrice before ascending toward the moon, diminishing until only the ivory plate with the sparkling blue crystal remained.

Instead of walking all the way to my home in Cudahy, I doubled back to the laboratory after my shift. With the insinuation of peril, it was off limits to all sentries. According to an oral tradition passed down through generations of guards, the whole perimeter had been sealed due to a mishap involving noxious potions. One night when I undid the lock, I noticed a distinct but not unpleasant ether-like fragrance, but I did not perish from any baneful concoctions.

With my lighter I lit the candles Sandy had spread around the couch in the reception room. Apparently fleshly unions are impossible in the absence of burning wax, which acts as an offering to some melting deity of Eros known only to women. I removed my filthy uniform and began a search for warmth and comfort in the fetal position. The calmative vapor teased me with hazy remembrances of salacious times as I closed my eyes and the couch began to fall ...

I sat up at the foot of a marble altar carved to resemble a skull, upon which sat a glass bowl filled with coins of many colors. Behind it stood two bald men in green robes. A giant prism looked out on a garden where swordfish flew from a pond and beached themselves. They bounced ten feet and higher but none perished. In lieu of a ceiling, a purple cloud remained fixed by unseen forces.

Both men put their heads down as though taking naps. I scooped up some coins and threw them across the room. They transmogrified into a buzzing swarm of gold and silver insects. Coalescing in the center, they returned to their native form and landed on their sides. I tiptoed a zigzag path until I found one on its face. Before I could read it, the strange votaries chanted, "The coin is not for sale. Time creeps on, no faster than your snail." Honey dripped off their faces, a milky film covered their eyes, and their bright robes billowed from a breeze I could not feel. Metal bricks composed the wall behind them, reflecting a thousand twisted images of me.

On the coin an armadillo stood back to back with a zebra above the inscription UNITED IN THE DRIVE TOWARD PERFECT EQUILIBRIUM. I turned it over and examined a Latin inscription beneath a pterodactyl when a swarm of coins blasted me in the head. I looked up and another iron fist struck. The votaries were pitching them at me. I covered my face and growled, "Stop." The voice, not my own, echoed across the room, slowing with each enunciation.

They raised their hands and looked to the cloud and grinned. A hole appeared and grew as they chanted, "What is perfect does not come from practice. The time has come, now, embrace the cactus." The coin scalded me. When I dropped it, tiny hands pierced the floor and grabbed my feet and I began to sink.

I sat up on the couch and slapped my cheeks. Thinking the two eccentrics were in the next room, I looked about for a sharp object. "It was just a dream," I said. "Perhaps this place *is* contaminated."

On the cliff I sought Quietude, affirming the course of events rather than beseeching the inexorable arrow of Time to make a U-turn on my behalf. But even my excellent lessons failed to bridle my foreboding and despair.

"Fret not Petronius Jablonski, the Venerable Horned One of the Lake has heard your lamentations and has deigned to grant you council," said a voice. A feathery arm plopped down on my shoulder. It was the bird, only he did not seem ominous in the light of day. His baggy red overalls were obviously intended to disguise his corpulent state, but it could scarcely be concealed. That he could fly at all thrust a damning accusation of inequality at gravity: If a beast in that condition is permitted to transgress aerodynamic mores, then why not I?

"Prepare to be comforted," he said, making pecking motions with his yellow beak, which, in conjunction with his button eyes, brought me the opposite of solace.

A gale-force wind swept the cliff, ambushing us. I clung to the sanctuary of the bird's stalwart belly. The earth trembled and the sun split in two, amoeba-style. My comforter pushed me away and let out a frightful shriek, "Brace yourself Petronius, and behold the Venerable Horned One of the Lake," before launching himself with a flap of his wings.

Half of the sun remained in place; the other half slid down and stopped above the lake. The water bubbled as millions of knives arose: a rack of colossal antlers. I recoiled at the thought of what monstrous creature from the deep they preceded.

A figure one-hundred times the size of a man took shape behind a wall of steam. In one hand he held a golden scepter with a red tip, in the other a stone tablet. The dense brume shrouding the surface of the lake coalesced with the hem of his vaporous robe. He glided to the edge of the shore, his robe undulating hypnotically, his hair and beard flowing like tentacles. He navigated the scepter around his antlers, raised it over his head, and looked upon me with eyes like wells of fathomlessly deep water. In awe I held my breath.

"*Ahhchooo!*" His sneeze knocked me to the ground, uprooted trees, and sent avalanches of sand hurtling down the cliff. He looked at his tablet and cleared his throat. "Petronius Jablonski, Son of Cudahy, Third Cousin of the Four Elements, Potator of Pabst, Student of Silenus, *ahchoo!*"

Emerald meteorites exploded all around. I covered my head from the gelatinous shrapnel and clung to the cliff amidst hurricane winds. It must have been the chilly lake air. I, too, suffered from a bit of a cold.

"Master of Sheepshead, Heir to Porphyry," he continued, reading from the tablet and waving the scepter to punctuate his declarations. "Apprentice of Sisyphus …"

Be done with it already, I thought. The histrionic address became monotonous, especially given my unfamiliarity with the strange titles, but I said nothing for fear of offending him. As he prattled on, I stole a glimpse of the half-sun above. Something whirled within. Though obscured by the orange haze, it looked like a huge brick of gold.

"Summon your courage. You will need it."

The imperious gaze from his ancient face filled me with a haunting sense of my insignificance. His permanence mocked the brevity of my existence. I summoned what little bravery I could in the presence of such a being.

"I, The Venerable Horned One of the Lake, have summoned you so I may offer my condolement and recompense an injustice." He pointed the scepter at me and stifled a sneeze. "My impudent nephew, Lunis, abducted your car. As you may have noticed, he has been coveting it. I am prepared to return it, absent the stereo. Or, hear me, Petronius Jablonski, I am prepared to make you an offer, one a chary man would long ponder."

I moved my lips and tongue in an earnest attempt at speech but the words failed to congeal.

"In exchange for your Bonneville you will be sent on a journey. Many times I have seen you pace the edge of this cliff in earnest perplexity. You fervently scour the heavens for answers, fretful of not finding them. The answers you want come from the lake. I am prepared to grant you the understanding you seek."

The gold bar slowed its rotations and I discerned its nature. I beheld a car, a great and glorious car, an enormous Cadillac, shining like the sun from whence it came.

"You will make this journey in the Chocolate Chariot," he said.

"You mean a black Cadillac?"

He checked the tablet. "Not chocolate, I meant *chosen*. You will make the journey in the Chosen Chariot, a chariot of gold, as bright and powerful as the sun."

"Oh most Horned One of the Lake, is that the Chosen Chariot?"

"That's the showroom model. You will have to supply the car. But it must be a great and noble Cadillac, and it must be colored gold. On your journey you will see many signs. Some will guide you. Some will confuse you. You must summon your wisdom to tell them apart."

"What kind of signs?"

"Stop signs. What kind do you think? Visions, dreams, aberrances in general. If you focus on the guiding ones the journey will teach you all that a man needs to know and your arrival at the Point of Percipience will consummate that enlightenment."

"The Point of Percipience?"

"The Point of Percipience."

"Is it on a mountain?"

"No."

"Is it high upon a hill?"

He scowled.

"When must I begin the journey? Many grains of sand must pass through the hourglass before the reins of a new chariot feel natural," I said, knowing he did not hear such dialect from any mortals in this feeble age.

"What the hell are you talking about?"

"The car and I will need some time to become acquainted before we embark on any journeys."

"Yes of course," he said, nodding his head and antlers thoughtfully. "You'll be given plenty of time to -- *ahchoooooo*!"

A vast section of the cliff fell to the shore in crumbs. Dazed and prostrate, I stared longingly at the heavenly brick. I could have watched it spin forever.

"Where was I? Oh yes, on your journey you must pay close attention. For this there are two reasons. Carve them on the picnic table of your heart. First, I am spending a fortune on special effects and I do not want it wasted. Second, not all of the signs are important, only some will lead you to enlightenment. You must be very careful about which ones you attribute importance to."

The rotations of the Chosen Chariot had nearly ceased, permitting me to ascertain how its rectangularity surpassed that of my Bonneville. Contrary to nonsense inflicted on the Reader by geometry teachers, this property admits of degrees. Whereas it is the primary criterion for automobile greatness, such a car inflamed me in the way finches inflamed Darwin.

"Petronius Jablonski, do you understand?"

"And if I choose the right signs?" I said, returning to my feet.

"You will obtain the deepest wisdom a mortal can possess."

Wind lashed the cliff and the Cadillac quickened its rotations. I knew the Venerable Horned One of the Lake would soon depart and there were many things I needed to clarify. In all the furor I could only articulate a few. "How will I know when to leave? How will I know where to go? How will I know if I am paying heed to the right signs?"

"When the fruit of the mind is ripe, it's time to go. You'll receive a map in the mail."

The wind blew furiously and the brick returned to a blur. With a terrible crash of thunder the Horned One entangled the scepter in his antlers. "Damn this thing," he bellowed. He raised the tablet and threw back his head. The half-sun replaced the brick and the water bubbled and made an earsplitting hiss.

"But how do I know if I am interpreting them correctly?" I said, silenced by the wind and steam.

"I, the Venerable Horned One of the Lake, bid you, Petronius Jablonski, an enlightening journey." A funnel engulfed him until only his fearsome antlers remained. He and the ball of fire descended beneath the boiling surface. A subaquatic glow moved to the horizon and disappeared.

Brooding, I paced the edge of the cliff until Reason surrendered to the outrageous demands of my senses. In such a position a man may either fret over what he cannot control and torment himself with frivolous regrets, or he can embrace and affirm the unexpected (but, as per my wondrous Shovel, not strange) turn of events.

"The confetti of fugitive passions cannot influence the purchase of a car," said Reason. "To select the proper chariot your will must have the strength of Hercules, your mind the clarity of vodka. You must prepare, cleansing your heart of every iniquity, your armor of every tarnish. In solitude, digest the implications of the past and nourish your spirit for the journey ahead. Become a thread woven into the lush tapestry of nature, away from all remnants of civilized life and the illusions of security they bring. Like a general camped out before a battle, listen to your soul and organize the scattered notes of your thoughts into a cohesive plan."

When my spiritual mentor, Marcus Aurelius, defended the Roman Empire against barbarian hordes, he often sought solitude in his encampment to fortify himself with Stoic philosophy. As a testament to this practice, the fruit of his reflections represents, beyond certainty, the greatest gift ever bequeathed to mankind: his *Meditations*. Surely my situation demanded the same approach.

Submerged in the living waters of nature, I could check the compass of my heart and trust its reading. In a city, the shacks and shanties and all the abscesses of humanity distort the guiding forces of Beauty and Truth, pummeling the sensitive needle. But in the woods, the maternity ward of life, when a man sits beneath tall trees like a child in his mother's lap, it does not waver. He can listen to the sad song of his soul and comfort it by wading through a virgin stream. The fragments of his thoughts become sonnets and the gentle forest breeze blows away the dust accumulated on the mirror of his mind. As the sunlight speckles the ground beneath the trees his troubles become a comedy, and the sparks from his campfire kindle the flames of long-forgotten dreams.

***

Upon returning home I awakened Zeus from a nap and removed my family's six-man tent from the attic. An extended porch with mosquito netting made it ideal for quiet meditations. Deprived of any prolonged access to a car, I pitched it in the backyard between our two pines. Unfortunately, I had to position it facing the house for the extension chord to reach my stereo. While I assessed my progress, Zeus frolicked through the remaining piles of snow, covering his black and gold coat with slush. A recent haircut revealed the unmistakable carriage of a tiny yak. (Though the popular legend contends that Shi Tzu were bred by Tibetan Buddhists to resemble lions, they in fact resemble yaks. This matter, including an innovatory thesis explaining it, will be addressed later at some length when it will not disrupt the euphony of my narrative.)

Wearing only a housecoat and slippers, my mother walked across the yard and stood beside me. "What are you doing?"

"I am becoming a thread woven into the lush tapestry of nature."

"Sandy's not talking to you again, is she? Now what have you done? This is no way to --"

"This has nothing to do with her. I am faced with a decision that will have consequences of epic proportions and I must be secluded while I prepare myself to make it."

I hoped she would hear the pathos in my voice and leave me to my solitude to check the compass of my heart. My bearing was stern but respectful. The decision to remain at home was entirely a function of her culinary genius. While my "peers" subsisted on scraps the Donner Party would have refused, I dined on masterpieces that could drive any chef mad with envy.

"What's going on?" she said, fixing me with a frightened stare.

Obviously I could not share all of the proceedings. "I am poised to purchase a car, a Cadillac," I announced, revealing a glimpse of my inner turbulence. "My Bonneville has already changed hands."

"Wouldn't it be easier to check the classifieds in tonight's paper? If you're looking for a car that's the best --"

"I am familiar with the broad outlines of the procedure," I said, brushing the snow off of Zeus. "But I need to steady myself before I check them. I do not wish to peruse them until I am on the porch of my tent, woven into the lush blanket of --"

"Okay, okay," she sang, heading back to the house. She paused. "Are you sure this has nothing to do with Sandy?"

"Yes," I gasped, my composure forsaking me.

"I think it will be too cold for Zeus to spend the night out here."

"I will check the globe in my study, but as I recall Tibet is not a tropical region."

"Look at little Zeus. He's shivering now."

I rubbed his giraffe-spotted belly. "Though his rugged constitution is more than a match for this weather, the task at hand demands solitude."

"Dinner will be ready in an hour. Two of Hieronymus' friends will be joining us."

I winced at the thought of my obstreperous brother and his oafish cronies. "I shall have my dinner here."

Zeus followed my mother inside and I finished stocking the tent with supplies.

***

Giant pines swayed beside me, bedposts supporting a speckled canopy. Atop my stereo, a kerosene lantern shed its humble light. Beside my adjustable lawn chair, the warmth from a propane heater rose to my hands. In my mouth, a big black cigar from the Dominican Republic supplied incense for my meditations while a sad, sad opera by Puccini filled the darkness with the sorrow inside me. The paper was crumpled up in a corner. Nada Fleetwood, nada Sedan DeVille. The classifieds were a nothing and a man in a tent was too and all he needed was a canteen full of bourbon and a porch with mosquito netting.

The opera's peak loomed, a mountain of woe so harrowing the night itself seemed to weep. A raccoon lumbered toward the tent, eclipsing the house and stopping no more than three feet from the unzipped flap. He looked into my eyes; I into his. I saw, not some wild garden-raiding beast, but a fellow traveler on the anfractuous road of life.

Madame Butterfly's voice climbed the jagged peaks of despair and the raccoon, as if to surmount the anguish flooding the forest, stood upon its hind legs. The light next door came on and the door flew open. Mr. Burzinski stuck his brutish head out.

"Jablonski! You turn that damn opera-shit down or I'm calling the cops," he hollered, rupturing the delicate veil of tragedy.

I struggled to remember that the insolence of fools is the wise man's burden. "On what possible pretext will you seek an intercession from your infernal god, the State?" He predicated the last totalitarian atrocity upon an absurd and wicked law which arbitrarily restricts the hours when a man may play Frisbee with his own dog on a public street.

"It's three o'clock in the morning," he said, jowls flapping. "I'm not gonna tell you again."

"And I shall not tell *you* again. Each time you invoke your dark lord as a mercenary you diminish the liberty of all free men. Your supplications nourish this Moloch, this Baal, this --"

He slammed the door. The climax ceased. The raccoon had vanished, absorbed by whatever dense thickets could contain it. My faithful canteen provided little comfort, its contents bitter in the wake of Mr. Burzinski's savage penetration of the operatic hymen.

***

I awoke early the next afternoon and sought sustenance, hunting and gathering some leftover casserole. I spent the rest of the day in meditation, nourishing the dauntlessness needed to select the chariot, suspended in the crystal aether of Bruckner's symphonies, freed from the isolation cell of Time. When darkness tinged the forest, the stealth Burmese cat stalked the encampment, carrying the evening paper.

"This is necessary before buying a car?" Sandy said, entering the flap to my porch, her feral eyes illuminating the shaded enclave.

"It is different from ordering a pizza. I suppose I could stumble onto a used-car lot plastered with twenty-dollar bills, trusting in the inherent mercy of vultures."

"Your mom sounded surprised to hear from me," she said. By default, she seated herself Indian-style and began wrapping a strand of her long hair around a finger. "We can't believe you sold the blue bomber."

I groaned at the epithet. "You had the finest moments of your life in that *blue bomber*. Maslow would have characterized them as peak experiences. You should be wailing in torment."

Predictably, she giggled and offered a revisionist account. "Getting laid in a backseat listening to Mozart is not what he had in mind."

"Beethoven. And if those were not peak experiences then that concept has no meaning. Your derogation of those transcendent encounters is understandable. When man encounters the eternal he is humbled. The cheap comfort of denial is more tolerable than the anguish of uncertainty."

"So who'd you sell it to?" she asked, studying my encampment: cats' eyes widening with perplexity on the emanation from my speakers; cats' eyes narrowing on my canteen, detecting the forbidden liquid within.

"Mr. Horn is an upstanding but somewhat eccentric acquaintance from work. His generous offer was clearly the child of impulse. Consequently, I had no time for lengthy deliberations."

"Cash on the spot?"

"Something not unlike that. But more interesting is how his offer was part of an extraordinary coincidence. At exactly the same time I arrived at the conclusion that a car superior to my Bonneville existed."

"Your mom's concerned about the price of a Cadillac. She thinks you should wait until you graduate before rewarding yourself with anything extravagant."

"Rewarding myself? This car is my inalienable birthright. Does she think I am contemplating the acquisition of a new Cadillac? I would crawl through broken glass before driving any of the abominations excreted from Detroit after 1977. Is she equating perfection with extravagance?"

Zeus scampered through the porch flap onto Sandy's lap and displayed his exquisite belly for rubbing. "Puppy Zeus, how do you run so fast with those little mushroom stumps?"

"He could just as well ask how you can walk at all on those ungainly celery stalks. If Mother Nature has ever graced creation with a more harmoniously designed creature, I have yet to see it."

Before inflicting a veritable fit of baby talk on him, Sandy told me to look at the paper. One ad in particular had fetched her eye. The heading read, "Huey Tozotli's Smoking Mirror Special. We've got the Boats. Cadillacs & Lincolns. Huey's got the Wind. The Sale is up to You."

Like something from a dream, one of the models advertised was from the mid-seventies. I would not be able to afford a full load the following semester, but I reasoned that possession of the greatest wisdom possible for a mortal mitigated the urgency of such hoop-jumping. (In candor, dismay characterized my impressions of university. Home-schooled by my father, his exemplar cultivation my beacon, I had acclimatized to excellence in all things. The question I struggled with daily: What had everyone else been doing for the past twenty years? Was I the sole survivor of a generation of feral children?)

"After I acquire my car, we shall make an excursion to facilitate the bonding process."

"I pretty much assumed we'd be doing little else for the next few years."

Though she did not understand the meaning of cars (hers, stitched together in some back alley of the world, contained only two doors and could have fit in the trunk of my Bonneville), Sandy lacked the *tabula rasa* quality I sought when selecting a concubine. I often marveled at how she took for granted precious gems of wisdom that I had only procured after grueling episodes of cogitation. Given her gender's feeble deliberative faculty, this could only be explained by the indulgence of Fate.

"Well yes, but those will be normal trips. I am speaking about a special excursion. With the thoughtfulness that often accompanies eccentricity, Mr. Horn spoke favorably of a destination of interest. The Point of Percipience, as I recall."

"What is it?"

"He was vague, but it sounds akin to the Cadillac Ranch, or at least not completely unlike it."

"Cool. Where is it?"

"He promised to send me a map."

Per my instinctive disdain for dramatics, I severed the ostentatious dross from my explanation. One can scarcely be faulted for such a beneficent trait. Before her inquiry gained momentum or specificity, I led her into the tent and zipped it shut. Zeus stood solemn guard.

"Your mom's home," she said, displaying a rare moment of disinterest, which passed quickly.

***

"So how much were you lookin' to spend?" Huey asked while I analyzed the rectangularity of my betrothed. The problem was twofold: it was green and priced over twice what I could afford.

I turned to inspect the ground behind me. "Do you see a placenta? Did the nurse not remove it when I emerged this morning? Why else would you ask such a question?"

"Gross," said Sandy.

The human wall of flesh, unimpressed by my jest, continued his estimations of me, not yet certain if Barnum had prophesized my arrival. "I'm firm on this one," he said, slapping a doughy mitt onto the hood. "This car is like brand new."

"The only tiny, insignificant difference is that it was made in 1976. But aside from that irrelevant consideration, brand new. Has it been traveling at the speed of light?"

"Odometer ain't even been turned over."

"Is this a car dealership or a revival? Is there a tent where your customers gather to further demonstrate their faith by dancing with rattlesnakes? What flavor is your Kool-Aid? I hereby offer you twenty-five. Reject it at your peril."

At a third the asking price, this constituted a major lowball: tactically bold but strategically reckless. If wise, Huey would have spit on the ground and returned to his office, forcing me to grovel with a more generous offer and establishing his regnant role in the interrelation of salesman and buyer, a position best likened to the alpha male in a pack of dogs.

He blundered thus: "Hell, I got a fella comin' this afternoon with five in cash."

"Ah yes, the Man with Cash," I said triumphantly. "I shall finally meet this legend. Clad in black with a stovepipe hat and waxed mustache, he roams the earth with a suitcase of bills, eternally in transit to close deals at just below the sticker price, making intermittent stops to tie damsels to train tracks. Sandy, remember when this villain almost bought your car out from under you? He has returned to --"

"Forty-five" Huey grunted, finally recognizing that I was not among Barnum's majority.

"Am I covered with bruises? Does it look as though I recently fell from a turnip truck? My terminating, unappeasable offer is thirty-five."

"Mine's forty. Take it or leave it."

"Like Caligula, I pride myself on my inflexibility. Come along Sandy. That dealership down the street had a newer Fleetwood that caught my eye." My historical reference was based on the celebrated Madman Theory. In any dispute, it profits one if his adversary thinks him less than fully stable. Sandy watched in adoration as I took her hand and led us away.

"Alright, alright," Huey called.

With the pride of the victor I turned to Sandy and put my hand on her forearm. "You do know that you are the luckiest girl in the world?"

***

At the body shop, I based my decision on solar considerations. "The sun is more orange than gold, is it not?" I asked the technician. After a long pause, he looked into my eyes and nodded in silent agreement.

Part II:
Addendum

If the Reader's understanding of the occurrences and ideas in Part II are in any way imperfect we have reached an impasse. Like an injured hiker attempting a perilous passage, he will struggle to remain abreast of me. Soon he will hobble behind, calling for clarifications with each painful step, begging me to lessen my pace. Inevitably, he will collapse and watch in despair as I vanish beyond the horizon. For a corrective we must turn to an old Russian proverb: repetition is the mother of learning. Solicitous of his welfare, I beseech him to return to the beginning of Part II.

Ideally, the second reading should be performed aloud. Of necessity, it must be performed at the time of day when the Reader's mind is at its zenith. I fear we have grown accustomed to collocate reading with the basest means of relaxation. No doubt other books he whores around with are tantamount to sedatives and television, but make no mistake: the reading of Part II is neither. Like a swim upstream in a cold river, it demands strength, precision, courage, cunning, and endurance.

Dear Reader, if you do not feel invigorated and stronger, how will you bear the weight of what is to come? As a historian and philosopher my role is not to carry the load, but, like a trainer in a gymnasium, to ensure that your muscles are capable of sustaining it. After you re-read Part II, I will perfect your physique by addressing the obvious questions sparked by a fastidious reading.

***

At this point the student must be aflame with one primary question and at least one auxiliary question.

"Scholar, regarding the first breathtaking appearance of your mighty tool and your subsequent handling of it: there exists a discrepancy, possibly a logical contradiction. When you introduced your Shovel, you demonstrated how it penetrates the illusory surface and digs straight to the root of Reality to reveal the primordial strangeness of all things. This was not given as an example of a particular act, but as a general antecedent of all penetrations performed by your invincible tool. Yet posterior to your demonstration, you cite several examples of particular penetrations, one which occurred anterior to your demonstration. Have you not blurred the critical line betwixt a *general anterior* and a *particular posterior*?"

The student was not sent to forage through Part II like a ravening bear, but to perfect his comprehension of its essential concepts and occurrences. Nonetheless, a fair point is raised. Aristotle first warned of the hazards inherent in confounding these concepts, and if I have done so I am guilty of nothing less than a logical felony. My defense will consist of two parts. First, a brief comment on the possibility that a misperception of ambiguity occurred -- understandable given the enthralling nature of the text.

It is conceivable that the Reader, shattered from his initial brush with Part II, became overwhelmed with dread by the grave warning at the beginning of this addendum and slipped into a delirium. I implored him to attempt Part II again when his mind was at its zenith. In the course of a day, this period usually corresponds to a time subsequent to the consumption of a caffeinated beverage. Apparently some men do not differentiate between one such drink and twelve. Consequently, no distinction is drawn between a state of enhanced cognitive agility and a pathologic condition where the mind paces a cage like a tiger. Students, far from being an exception to this tendency, are more likely to succumb to it. I insist the Reader again attempt the glorious summit tomorrow with a clear head, having consumed only one. He should perform his next reading standing. During the more intense passages, pacing is advised: book in one hand, chin in the other.

***

At this point the Reader might accuse me of avoiding the singular thrust of his objection. Patience is advised. I have been limbering up before entering the ring with Aristotle. My philosophic muscles supple, I am prepared to grapple with him. Now, as both he and Thomas Aquinas conceived of the concept, a *particular posterior* is distinct from --

A bitter and melancholy dagger pierces my heart. The Reader used his prima facie intelligent question to stage a crude burlesque, hoping that I, entangled in nets of logic, would remain oblivious to the coming pratfall. And where had he hoped to go with this? To Sandy, no doubt. Fast approaching was some utterly craven punch line about how "he'd love to penetrate *that* particular posterior." The poor girl has been free of her terminal disfigurement for all of a few pages and the Reader cannot abstain? If such was his intention he has succeeded magnificently -- in making a *particular posterior* of himself. Metaphysical jokes work on many levels, dear Reader, many levels.

***

After hours of skeptical brooding, a vigorous walk with Zeus, and several fermented elixirs, I have reluctantly come to recognize the necessity of bestowing the gracious benefit of the doubt to the Reader's intentions. With this unpleasantness behind us, we shall turn to the auxiliary question.

"Scholar, regarding the brevity of your mother's appearance in the text: Are we to assume her role is peripheral?"

Gorged on sci-fi trilogies, vampire novels, and worse, the Reader expects another FBI profile, that lazy contrivance of modern scribblers. Does he perchance want to subject me to the obtuse instruments of Freudian analysis? And now, absent any details regarding my mother, his analysis is arrested? Dear Reader, your reverence for Freud is most disconcerting. His plagiarism from Schopenhauer is opprobrious. The following comparison has the dual virtues of putting their relationship in its correct perspective and being easily accessible to the common man. The Reader is urged to underline or highlight this illuminating passage and, as soon as he is able, make use of his internet to confirm and study it.

Freud's "originality" compared to Schopenhauer is analogous to Burger King's "originality" compared to McDonald's.

An even darker crime can be laid at the clay feet of Freud. He and mystical doodlers like Jung distracted generations of earnest students from the work of men who deserve emulation. Instead of revering the rigorous scientific approach of Emil Kraepelin and his noble quest to help those truly ill, they have been wheedled by debauched ravings concerning archetypes, anuses, incest, and complexes.

I do not mean to scold, but I simply will not be the subject of any Freudian butchering. My mother's significance vis-à-vis my annals can be summarized -- nay, exhausted -- thus:

1) My mother came outside.

2) She wore a housecoat and slippers.

3) She asked me several questions and made a suggestion.

4) She informed me that dinner would soon be ready.

5) She returned to the house.

6) She informed Sandy of my intentions and shared a misgiving regarding them.

And that is all there is to it. There is nothing to analyze, deconstruct, read into, or fathom here. Intellectual flavors-of-the-day need not apply. A logical mind, instinctively recognizing that no deductions or inferences are possible, moves on.

This is one of the cardinal virtues of an Objective narrative. Given its timeless nature, there is no need to assemble it with rackets and ruses. With the envy of eunuchs and ingenuity fanned by resentment, men incapable of profound insights deny the Objective nature of the written word in the despairing hope of dissuading those who know the Truth and have the courage to write it.

After I make it official, we shall proceed.

I, Petronius Jablonski, hereby forbid any and all Freudian, structural, post-structural, post-post-structural, post-colonial, post-*anything* analysis or deconstruction of my annals and condemn any and all such enterprises. All theorizing based on class, gender, and ethnicity is strictly prohibited.

An Objective narrative is not a Rorschach blot for one to project his pathologies and sundry whines. If the Reader insists on "reading into" the narrative, he should fill the margins with sketches of penises, vaginas, and stick-figures engaged in coitus.

III:
The Journey to the Light at the End of the Tunnel

"Are you hungry, friends?" said the gas station attendant.

Sandy poured a coffee while I examined a pack of Night Light glow-in-the-dark condoms for warnings or liability waivers.

"What do you think, Petronius? Let's eat."

The attendant gazed at the harsh fluorescent lights without blinking or squinting. "Friends, there's a restaurant down the street. It's wonderful. But you'll have to walk to it. There is no other way."

"Permit me to make a conjecture," I said. "Your family owns it."

"No, it's not like that."

"How do we get there?" said Sandy.

"There's a road behind this station," he said, his gentle voice tinged with enthusiasm. "It's closed to traffic but you can walk on it. Keep going until you come to an intersection."

"We cannot drive to it?" I said.

"No. You must take the road. There is no other way." He smiled. "It has everything you need."

"Should we?" said Sandy.

With a nod of my head I permitted my ever-scheming stomach to dethrone Reason.

"You can park your car on the side over there under the light," he said, somehow sensing my reservations. "I'll keep an eye on it."

Had any other stranger suggested that I abandon my car for him to watch I would have laughed in his presumptuous face, but the attendant radiated sincerity and benevolence. The discovery of an altruist, a living counterexample to the truism that men are wolves with manicured claws, disarmed me no less than an encounter with a griffon would have.

Sandy thanked him and I moved my car. Walking past the station, we basked in the warmth of his eyes. At the bottom of a steep hill, a winding snake of flashing lights marked the closed road. The orange serpent slithered into the fog, its precise length unknown.

"He said nothing about a hill," I said.

"He probably forgot. At least the road's lit up. It's probably a little bit past where the barricades come to an end. Let's go. I'm starving."

With arms outstretched for balance, we determined the topography of the ground lurking beneath the soggy grass before committing our feet. At the bottom we hopped over a drainage ditch and onto the freshly paved road, which was safe to walk on but not ready for traffic.

After passing each barricade we quickened our pace, awaiting the next throbbing splash of orange to appear in the static. In hazy increments they became distinct, joining reality as we approached.

We walked until our feet rebelled. I could not remember the attendant discussing a specific distance -- indeed, his endorsement was altogether free of circumstantiates -- but I did not recall him dispatching us on an odyssey. What manner of eatery would be on a road such as this? I wondered. Must all of its clientele abandon their cars and make a pilgrimage?

We peered through veils of gauze for our next beacon as the fog extinguished the last light behind us. We approached something big and dark.

"He said nothing about a tunnel," I said, expecting Sandy to share my conviction that something was fishy.

"So he forgot. When you give someone directions you don't mention every little thing they'll see along the way.

You just tell them as much as they'll need to get there, the important stuff. That's probably the light from the restaurant on the other side. C'mon."

I often marveled at how her tiny stature could harbor such grandiose authority. Dissuading her, though not impossible, frequently represented the path of greatest resistance. My acquiescence to her in matters of irrelevance was therefore no sign of weakness but merely pragmatism.

"Perhaps we can walk around it," I said, appalled at her immoderate indulgence of a stranger's testimony. I wondered if he had been to the restaurant himself. Maybe he was parroting what his enthusiastic manager had said. Maybe both men were links in some rapturous Chinese whisper.

Far steeper than the one we descended earlier, the hill the tunnel bisected would have been impossible to safely traverse. In all likelihood it shielded traffic from falling rocks. "Their coffee better be good," I muttered as Sandy pulled me in and darkness consumed us.

The tunnel's length mocked my initial estimate. The light at the other end looked like a pinprick on a black sheet covering a window. I wondered why the air seemed unnaturally thin and odorless until the inability to inhale smothered my reflections and forced me to gasp for breath. "Let's get out of here," was on the tip of my tongue with nothing to discharge it.

Faced with an imminent collapse, I became cognizant of a structural problem. The tunnel's circumference, initially generous, began to shrink. I could not see the walls, but I felt them constricting while the light at the other end darted away like a firefly. I tried to grab Sandy's hand but nothing below my neck heeded my requests.

My bowels turned to ice as I realized that even if we could turn and run we would never make it out in time. With the tunnel's increase in length proportionate to its decrease in width, we would need to run several times as far to leave. I envisioned the gruesome folly of an escape attempt: scrambling like monkeys, one behind the other with hands pressed against the encroaching sides, then crawling like moles until the concrete crushed our shoulders and the pipe stretched out into a thin tube.

Soon, my forehead will scrape the ceiling, I thought, accepting with noble indifference the asinine role Fate assigned me. Fate, that blue-haired dingbat running a crooked Bingo game. Is there greater outrage than the recognition that the world will continue in your absence just as it did before your birth?

Numb from a lack of oxygen, prepared for an encounter with those remorseful and incompetent creators who erase their work so soon after it is finished, I felt the walls recede until we were crossing a bridge above a black sea beneath a starless sky. The air became so rich that more than a tiny breath induced the delightful giddiness of nitrous oxide.

One might suspect that the terror of being buried alive would promptly be replaced by a new but contrary horror: agoraphobia from the sudden and complete exposure. Such was not the case. Soothing warmth surrounded me as though we were floating through dark water to the light above the surface. A clanking sound, faint at first, became pronounced as we approached.

Unlike the sun, it did not hurt to look upon this light. It felt good in a curious fashion: the way a man feels after reconciling differences with an old friend, or how he feels when he is lost and discovers a sign. Brighter than anything I had seen before, it was of a different genus of illumination. Bereft of adequate descriptions for this extraordinary phenomenon, I can only say it was white, almost clear, and I could feel it as much as I could see it.

Like a lucid dreamer discovering his powers, I clasped Sandy's hand and marveled at the wonderful electricity conducted through her skin. With an understanding bypassing my senses, this simple union communicated more than we ever could with the primitive tools of language. The formidable barriers that make complete communication impossible melted away, dissolved in the purifying bath of the light.

I could not tell if we were running or flying and I did not care. The space in the tunnel rushed past us, increasing to a roar, and the clanking noise thumped like a heartbeat. Everything throbbed in unison and it pulsated through me, sustaining all existence from instant to instant, something I normally took for granted.

An almost lustful yearning to be with the light made even our breakneck speed too slow. It seemed we were no longer moving at all, that it was coming to us, accepting us. I felt consoled, as though returning to my home after a troublesome voyage. The heartbeat changed back to a clanking sound and the light absorbed us. The crude and arbitrary boundaries of words could not map its nature. And there was clanking, clanking, clanking …

The light went out.

Our eyes adjusted to the exiguous glow cast by a lantern in the middle of the road. A decrepit old spotlight stood before us, the kind commonly used for the grand openings of bowling alleys. A spiderweb crack filled the glass and rust grew over the frame like moss covering a trellis. Something stirred behind it. I dropped Sandy's hand and we approached. The air felt cool against my sweaty palm.

A man hoary with age and wretched like some deposed king pounded on a little metal box with a wrench. Wires of many colors sprouted from it, some going into the base of the light, others remaining unattached. He mumbled profanities, completely engrossed in his toil. On the ground behind him stood a bottle of wine, its purple surface quivering with each furious pound. When he finally looked up, our presence took a few moments to register.

"You kids in the tunnel? See the light? Pretty bright, huh?" He smelled like stale milk and the curls in his gray main, sodden with grease, hung limply against his head. "Sellin' it to the contractors fixin' the road. Gotta fix it first. Damn thing goes on but she don't stay on."

He picked up his bottle and took a sip. The lines across his grizzled face looked like greasepaint but they persisted after he wiped the sweat from his forehead with the tattered sleeve of a flannel shirt. His glazed eyes staggered up and down Sandy. With considerable difficulty they found their way to me. He grinned. There were slimy almonds where his teeth should have been. "I know what you were doin' in there. Can I sniff your finger?" He began wheezing and cackling. Sandy stepped back and stood behind me.

I would not normally have bestowed mercy upon such a scurrilous inquisitor, but given the infirmities of this hideous thing I decided to remove Sandy from its noxious presence rather than beat it senseless. As we walked away, an explosive hiccup interrupted the creature's chortling. We listened as it shared its wine with the earth.

Instructed to be on the lookout for visions and to interpret them carefully, I scarcely expected something so crass, so shallow.

"What an awful man," said Sandy.

"Just a mammal like us, ravaged by age and drink," I told her, extending my Stoic tolerance to even the lowliest organism.

"*Hmmm*, ravaged by drink. Maybe there's a lesson."

Maybe you should shut your damn mouth, I thought. (This baffling, irksome phenomenon -- the universal proclivity of the fair sex to deprive man of life's simplest, most decent pleasure -- will be enlarged upon and analyzed in Parts IV and V of my annals.)

"That light made me dizzy," she said.

"It was disorienting."

We approached a distant streetlight and I begged the restaurant to be nearby. A barricade blocked the road at an intersection. Nothing loomed from every direction.

"It's not here," she said. "This is where he said it would be and there's nothing. He lied to us."

"I think he was sincere but mistaken," I said, recalling his demeanor.

"Perhaps that is a species of lying," said Reason. "Is there no little dishonesty involved when giving directions to a place you have never been?"

I sat on the immaculate concrete and sighed. "All this way for nothing. It is enough to make you sick."

Part III:
An Appurtenance

When assessing a portion of a text, even the finest student, entranced with the wondrous realms his reading transports him to, can drop his compass and forget that the best questions are not always the obvious ones. And (depending how "obvious" is defined) that the obvious questions are not always obvious.

How should the Reader excavate practical gems from the theoretical diamond mine in the prior paragraph? Before making an inquiry, *digest* what you have read. This process does not occur of its own dynamism. One needs to be actively involved. To aid the digestion of great writing one must, in addition to reflection and repeated readings, turn to the time-proven methods that facilitate the digestion of great cuisine: fermented beverages and fine tobacco, fugues by Bach, a brisk walk with a hearty dog, an aimless drive in a rectangular sedan. The birth of a penetrating question requires the services of a midwife.

Once the Reader has fortified himself he must ask: What is it I most need to know? Do I need any additional information, or is what I have read so complete unto itself, so self-contained that no further details are required? Was my reading a sumptuous feast, more than sufficient to nourish the tendons and muscles of my mind, or is an additional serving required?

A student plagued with indigestion, one who has failed to recognize the full course of Part III, might fire off a series of "obvious" but needless questions.

"And what occurred on your way back through the tunnel? Did you again encounter the unpleasant spotlight owner? Were words exchanged? How did you find your way through the tunnel in the dark? How did you locate the point where you had to mount the hill to find the station? And regarding the attendant: surely Sandy reprimanded him for his deception. If not, how did you restrain her?"

Enough! Cease and desist, I beg you. Stop pummeling me with questions. Obviously we made it back. Or is the Reader entertaining the possibility that I composed my annals while seated at the deserted intersection? Does he imagine I carved them on the fresh concrete while Sandy communicated with prospective publishers via smoke signals? How on earth would smoke signals have penetrated the fog? Does the Reader think my story ends there, and the remaining pages consist of acknowledgements and appendixes, or that the rest of my story is one very long chapter titled My Day-to-Day Struggles Seated at the Foggy, Deserted Intersection?

Had such particulars been of any magnitude I would, as the humble and obedient servant of Objectivity, included them. Does the Reader doubt my judgment? Perhaps he misconstrued my advice on how to improve his digestion. How many fermented drinks has he consumed?

So that something good may arise from something bad, the answers to the Reader's frivolous inquiries will be the subject of an addendum to this appurtenance. Its spectacular lack of merit will serve as an enduring testament to my judgment.

***

The remainder of this appurtenance concerns an editorial point of intermediate importance. If he was not in any way dissatisfied with the prior paragraph, the Reader should proceed forthwith to the posterior section.

***

While reading the prior paragraph (not including the one immediately prior to this paragraph), the Reader may have expected some lavish reference to "a Phoenix arising from these ashes" rather than the simplistic "good may arise from something bad." The following considerations should assuage his disappointment.

On principle I avoid all references to Egyptian mythology. As clever as they were in covering a desert with giant triangles and gruesome half-cat half-man monstrosities, their obsession with the afterworld was preposterous. How did they expect a mummy to untangle himself once he arrived in the next kingdom? Did not the removal of his vital organs and brain bode ill for his health and vigor? What were those silly people thinking?

As the legend has it, after the Phoenix set its nest afire and burnt itself to a crisp, it was reborn. Why can no modern hack go within a mile of a keyboard without making a reference to it? Verily, it is the true curse of the Pharaohs. That such a story persisted longer than one generation bespeaks the appalling poverty of imagination rampant in Egypt at the time. Worse, it is frighteningly evocative of the Buddhist monks who practiced self-immolation in protest of the Vietnam War.

A conscientious writer will only use a mythic allusion to bring clarity. If there exists even a remote chance of it evoking irritating questions regarding mummies or horrific images of suicides, then he must look to other means to make his point.

Even ignoring the preceding (and utterly damning) objections, it is not clear a Phoenix reference would have been appropriate. I want something good to arise from inferior questions. There is nothing whatsoever in the Phoenix legend about a superior bird arising. It is the same tedious, self-immolating one each and every time.

A question we shall not pursue here is how a bird can set anything on fire. Did it strike a match? Did it rub two rocks together? The Egyptians were aware that birds lack opposable thumbs, were they not? Perhaps they should have spent less time carving gibberish on their gaudy tombs and more time observing the natural world. What manner of brain-disabling deadline did the author of this puerile legend work under? Had the Pharaoh commissioned him to write a new one by the morrow? Or did he compose it after hours in the broiling sun?

In summary: a reference to a Phoenix arising would have been inappropriate, subjected the Reader to needless trauma, quite possibly ruined my otherwise splendid appurtenance, and covered my hands in filth from the crime of perpetuating this cheap, contrived, and all-around deplorable myth.

A Bland and Unnecessary Addendum to the Appurtenance of Part III, Provided at the Reader's Insistence

The puddle of vomit next to the unconscious old man made me think of giant protozoa. The beam from his spotlight now struck the interior wall of the tunnel, illuminating most of the walk for us. I put my hand above Sandy's head to alter the appearance of her shadow.

"Knock it off."

"It would have behooved us to ignore that deluded attendant," I said. "Look at the time and energy we wasted."

"How *behooving* it would have been. It would have been the *behoovingest* thing we ever did," she said, succumbing to a sudden downpour from one of the sporadic thunderclouds typifying her internal weather.

"It would behoove you not to mock. The word used felicitously."

"Would it *behoove* me felicitously, or felicitously *behoove* me? Why can't you talk like a regular person? Do you think it makes you better than others?"

"You are mistaking the effect for the cause."

"Because it doesn't."

"All hail the common denominator, all hail," I said, waving my hands over my head. The shadow cast on the tunnel wall looked like a giant bat. "Bach, Beethoven, Bruckner, hip-hob, breaking wind to the tune of 'Dueling Banjos' – it is all good. How arrogant of me to imply that anything is superior to anything else. All ye unwashed, rap-listening, reality-TV-viewing masses: fear not, bathe not. Come, join us in the parlor for a belching competition. Have you not heard? A revolution has occurred. There is no high or low culture. We are all one. My elitist scorn is naught but petty judgment, certainly not righteous indignation against Vandals ransacking the remains of a once glorious culture."

"It's snootiness, that's all."

"Clearly you were not home-schooled by my father. Condolences. Taking pride in the mastery of one's native tongue, using it like a violin rather than a hand under an armpit, is not arrogance. Rather, it is the pursuit and joyous acquisition of excellence. Deciding that one word is more felicitous than another is no more arrogant than deciding that a New York strip is superior to a plate of cockroaches. Who shall help me defend civilization from the barbarians? I shall not surrender. Like the great army at Masada I would sooner die by my own sword than …"

I continued my excellent discourse throughout our walk. This oxymoronic counter-"culture" has spread like gonorrhea at a naval port and it is high time a true philosopher armed with rhetorical penicillin cured it. My discourse soon became a soliloquy, as Sandy was wont to tune out ideas she found disagreeable. (This particular theme had, on other occasions, been condemned as "old fogeyish.")

My concern that we would be unable to locate the spot where we needed to surmount the hill proved to be unfounded, a child of panic. As we approached the top I took deep breaths, afraid of what mayhem would ensue if any harm had befallen my car. Though Aristotle taught that for a punishment to be just it must be proportionate to the crime, I had logistical reservations about nailing the attendant to a tree.

Aglow beneath the votive light, it appeared unharmed. Sandy stormed into the station. "You asshole," was all I heard before the door closed behind her. I walked to my car and inspected it. With the weight of the earth leaving my back, I enjoyed the symphony of crickets while emptying my bladder.

Sandy slammed the station door and walked outside. She pounded on the glass and displayed a universal gesture with both hands. The attendant's face glowed with compassion. His eyes were windows into a world of absolute stasis. He smiled.

Contrary to my expectation, to the extent that I invested any thought at all in the matter, she chose the longer of two possible routes to arrive at the passenger's door, thereby ensuring a walk through the fresh and far from negligible pool of urine.

"What the hell."

"You will have to take your shoes off and store them in the trunk, I am afraid."

"Why couldn't you go over there?"

"Am I psychic? Do I know what path you will take? Please remove them. What did the attendant say?"

"Petronius, this'll kill you. He says he's never been there but some friend he trusts told him all about it. What an idiot."

"Could you perhaps purchase a new pair? I am not sure I want them in my trunk in their present condition."

In a gruesome exhibition of unladylike behavior, she cussed repeatedly, misdirecting her anger toward me as unenlightened persons are wont to do. Rather than embrace all that happens as thread spun from the spool of Fate, they fulminate against fellow non-combatants. She searched her backpack and tore several pages from a magazine that consisted entirely of advertisements for cosmetics. Under my supervision she carefully wrapped each shoe. As we drove out of the station she used one of Freud's eye-crossingly inane theories to accuse me of being inordinately concerned with my car. By means of a dialogue, I attempted to demonstrate that the quest for cleanliness and order in a world of chaos and filth has nothing to do with a man's anus.

***

The remainder of this bland and unnecessary addendum to the appurtenance concerns an editorial point of minor importance. If he was not in any way dissatisfied with the reference to the army at Masada, the Reader should proceed forthwith to the next section.

***

The Reader, if he read the bland and unnecessary addendum to the appurtenance in a doctrinaire cast of mind, may have objected to my comparing myself to both the Romans fighting against the barbarians *and* the Jewish army fighting against the Romans. There are two main schools of thought concerning mixed metaphors. *Classicists*, such as myself, consider a mixed metaphor to be as venomous and bulky as a poorly mixed drink. On the other hand, English-sacking Huns (or *pragmatists*) believe the evolution of language leaves us with only one criterion when judging mixed-metaphor cocktails: the proof is in the pudding.

"But how can you possibly reconcile your laudable stance with your egregious metaphor?" the incredulous Reader demands.

The Reader has to remember that we classicists are not unrelenting tyrants. Indulgences are granted when circumstances warrant them. My reference to Masada did not occur in the ambrosial peace of my study with a snifter of cognac in hand and Zeus curled up next to my oak desk. It occurred in a dark tunnel next to Sandy in the throes of one of her spells. Under the circumstances, I believe my discourse was more than satisfactory. Its ardency more than compensated for what it lacked in consistency. Would the Reader have behaved differently, perhaps composing and whistling a rondo? I thought not.

The identification and critique of mixed metaphors is a worthy pursuit. (And I hereby challenge the Reader to find another in my annals.) But it must be tempered with an examination of the conditions under which they arose. If the conditions were severe, clemency must be granted.

A Supplement to the Bland and Unnecessary Addendum to the Appurtenance to Part III

Does the Reader feel edified? Is his life now complete? Has the knowledge that Part III ultimately ended with Sandy walking through a puddle of pee and accusing me of being "anal-retentive" transformed him? I insist that he place a separate bookmark in the previous section. As often as he questions my judgment he may turn to it and remind himself that initially I chose not to include those inconsequential factoids.

And did the rigors of my Socratic dialogue disabuse Sandy of her psychological theory? (I assume the ever-consistent Reader insists on "closure" here. No doubt an inquiry concerning her shoes is next.) In the topsy-turvy world she inhabits, the rational extirpation of fatuous theories is becoming impossible. If only Freud were the worst of her mentors. The trend of late is the denigration of History and Reason, with wariness fertilized by the manure of multiculturalism. How on earth does the merit of an idea, practice, or work of art have anything to do with its origin? Culture should be defined as the greatest things that man has created and done and thought and dreamed. Those obsessed with subdivisions missed their calling in set theory or classifying beetles. (Do they pine for the days of "German science," I wonder.)

"But scholar," the Reader pleads, "doesn't the scant contribution from Greece, Rome, Europe, and North America warrant the unbounded attention lavished on the other major players?"

Dear, sheltered Reader, multiculturalism erroneously assumes -- nay, demands at gunpoint -- the ludicrous notion of equality between groups. (In the absence of cloning, no two humans are equal. How could groups be?) Before any group may bask in the illustrious torch of History, it must contribute something of value to humanity. Contrary to contemporary "historians," most merit little more than a footnote for being plundered. Victims are not heroes, and history is not a sanctuary for ne'er-do-wells. Multiculturalism is analogous to the Special Olympics where prizes are bestowed upon all.

We once took a vapid class to satisfy the benighted diversity requirement -- as though exposure to "the greatest things that man has created and done and thought and dreamed" would not, of its own dynamism, erase all parochialisms. Surrounded by students deprived of Homer and Horace in favor of cryptic gobbledygook, I succumbed to labor pains of exasperation and birthed the following revision: when Dorothy, the Scarecrow, Tin Woodsman, and Cowardly Lion discovered that the much-ballyhooed Wizard was a fraud, they should have castrated him with the Woodsman's axe. That is how I would have ended the novel, sending an unequivocal warning to all charlatans seeking power. Then the Lion, crazed from the scent of blood, would tear the Wizard to shreds. Dorothy would grab his head, walk outside the castle and hold it high, proclaiming, "Sic semper charlatans." This delightful vision was my only solace during the gloomy nights when I endured the grandiose, multicultural babbling of Professor Oz.

IV:
I Find Myself in a Tavern, Fail to Initiate Two Sprites, Dream My Second Dream, and Suffer a Ghastly Dizzy-Spell

My sobriety had abandoned me. I sat with my back to the bar looking at an empty lot beyond a quiet street. Normally I deemed a big window in a tavern to be analogous to a horseshoe mounted on a wall with its prongs pointing down: it lets all the magic seep out. But this view filled me with thoughts, as though they had been waiting and would not have found me elsewhere.

After a delightfully digressive telephone conversation with my mother wherein I became *au courant* with the latest adventures of Zeus, I studied the field from my stool while the sun slid down the sky. My ghost joined me at twilight, staring back from the window, more vivid than the vacant lot but not as interesting. The barkeep's ghost joined him and together they watched us.

"Someday all the grass will look like this," the barkeep said. "When there's no one round to cut it, it'll just grow and grow, all long and messy."

"Please do not feel that you are in any way obliged to regale me with quaint colloquialisms or synopses of your *Farmer's Almanac*," I said. Earlier, the brash and dour lout interrupted my telephone conversation during a particularly enchanting anecdote to remind me that I had been using his phone for over an hour.

"All long and messy," he said. "No one to cut it. Doesn't that bother you?"

To what galaxy must a man travel to enjoy his own company? I turned around and braced my elbows on the bar and my feet on the rail. "Very well, would you prefer a discourse pertaining to sports or the weather?"

"You like a stool with a view."

"Not generally."

"Don't let me disturb you," he said and took a sip of red slush that reeked of strawberries. His eyes, white lights in dark craters, bounced between the window and me. The tributaries surrounding them suggested that he perceived the world with reckless humor. Short black hair stood straight up in places and lay matted in others, as though Lilliputian and misguided aliens had inscribed a crop circle on his head. The red ring around his mouth conspired with his raccoon eyes to give him the lineaments of a macabre clown.

Visions of Zeus emigrated to accommodate expansive but enigmatic thoughts conducted by the empty field in the key of the Petronius Sensation: reflections slipping through the stubby fingers of language despite the itching allure of their existence. Though strongly tempted to deny and ignore the indescribable, I could not turn them away.

"It is too dark in any event. The view is ruined," I said, slurring my thoughts, each bleeding into others like the colors on a slick of oil, few remaining distinct long enough to name. One notable exception was the concern of suffering from a dizzy-spell. A marathon bout of abstinence had wreaked havoc on my health, my legendary tolerance in particular. The possibility that my thoughts might soon be lost forever, buried in a landfill of cocktail napkins and swizzle sticks, instilled a most peculiar trepidation.

"If the sun never again rises on these reflections, they might as well not be here now," Reason blurted. "What is the difference?"

My preemptive summation involved the necessity of seizing the moment. After all, a dizzy-spell is a paltry debt when measured against the immeasurable boons of so wondrous an elixir.

The barkeep watched me think about the precarious nature of thinking. "From around here?" he said, leaning on the bar with his beefy arms. His breath emblazoned a strawberry on the oil slick. Oleaginous eddies annexed its borders and morphed it into hundreds of dark eyes peering from a red cloud.

"Passing through," I said.

"You and your better half?"

I nodded. Sandy's face, contorted in a furious scowl, flashed atop the puddle. Her flesh became red from the barkeep's breath, then dark green as she transmuted into a dragon before dissipating into a field of grass. I prayed she would be sound asleep when I returned to our motel room.

"Where you headed?" he asked.

An orange rectangle and a blue rectangle appeared against a dark background. They collided and bounced away undiminished, each striking invisible boundaries and caroming again and again with trajectories predictable in principle but not in actuality.

"Enjoying the scenery," I said.

"Not *all* the scenery, I hope. Aren't some sights more important than others?"

It felt as though the thoughts in the field behind me had accumulated and I could not possibly attend to them all. Since most men spend their lives fleeing their ideas, perhaps others are obliged to contend with them. This responsibility often made me thirsty. I studied a tiny glass containing a brown potion. The sight would have sent Ovid running home for his pen. Reflecting on the greatness of Epicurus, I flicked my wrist and it vanished, warming my face and body like a mouthful of liquid sun. I basked in the warmth like a lizard on a rock until the door opened and everything changed.

The petite twins had brown skin and curly blond hair. A green dress and a blue dress tightly wrapped wonderful things. At the behest of an instinct honed and perfected long before elaborate gizmos like consciousness were even a twinkle in Mother Nature's eye, I followed them to the other side of the bar and negotiated a stool between them. The barkeep stood before us, scowling at me. His crossed arms formed a barrier between the lesser bulge of his chest and the massive monument to Bacchus below.

"This is how a book must feel," I told him with a wink. "Drinks for everyone."

The green sprite touched my forearm and smiled. "We have been spoken for."

"You most certainly have, and I am the luckiest man alive," I said, returning the caress. One type of Ovidian musing supplanted another: all metamorphoses solidified into the granite conviction that the redundant nature of this conquest would in no way detract from it.

The blue sprite put her purse on the bar and turned to me. "Speaking of books, there's one you have to read. It's at a book party."

My head, suspended by their heavenly scent, hovered far above my shoulders until I moored it with a cigarette. "Book? Are you familiar with *Gargantua*?" I said, confident my double entendre could scarcely fail to amuse a lady with literary inclinations. "How thoughtless of me. I should show you rather than tell you."

The barkeep brought two glasses of water and another of the brown elixir. "Don't forget to read it," the green sprite whispered, her lips touching my ear. I inhaled my shot and turned to her and a gelatinous strawberry lagoon shimmered in the moonlight. A zebra approached the edge and stood beneath a palm tree. In the distance a police siren howled. The zebra, his stripes blurred by a neon moon, looked left and right before lowering his head and slurping up the sticky jelly, globs of which dripped off his snout. As he entered the lagoon, the wind picked up, rustling leaves and creating waves. Tires squealed in the distance. After paddling halfway across he stopped, ensnared by something lurking below. The rising jelly splashed against his head and he brayed, "Help me you coward. No one is seeing this but you." The struggle made a *sloshing* sound, which soon muzzled his denunciations as the lagoon consumed him. All I could smell was strawberries.

I sat up in the dark, scared and confused. *Why did I not do something? I could have saved him.* These concerns receded as a more pressing terror barged into the foreground: Where am I?

I was in a motel room. A beam of light dissected the drapes, erecting a paper-thin wall of gold mist. Sandy slept beside me, her snores as unique as fingerprints. I composed a hymn to the Persistence of Memory. I addressed a prayer, "To whom it may concern, please, no dizzy-spells." And I undertook the arduous archaeological excavation of unearthing the previous evening, brazenly beginning with the question of how poor Odysseus made it home.

I caressed my temples and raced down the streets of the prior night with no steering wheel or brakes and a peephole for a windshield, careening off things I could not discern and never stopping long enough to permit a reconstruction. I should have started with a less ambitious question: Under what circumstances did Odysseus leave his home?

My thought process, normally analogous to a crystal temple where irrationality withers from the radiance of Reason like moss in the sun, resembled a swamp crowded with haphazardly situated funhouse mirrors. As often as a recollection flashed behind a dense patch of foliage, I splashed after it and lost it amidst teeming vines and vertiginous reflections.

My survival instinct chimed, "Shower, coffee, breakfast, swim, sun, perhaps a revitalizing elixir -- No! We must return to the road as soon as possible."

This improvident desire evinced mathematical certainty that I had suffered a dizzy-spell. Assuming the continuity of the self (which Buddhists deny, perhaps correctly, though for the sake of narrative cohesion it shall be granted asylum in my annals), a dizzy-spell has six primary effects, eleven secondary. In addition to the ravages withstood by the recollective faculty, the prioritizing faculty undergoes states of discombobulation. At times it is as though a change of command has occurred: an emperor was poisoned at dinner and his successor has drastically different plans for the empire. In extreme cases, one could just as well have a Siamese twin afflicted by chronic flatulence and Tourette's syndrome. Some mornings, graciously sparse, it is akin to being conjoined to a huge tarantula when one is deathly afraid of spiders.

I stood. The change in altitude popped my ears and churned my stomach. Shallow breaths forestalled fainting. Using four packets instead of one, I prepared a formidable brew in the coffee machine next to the sink. By bending over to remove my shoes, I provoked the anaconda coiled around my head to constrict, which splattered the white tiles with gray soup. I found my way back to an upright position and resolved to proceed with greater vigilance.

Keeping my head and neck perpendicular to the earth, I disrobed and examined my body for bruises and other clues about the ancient past (a good archaeologist always checks his knuckles first). Reaching for the shampoo, I unwittingly knocked it on its side. The translucent gel oozed down the wall to the floor of the tub where it came in contact with the water and generated a multitude of bubbles. They persisted for a moment before disappearing down the drain. Generations formed and perished. Though labyrinthine passages characterized their brief existence, their destiny remained fixed and remorseless. I watched the absurd little procession until it ceased. I do not know why. After seeing it once I extracted what little essence the insipid phenomenon contained. Based upon studies in physiology, I suspect my sensitive condition augmented my perception, calling my credulous attention to stupid and monotonous details.

I dressed, inspected the tar-like consistency of my ferocious distillation, located my Ovals, and tiptoed to the balcony with wistful dreams of exhuming the previous evening without any prompting from Sandy. Like many of her fragile gender, she did not comprehend the hearty and rambunctious training a man requires to vivify his being. This was not her fault, as she saw only the coarsest by-products and not the inestimable blessings.

The chlorine from the pool below, redolent of idleness, bathed me in wonderful memories, a cascade of bikinis and martinis. Beneath the warmth of the sun I read the depth markings and shuddered upon realizing it was not even open yet. "Impossible. I have been awake for aeons," I cried.

I lit an Oval, leaned on the rail, and tried to resuscitate my memory: I sat with my back to the bar, looking out a large window at an empty lot beyond a quiet street -- that much was clear. Wild grass and an ogre-like creature reverberated around the funhouse mirrors, evading a persistent view. *Someday all of the grass will look like this, all long and messy.*

After days of backbreaking toil, digging through ruins without finding any noteworthy artifacts, I summarized my excavation thus: consign it to the underworld. After all, what is the difference between what has happened and what never happened? At first there is a superficial discrepancy, which historians strive to clarify. But as the days flow past it becomes less and less clear. The difference starts to fade. Eventually it is bleached clean. With repeated washings the fabric itself disintegrates until there remains no difference at all. Besides, I will never return to that tavern.

Satisfied with my findings, despite their uncanny similarity to other excavations of this sort, I sipped my coffee and stared at the cloudless sky, perplexed by its misleading appearance of proximity. Looking over a cliff fills a man with dreadful insecurity, a fear of falling, but when looking at the sky he feels calm, as though he can only find succor from the sight of his essence, which is not the substance of earth but the nothingness of space. "Between now and the drain, what to do?" I said. After a wave of vertigo, I fixed an uneasy gaze at the endless blue. "Just swish around for awhile."

The door slid open and Sandy stepped onto the balcony wearing a baseball jersey that revealed legs muscular and long relative to her height. Hair veiled half her face. The other side twitched in silent contention that regarding the previous evening there was indeed a difference between what had happened and what never happened. Like a condemned man with amnesia, I stood at the gallows and waited for a list of crimes to be read before the trapdoor opened.

"So when did you come in last night," she said quietly, trying to disguise and delay the impending explosion.

She was testing for echoes, trying to determine if I had suffered a dizzy-spell. Once she determined this, she could exaggerate (or even embellish) details until her malevolent little heart was content. By means of evasions and ambiguities, I hoped to conceal that my comprehension of the previous evening was characterized by anything other than clarity and self-assurance. "I do not recall looking at a clock. You were quite exhausted when I left."

"When did you slink away?"

"I did not *slink away*. I wanted to enjoy an invigorating drink while I listened to the latest adventures of Zeus. I then wanted to enjoy a drink or three while savoring the news, the way a man relishes an enjoyable story he has read."

"The way a man relishes his little bookends!" she screamed and began crying. "*You,* you asked me if your little bookends could come back to the room with us, so they could see *Gargantua.* But let me guess, let me fucking guess: you don't remember."

"I spoke of literature. It is Rabelais' masterwork," I said, receiving what felt like a snap from a towel behind my eyes and a flash of blue little blond and green little blond. Another snap consoled me: thank the gods they did not return with us; to forget such a tryst would be beyond tragic.

"It sounds as though I fell victim to a dizzy-spell," I conceded thoughtfully. "A man can scarcely be faulted for his reflex-like actions and words when helplessly in the throes of one."

"They're called blackouts. You introduced me as your spicy little egg roll. I've never, *never* been so humiliated."

"You certainly have," I said, thinking quickly but not clearly. "At your sister's birthday party, at the Christmas party in your dorm. These girls were strangers, mere bar wenches. Who cares what they think?" But at this she burst into sobs and left the balcony.

I peered down into the cloudless, almost blue sky, a little queasy, but transfixed by the view.

The Anticipation and Refutation of an Utterly Incorrect Objection to Part IV

We strive to harness our thoughts so they resemble the linear clarity of the written word. Concise segmentation is a presupposition of rationality. We toil with the futility of Sisyphus, however, to reproduce the chaotic bric-a-brac of our inner lives by these same means. An asymmetric relationship exists between them. Consciousness is, beyond certainty, the most inexplicable phenomenon in all of existence. Just as the essence of Rachmaninoff's piano concertos cannot be captured with oil paintings, the ineffable nature of consciousness eludes transcription to markings on paper.

If only this asymmetry had served as a deterrent, a grim sentinel barring entrance to all. Instead, it has inspired waves of scribblers. The history of the written word is as checkered and stained as a tablecloth at an Italian wedding, but the darkest blotch by far is the reviled literary technique known as stream-of-consciousness writing, where normal rules are dispensed with to provide the reader with an allegedly perfect view of a character's inner world. That this migraine-inducing stunt has been attempted is not surprising. To a modest extent, most writing hopes to frame images from that strange land within. What is objectionable can be divided into eight parts, the most serious of which is the Reader's accusation that I employed the notorious gimcrack in Part IV.

First of all, *stream*-of-consciousness is a misnomer based on a stillborn metaphor. It is far from clear what, if anything, consciousness can be likened to, but a stream is preposterous at best. The non-linear, too-many-things-happening-at-once nature of it slays this metaphor in its cradle. Cleary, an overwrought writer coined the phrase, not a philosopher.

The phenomenon could more accurately be compared to an exotic growth that arises under special biologic conditions, a mushroom for example. Now, *mushroom*-of-consciousness has the dual virtues of accuracy and prophylaxis: no writer, no matter how unbounded his ambition, would inflict on us a novel based on a mushroom-of-consciousness technique.

Another metaphor submitted for the Reader's contemplation: consciousness is a chaotic gaggle of geese. They rarely fly in unison. Some fly north as others go south. Their characteristic feature is a perpetual state of commotion, not unity or linearity. Indeed, the only sense in which they are an undivided unit is conceptual. It is convenient for us to speak of them as a single entity, just as it is convenient for us to speak of "consciousness" rather than the motley flock of ideas, sensations, memories, and all manner of what-nots perpetually fluttering about inside our heads.

Second, we are inclined to believe that our language mirrors our thoughts, from which it appears to follow that language can paint accurate pictures of them. In fact, it is the latter that occasionally mirrors the former, simply because we are often forced to think according to its rules. This does not work in both directions. Thoughts are lawless gangsters roaming a wild frontier, behaving themselves only when the sheriff is nearby.

Does this explain the pretension of forgoing the rules of language to unveil the nature of consciousness, its very mirror image, page by page? Nay, a realistic account goes as follows. Twentieth century writers, unable to compete with their betters from the eighteenth century, resorted to all manner of shenanigans. Their rationale was simple: in lieu of a good book, stupefy the reader, confound and disorient him, induce in him a profound sense of his own stupidity and unworthiness and he will be unable to stand in judgment of your masterpiece. After all, not understanding something is an admission of ignorance. Contrariwise, through feigned understanding and enjoyment of inscrutable tomes one joins the esoteric enclave of the cognoscenti.

One reason we turn to great writing is to free ourselves, however fleetingly, from the burden of consciousness with its peculiarities and uncertainties. A good book offers us a glimpse of a fabled world where effects can be traced to causes, conclusions follow from premises, complex situations have a unifying meaning, and a moral can be derived from any bundle of circumstances. Now why would a man pick up a book whose contents are more incomprehensible and higgledy-piggeldy than consciousness is in the first place?

The Reader's accusation that I used the abhorrent gimmick in Part IV shall not stand. What need have I of experimental techniques? The following formula is the only one my purely Objective narrative follows: 1) X happened. 2) I write that X happened.

Regarding the passage in question: one moment I spoke with a set of comely twins, hoping to initiate an act of libidinous redundancy with them. The next moment I dreamt of a zebra drowning in a lagoon of jelly. Then I awoke beside Sandy. How much more clearly, how much more *objectively* could this have been conveyed? Would the Reader prefer a timeline, a flowchart perhaps? If he wishes, he may return to the sequence that so befuddled him and number (with different colored crayons) the events one, two, and three respectively.

Regarding other parlor-tricks the Reader suspects I foisted upon him: the oil-slick simile provided a consummate description of intoxication. If the Reader has a superior one he should send it to my publisher and we will incorporate it in the next printing. I shall not hold my breath.

And the hyperbole used to describe my dizzy-spell? Given its ferocity I am scarcely convinced my description was exaggerated. Instead of brandishing baseless accusations, the Reader should take comfort in my principled refusal to stain my hands with any modern ruses. Imagine every thought expressed throughout my annals appearing and dissolving, just to make the sophomoric point that consciousness *per se* is an oily puddle. Clearly some gratitude is in order.

To diagnose the cause of the Reader's inappropriate attribution, we need look no further than the septic standards of contemporary writing. Lobotomized by intellectual lacerations from an onslaught of pulp regarding lawyers, serial killers, wizards n' witches, family sagas, and celebrities, the Reader became unduly dazzled when confronted with the scintillating, but not experimental, prose of Part IV. All is forgiven, dear Reader. And what an excellent lesson has been learned. The freak shows of modern books cannot compete with the Big Top of Truth.

V:
I Introduce My General Potation Theory and Petronius' Third and Fourth Sensations, Attain Oneness with My Fleetwood, Compose a Hymn to Aristotle while Sandy Constructs a Bridge, Behold a Town of Ghosts, and Begin Composing My Magnificent Annals

Like some mad captain obsessed with hunting a chameleonic sea serpent, I took the helm all afternoon and chased the highway. The salty spume from hangover waves stung my eyes and the sirens' call of rest areas sang to me. After dinner, a nap generated a vibrancy I would not have felt had I not irrigated myself the previous evening. Imbibing polishes the marble halls of a man's mind, but until it dries he cannot see the shine. As the ambitious playwright, Sophocles, once said, a man must wait until late in the afternoon before he can determine how splendid the previous evening has been.

Seeing how he took no credit for the ascertainment of this phenomenon and, in any event, did not connect it to the consumption of fermented beverages, I humbly submit my maiden discovery in psychology: Petronius' General Potation Theory. (The requisite justification of counterfactual analysis will be provided later when it will not delay the Reader's fantastic journey.) This is distinct from my Special Potation Theory, which shall be submitted in due time. Both illume heretofore ignored boons of a much-maligned elixir.

In grateful possession of the necessary preconditions for night driving, an exacting blend of tranquility and diligence, I longed for an interstate to Alpha Centauri. My car, the Taj Mahal with an orange glaze and hovercraft engine, glided along with the windows down. Atop the side mirror perched my hand, slicing through the warm butter of air resistance. Sandy hung her bare feet out the window, resting her head on the armrest.

The assurance of steady progress soothed our journey's colicky infancy. Once a man begins a grave undertaking some of the urgency dissipates. He can savor the rapture of completeness: nothing more is necessary or even possible for the acquisition of his goal. Though many throughout history have experienced this sensation, shamefully no one has named it. I hereby christen it the Third Petronius Sensation.

Upon conquering the globe, Alexander expressed sorrow. He had no further frontiers to tame. He had deprived himself of ever again tasting the bliss of the Third Petronius Sensation. Commonly it is assumed a man's greatest joy is the attainment of his heart's desire. This is folly. Satiety is a glacier that leaves a chasm of yearning in its wake. On life's many journeys it is not the arrival that thrills us: we wait in line to check in, discover our room overlooks a gas station and the bar doesn't sell carry-outs, learn our girlfriend "just wants to cuddle." Nay, the joy is the journey. How regrettable that such insights cannot be perceived without hindsight, thus sparing a man from commitments to dead-ended paths, permitting him instead to pursue the mastery of fly fishing or any quest approaching its kingdom via an asymptotic curve.

***

The elegant lane shifts of my Fleetwood, the Renaissance curls of its turns, even its smooth course down a straightaway, were these not calligraphy flowing across the pages of the road, composing poetry that could make the hardest man weep? Though it hurled through space at 120 miles-per-hour, I experienced it not as motion but the exaltation of surfing a tsunami in a luxury liner. As my toe brushed the landmine gas-pedal, the ravenous hood devoured the road and the distinction between us blurred. "I" became the rational faculty of a mythic being: half car, half man.

As if mocking the distinction between transcendence and immanence, the soul of this latter-day satyr neither existed apart from us nor was it pantheistic. Though the product of a synergy, it could not be equated with any sum. When the dichotomy between my car and I collapsed, when we attained oneness, our coalescence became irreducible like an elementary chemical. Any insinuation of my cognizance of this unity would be fraudulent. Something infinitely greater than man's powers of reckoning absorbed me. More cannot be said. Some experiences (per the First Petronius Sensation) cannot be contained in the cheap Tupperware of language. You cannot take a shining star from the heavens and place it in a meatloaf dish.

***

Sandy awoke at dawn and took the first tentative steps toward building a bridge across the awkward distance between us. "We need to talk," she said. The declamation resounded like a seventh trumpet, a certain augury of "lightning, rumblings, peals of thunder, an earthquake and a great hailstorm." In fact, *she* needed to talk while I occasionally nodded my head in thoughtful agreement.

Reduced to its elements, the reconciliation ritual is a matter of forbearance during the verbal stage. After enduring it unscathed, a man may savor the remainder of the ceremony, which is blissfully free of verbiage. As that clever but overrated poet observed, "Love quarrels oft in pleasing concord end." Pleasing concord indeed.

I fixed Sandy with repentant grimaces. She chose her words with a circumspection necessitating frequent pauses, giving me ample time to retreat my eyes to the dash whenever they met hers for more than an instant. No doubt she had been rehearsing since we left the motel. The harsh taskmaster of experience had long since demonstrated to me the strategic superiority of silence in these situations.

My unspoken defense stood upon the eternal pillars of physiology, biology, metaphysics, and moral philosophy: a man lost in the throes of a dizzy-spell cannot be held morally culpable for his words and deeds. He is as blameless as a man whose actions were caused by the winds of a tornado. But Sandy, impervious to Reason, would only become inflamed at this. Like most people incapable of distinguishing an excuse from an explanation, she condemned any list of causes with the incoherent epithet "rationalizing." Not languid in my silence, I composed a hymn to Aristotle:

O Great One, how far we have fallen in our headlong race from Truth. You taught us "... as regards the sexes, the male is by nature superior and the female inferior, the male ruler and the female subject. And the same must necessarily apply to all mankind." Oh Master, in the dreadful night of the present era I cannot, on pain of death, even repeat your wise teachings aloud. How shall we return? Who will show us the way? Anoint me, o Great One, and I shall lead *man*kind back to --

"I never intend to hurt you," I said instinctively, my paean interrupted by a long pause from Sandy.

"But you always do. And you words words words words words words words words words words words words words words ..."

She constructed the bridge in earnest. As with countless scourges endured before, the fortification of Stoicism (modified by my innovatory Blender) sheltered me. During her meandering diatribes -- critical of fermented drinks, the consumption of meat, the appreciation of music composed before 1900, polygamy, and the gods only know what else -- my eyes remained sad and thoughtful, my hand stroked my chin, and my mind freed itself with meditations on the miraculous fine-tuning of our universe described by cosmologists. Of all the ones that could have formed, in only an atomistic percentage of them would intelligent life have evolved.

(Willfully ignorant or congenitally obtuse, atheists overlook the mystical proportions of this. As a crystalline reformulation of the Anthropic Principle, in order to fill even the most hardened Skeptics with awe at the ingenious and philanthropic nature of the gods, I suggest the substitution of 'intelligent life' with 'sensate beings capable of enjoying fellatio and cunnilingus.' Verily, it will inspire all unbelievers to run outside and carve a graven image. O miracle most divine, what were your odds?)

We drove past a billboard that portrayed a sports celebrity with a caption bubble next to his head. Watching Sandy's mouth, I imagined the words floating out in little plastic letters. As they stretched over the hood and beyond the horizon, I wondered how long the line of them would be by the end of the day, how many miles. This whimsical inquiry may have had its place under different circumstances: pillow talk, for example. But raising the question aloud would have had devastating repercussions for the next stage of the reconciliation ritual, in all likelihood precluding it altogether.

I pondered how long a man's word-line would grow in his lifetime. If every utterance from "mama" to "Rosebud" were written in a straight line of refrigerator magnets, how long would it be? A thousand miles? A million? What difference would it make? From even a short distance it would be indistinguishable from one consisting of cigar bands and pop-tops. If anything, the latter would be aesthetically preferable. But all our words are not preserved,

I thought, bringing this amusing daydream in for a landing. What becomes of them?

The deluge of Sandy's letters suddenly stopped. Her eyes, concerned and earnest, met mine, signifying it was the part of the ritual where I had to add a few cigar bands and pop-tops to my line.

"I apologize for putting myself in situations where I lose control," I said, looking to my hood ornament for inspiration. "I assume responsibility for the initial decision."

Sandy kissed me on the cheek, concrete flowed under the car, and the earth turned to face the sun. We drove all morning until seeing a sign that said, "Township of All - Five Miles," when we agreed it would be a good time for brunch.

***

On sun-scorched pavement we meandered from store to store. "This one looks interesting," said Sandy. The dilapidated exterior concealed a cavernous depth. Rows of shelves displayed refuse not connected by any unifying theme except that the previous owners had quite understandably abandoned it, and the junkyard, with good reason, would not accept it either. She stopped to inspect a crystal ball.

"Be on the lookout for a monkey's paw," I told her before wandering off on my own. In the back of the shop I discovered actual antiques. Mounted on the wall were the head of a warthog and a swordfish. Between them stood a tatty mannequin of an old witch. I visualized how splendidly the head would adorn my study, how my comrades, even if not convinced I felled the beast, would nonetheless affirm its fierce grandeur. I then visualized the bridge Sandy had just constructed, what it led to, and saw it engulfed in flames as she watched in abhorrence while I struggled out to the car with my trophy.

"Can I help you?" said one of the antiques, launching me a foot off the ground. "Are you looking for anything special?"

My flight instinct made a rare appearance until I realized the witch was alive, human even. "Browsing," I said. "Are any of your treasured relics exalted above the others?"

"I'm so glad you asked." She burrowed through a pile of junk while I contemplated the tortile nature of the tusks. She handed me a pair of horn-rimmed glasses with absurdly thick lenses. "These are very special. You'll like them."

"I put these on and I can see what people look like without their clothes, right?" I said, insulted by the offer of a child's toy.

She cackled hideously. "They're more special than that. They make you see things more clearly, much, much more clearly. Go for a little walk. They work best outside."

In case they did enhance my ocular powers I waited until I was a safe distance from her. I walked through the cluttered rows and found Sandy still examining the crystal ball. She held it inches from her face, rotating it slowly, inspecting something preserved in the center. I went outside, slipped the glasses on, and turned my head every which way to initiate their effect. Stepping off the curb I sensed something huge moving above me. I covered my head and watched the sun zoom toward the horizon. It rose in seconds and soared across the sky and set again.

By the time I made it to the end of the block it must have flown past fifty times. Perhaps I will purchase these, I thought. I knew that Sandy, an aficionado of psychedelic phenomenon, would be quite taken with them.

Two men seated in front of a barbershop played chess, paying no heed to my approach or the sun's newfound velocity. When one of them reached to move a piece, I saw the board through his arm. I bent over to engage in a more circumspect analysis and confirmed that both were ghosts.

Stepping back, I shook my head and looked down the street. It seemed as though a deranged stage hand was flicking a blinding light in an amphitheatre. (On account of a misguided dig with my Shovel, I considered the sun's activity as "stranger" than the presence of ghosts. An important lesson arises from my error: it is not enough to be equipped with a mighty tool; one must know how to use it.)

I studied the complex endgame position: White had a king on d2, a pawn on d4, and a bishop on e5. Black had a king on d7, a pawn on d5, and a bishop on e4. The ghost-man playing the white pieces pulled at his thick silver mustache. Rage and longing filled his eyes. His hand trembled over his king. He vanished and another ghost-man, young and smiling, replaced him and confidently slammed the piece down. Likewise, his opponent changed with no disruption to the flight of the bishop. The successor completed the move and in a flicker of the sun another replaced him, this time a ghost-girl.

Ignoring the absurdly ephemeral players who scarcely existed long enough to have any significance, I concentrated on the game itself. White enjoyed what seemed like a decisive edge until Black turned the tables. Eventually, the status became uncertain. My own excellence at this divine convergence of art, science, philosophy, and religion came from incendiary middle-game tactics, which spared me the drudgery of grinding my opponents down in the endgame.

I glanced skyward at the orange streak, swooned, and looked earthward. It is a good thing these ghosts do not look up, I thought. They would never be able to concentrate on the game.

The pieces bounced around the board until something tugged on my shirt. A little skeleton with baby teeth grinned up at me. A baggy yellow shirt and gray gym shorts cloaked his pale bones. This phenomenon was more in keeping with the old comic book advertisements for x-ray glasses, which always depicted the wearer surrounded by skeletons and naked ladies. I hoped he would take me to the latter.

He clasped my hand in his cold little bones and led me around the side of a post office. His tibia and fibula protruded from black Nikes, shimmering like swords in a thunderstorm. He let go of my hand and pointed, shaking his little finger.

"Impossible." I said. "Absolutely impossible."

We stood atop a hill overlooking a field bordered by two ponds, between which thousands of ghosts toted buckets of water. So swift were the sun's revolutions that they appeared to move in slow motion. Some emptied their buckets in the pond to my left and filled them at the one to my right, others contrariwise. Some emptied *and* filled their buckets at each, which seemed odd. Awaiting their turns, they huddled impatiently. Whatever order the caravan possessed could best be attributed to an absence of chaos. Despite the commotion, the surfaces of both ponds remained smooth.

Individual ghosts changed in the same abrupt fashion as the chess-playing ghosts, supplanted before their buckets could hit the ground. An old woman hobbled past us in jerky segmented motion, water sloshing from her buckets, her face contorted in agony. In a flicker of the sun she vanished and the ghost of a young girl replaced her, laughing and swinging the buckets devil-may-care.

I was, of course, reluctantly acquainted with the puerile superstition maintaining how the foremost difficulty confronting ghosts is a lack of insight into the nature of their condition. As this rancid scrap of conventional wisdom has it, they are unaware of their ghostly status; they continue to labor under the misapprehension, the delusion that they are real. While regarding such preposterous ravings with the contempt they deserve, this was my independent diagnosis of these ghosts: they were simply ignorant of their condition. They mistook it for something else. They behaved as though engaged in something of great importance, as though the phantom twinkle of their existence mattered. I would have laughed but the spectacle engendered pity.

The skeleton-boy tugged at my shirt. He pointed to the ghosts, then to me, then back at the ghosts, nodding his head slowly.

"I most certainly will not go out there you scrawny little urchin."

He shook his head no, but continued pointing.

"Perhaps I will take a closer look," I said, "if only to discern the nature of this chimera." I made my way down, stopping short of the field itself. The multitude of ghosts homogenized into a fog that buckets appeared to float through. (Fear not, the oblique nature of this outrageous spectacle will be eviscerated in my excursus to Part V. If it becomes the Reader's most beloved portion of my annals no one shall blame him.) The strobe light above gave the field the offending ambience of the noxious dance parties Sandy often dragged me to. The ghosts, scarcely persisting long enough to fill their buckets a few times, much less make any observations about the nature of their surroundings, ignored the disorienting flash. This was in their best interest. Had they noticed it would have sent them clutching at the grass for stability.

The view from their level disturbed me and the sun devastated what remained of my counterpoise. Turning from the melancholy vision to surmount the hill, I fell. As I scrambled to the post office I saw grass and rocks through the misty outline of my arms. I screamed and looked away. The skeleton-boy towered over me, nodding and pointing and grinning sadistically. He reached down and held a bucket out to me. I tore the glasses off with my ghostly hands and shut my eyes, begging the gods for the return of my mundane vision.

"Are you okay?" Sandy called.

When I finally looked up the sun was anchored by an unseen tether. Sandy's face evinced a degree of concern I had not seen since her sister's birthday, when my festiveness, according to some eyewitnesses, eclipsed my sensibility. "Those glasses are worse than that so-called Ecstasy you poisoned us with last summer."

"The lady said you might need help, that you might get lost or something. What did you see? Let me try them."

"Your poor little brain has been through enough. I lost my way and fell down the hill. I could have been killed. They cause occular damage at the very least."

She took my hand and led me away. Before turning the corner I looked back at the field. The ghosts were gone and the water in the ponds stood unperturbed.

"Did you like what you saw?" the old gypsy said with a toothless grin. "Want to buy them?"

"That is not the kind of pageant a man would want to see more than once."

"Once is all you need. Most people never see it at all."

"And they are none the worse for it. If a man wore those glasses all the time --"

"He'd go mad," she whispered. And we looked into each other's eyes for a long time.

***

Sandy held her crystal ball up to the window, examining it in the sunlight while I drove. The size of a softball, it contained a tiny, rainbow-striped armadillo in its center, seemingly preserved like an insect in amber.

"Is that thing real?"

"Of course not, but isn't this beautiful?"

"That creature will contaminate the prophecies you receive, will it not?"

"What do you mean?" she said, putting the ball in her lap but keeping her eyes fixed on it.

"Oh great and mysterious ball, what are we having for lunch? Rainbow armadillo. Oh great and round crystal ball, what does the future hold for me? Rainbow armadillo."

"It's not for predicting the future. The armadillo is probably part of some cultural narrative. We'll have to look it up when we get home."

"Cultural narrative? Like the Phoenix?"

"Maybe, but isn't that one shared by many cultures?"

"Like a plague. I recommend not looking it up. The aesthetic value of mythical creations invariably exceeds whatever meaning they have, if any."

"Like your hood ornament and dashboard mascot?" she said with disapproval.

"Precisely. I could care less what outlandish tales they denote. The sight of them brings me joy. The only *meaning* that matters is what *meaning* they have to me. Besides, she said it was a real crystal ball with special powers of prognostication."

She raised the ball so the sun again shone through it. "What a character. Tourists love that shit."

***

At the fall of night we entered a rest area. Sandy climbed in back and gained immediate passage to the Land of Nod. The gatekeeper had always been fond of her. For reasons never disclosed, he despised me. Even the most excessive bribes proved insufficient to gain his favor. While I leaned against the trunk and reflected on the day's proceedings, an epiphany befell me: I must begin my annals, my history of this portentous odyssey. How else can I sift the revelatory elements from the dross? There can be no certainty while adrift in the middle, for the moment is always given precedence by the senses. And hindsight is a flighty harlot indeed, popular and acquiescent but scarcely faithful.

Grateful that my muse contacted me before any precious details were shipped off to the overflowing landfill of history, I retrieved a notebook from the trunk, located a pen in the glove compartment, and turned on the reading light. Sandy's snores indicated that no stimuli could awaken her (one curious and delightful exception being the corner of a bed sheet tickling her ear).

Not wishing to begin my chronicle in haste, I paused to gather my recollections, lit an Oval to vitalize my gifts of transcription, reflected on the accomplishments of my peers: Thucydides, Polybius, Livy, and Seutonius. And I began my annals, writing slowly at first, refusing, like any great historian, to permit vain concerns of style to interfere with the simple accuracy of my narrative. As my confidence ascended, a natural eloquence took over, and Truth joined splendor in an uncompromising union.

A ponderous yoke left my shoulders, a gratification common to all practitioners of this noble science. When a historian documents events he witnessed it not only confirms their ontological status for posterity, it endows him with a distance from which he may provide a level survey. I could not fathom how the self-evident necessity of this undertaking had evaded me.

I filled a third of the diary in an hour and made a mental note to purchase more notebooks the following day. I wondered if the signs had the same meaning by themselves that they did in the overall context. I footnoted this exegetical query, hoping the answer would be forthcoming once my annals were complete and I had time to meditate upon them.

Whereas the events of the afternoon were fresh in my mind, I devoted a disproportionate amount of space to them, secure in the belief that I could recount the other epic encounters at my leisure. The remembrance of the benighted phantoms slithered across my flesh. Though reluctant to relive the experience, I needed to purge it from my mind, to trap it safely behind bars of ink.

When cramps silenced my arm and the fog of enervation clouded my transcriptive faculty, I turned to the first page to peruse my annals, prepared to savor that sweet but guilty pleasure common to all great writers: the vicarious enjoyment of one's creation via the imagined bliss it will bring his reader.

The page was blank.

Frantically flipping through the notebook and not finding so much as a smudge, I felt the nauseating momentum of the earth hurtling through space. My voodoo doll mocked my failed authorship with his savage leer and a perverse and cantankerous determination overcame me. I turned to the first page and began again.

"So what if it all disappears," I whispered, bristling with defiance. "The transcription itself is ennobling. It preserves what happened for a moment, which is better than nothing. Indeed, it staves off the Nothing -- for an instant." In my fervent state I believed this to be important. In the coolness of detached reflection I often wonder if it is. How can a historian reconcile himself to the disappearing ink we delusively use to preserve our chronicles?

I went outside to stretch and smoke. Headlights on the interstate sliced through the night but always left it intact. I reeled from a sensation common to all eminent historians taking a rest from a momentous project: a wearying synergy of woe and agitation begot of the recognition that there is much to be done and one is not doing it. I hereby christen this Petronius' Fourth Sensation. With odium, I will tolerate its application to pauses from momentous projects in general. (The perspicacious Reader will recognize how it forms the yin to the yang of Petronius' Third Sensation.)

When I tried to sleep, my eyelids became screens where ignorant, pathetic ghosts marched back and forth. "Impossible," I said. "Completely impossible." I sat up, not frightened but enraged. (Do not worry, dear Reader, as you shall see in the excursus to Part V, the manure of this rage fertilized a most wonderful fruit.) I opened the back door and eased my way in. Though it provided extensive space for travel, the backseat did not comfortably accommodate two with the intention of sleeping.

***

Viewed with the detachment of satiety, the attraction between the sexes, the magnetism that mercilessly and inexorably drags them together, appears as nothing more than bizarre cajolery hoodwinking us to populate a madhouse with fresh inmates, something the distant murmur of Reason could never do. (Salubrious for the madhouse is that satiation rarely exceeds thirty minutes.) Considered from any other standpoint it seems the most lavish of tricks, magnificent chicanery, Mother Nature's greatest special effect: commanding the perpetuation of an existence that most of its heritors have grave reservations about, yet making the means of perpetuation its most redeeming feature. Bravo!

Sandy's arms gave me sanctuary from the ghosts. But where would that comfort be tomorrow? For what can comfort a man who has found himself in a town of ghosts?

The Dialogues of Supernatural Individuation

So that the Reader may fully share the perturbation I experienced in Part V, it is essential that he understand and fully acknowledge the theoretical impossibility of ghosts. To the philosophic novice, being theoretically impossible is a far graver offense than being physically impossible. The latter is a misdemeanor against the laws of nature; the former is a desecration of logic herself. Unfortunately, a straightforward descant would expose even the most learned to arguments intricate and arcane. Despite the technical perfection, my exposition would prove insufficient to infuse the Reader with the perplexities that assailed me or bring him to his knees with the unique awe of a grand philosophic revelation. His loss would be of tragic proportions: the argument I shall unveil is as original and profound as the introduction of amino acids into the primordial soup. Remember, I was not frightened of the ghosts; *the impossibility of their existence agitated me.*

To clearly elucidate and explore this point, I have decided to demonstrate it by means of a dialogue. If the format was good enough for Plato and David Hume it is good enough for me. The Reader is encouraged to imagine himself seated at the table with the participants, actively following (perhaps even participating in) the discussion.

***

The Participants

Sophia represents the voice of Reason. *Scatius* is a wily philosopher whose views are in diametric opposition to mine. *Cretinius* holds the views of the common man.

***

At a picnic table in Pulaski Park sat Sophia, Cretinius, and I. The morning sun or Sophia, which article of creation deserved greater reverence, which was more conspicuous and inexplicable in its beauty and power? Though she was barely eighteen, to look into her dark green eyes was to confront wisdom itself. We shared a bottle of schnapps (far from discouraging my enjoyment, Sophia filled my glass the instant it was empty) while giant but gentle Cretinius worked the morning crossword.

"Sophia, a fascinating problem vexes me. In the realm of the supernatural how, in theory, would we individuate things? How would we recognize one entity as being distinct from another?"

"What's a two-letter word for alternative?" said Cretinius, rubbing his salient brow.

After some thought, Sophia leaned forward, revealing cleavage from the plentidudinous bosom concealed beneath her toga. "It couldn't be the same way we individuate natural things. Consider five coins. What distinguishes each of them is their occupation of different spaces."

"Exactly," I said. "Now I am not asserting that spatial continuity is the only consideration, but it is essential."

"Cretinius, that's a terrible habit," said Sophia, her radiant, non-Asian features grimacing as his finger excavated his nose.

A loud belching interrupted her as Scatius staggered into the park. His spindly legs seemed incapable of supporting the humpbacked torso upon them.

"I fear he is in his cups again," I whispered.

"Those are sandals," said Cretinius, his lazy eye looking up and away from the crossword.

"I wonder what views Scatius holds on your position," said Sophia.

"And what position is that?" he said, taking a seat. The black caves of Scatius' eyes provided the only contrast on his forbidding face to his pasty skin. Though his hair was thin to the point of endangered, his skeletal arms were covered with dense patches of beastly fur. He helped himself to our schnapps, guzzling it from the bottle.

"I was maintaining the theoretical impossibility of ghosts," I said. "My critique is more severe than the assertion that they do not exist. I maintain that it makes no sense to even speak of them."

"Ah, the cheap solvent of logical positivism," he said with a hiccup. "That's about as original as breathing."

"Scatius! Don't touch me there," cried Cretinius.

"My argument owes nothing to the lazy and arrogant positivists," I said. "They assert that statements are only meaningful if they are verifiable. My position is that we cannot coherently speak of ghosts because they cannot be individuated by the criterion of spatial continuity. The difference between one and three of them is not a feature of the distinct chunks of space they occupy. By what criterion can they be separated?"

"Your argument is fascinating," said Sophia, cradling her chin in her hand and batting her long lashes.

"It is interesting," agreed Scatius.

"What about Casper the Friendly Ghost?" asked Cretinius. "He takes up space. So do the ones on *Ghostbusters*."

"That's the stupidest thing I've ever heard," said Sophia.

"Be patient," I said, stroking the celestial crop of sunbleached down on her arm. "Something good will arise, non-Phoenix-like, from his point. Cretinius has voiced the common perception of ghosts. Although we say they do not have spatial dimensions, we conceive of them as gaseous or luminous beings who occupy space in a mysterious fashion that allows them to float through walls. Unable to conceive of non-physical, non-spatial, invisible beings, we are reduced to the conceptual level of tabloid sightings and cartoons. Oh, what can comfort a man who finds himself in a town of ghosts, a town where the stern sheriff of logic is not obeyed?"

Scatius belched. "The answer is both obvious and devastating to your cute little argument. Ghosts can be individuated on the grounds that they have unique minds or personalities."

Sophia turned to me and put her hand atop mine. So soft the skin. So unequivocal the yearning in her eyes. The sun beamed on its masterful handiwork: sporadic freckles on her nose, shoulders, and in the heavenly valley of her mountainous bosom.

"What's a three-letter word for opposite of later?" asked Cretinius.

I winked at Sophia and clasped her tiny hand and prepared for triumph. "On the contrary, we cannot speak of distinct personalities unless individuation has already occurred. 'I have seven minds but my bother has only four,' is a ridiculous statement, but if physical embodiment is not a criterion how can we criticize it? From this it follows that we have no means of individuating disembodied minds."

"Sophistry," groaned Scatius, reaching for the schnapps. He finished the bottle and smashed it on the bike path. "Let me think," he said, massaging his temples.

"Oh Petronius, your arguments shine with the light of Truth," said Sophia.

"Here is the fundamental difficulty," I said. "Terms such as *two*, *many*, *some*, and *few* are coherent insofar as they refer to distinguishable items. If we have no means of theoretically distinguishing one ghost from another, what sense would it make to say that there are *many* of them as opposed to a *few*, or *one* as opposed to *three?* When we attempt to determine the autonomy of entities in a domain where spatial and physical considerations can not be applied we are, to put it politely, speaking gibberish."

"Gibberish indeed," said Scatius, pounding his fist on the table. "You would deny what all of mankind has believed since the dawn of time?"

"He's angry," said Cretinius.

"Mankind does not know that what they think they believe is conceptually impossible," I said. "It is the philosopher's task to demonstrate this, not to encourage their folly with trickery."

"Writer's throughout history have documented the tragic plight of ghosts," said Scatius, putting his head on the table. "Trapped between planes, ignorant of their condition ..." He began to snore.

"You mean cynical hacks know a good gimmick when they see it," I said. "The lost-ghost cliché is absurd on the face of it. After a full day without hunger pangs or trips to the restroom even Cretinius would figure out that something special had occurred. And what should we make of the supernatural dimension that stands as the basis for these tales? What could possibly transpire in a bodiless, non-physical realm? The traditional answer is the experience of bliss or a reunion with deceased family members. Has no one noticed these are mutually exclusive?"

"But wouldn't you want to see your father again?" said Sophia, running her fingers through my hair.

"Exceptions only prove the general rule. Regarding the plausibility of the former answer: compile a list of all the types of bliss you have experienced without the use of your body."

Sophia giggled. "There aren't many, and the best one isn't included."

"Something smells bad," said Cretinius.

"Oh my," cried Sophia, pinching her nose. "Poor Scatius has had an accident."

"He pooped," agreed Cretinius, and we all abandoned the table with its slumbering defecator. "Petronius, look at the bugs," said Cretinius with glee. Attracted to the sweet liquid from the broken bottle, a squadron of yellow jackets darted about the shards.

"No Cretinius, those are --"

I put my finger to her lips. "Sophia, when I establish my academy, Experience shall be granted an honorary professorship. Hopefully all my pupils will be as receptive to my teachings as you. And as lovely."

Cretinius screamed and lumbered away flailing his arms.

"Now, even if we can conceive of a disembodied state of bliss, what do we mean by bliss in this context? A state of schnapps intoxication? For all eternity? As much joy as that syrupy nectar can bring, would you want to feel like that forever?"

"Oh Petronius, let's go for a walk in the park."

VI: A Book Party, an Infernal Nightmare, and a Refutation of Vegetarianism

After losing our way we found ourselves on a nameless road heading into a nameless city. The architects guilty of the structures we passed must have conspired to design buildings as nondescript as human ingenuity permitted. Even pyramids would have been preferable. Instead of expressing empathy or maintaining a silent faith in my driving prowess, Sandy reveled in my fallibility.

"Columbus, where are you taking us? Are you sure this is the way to India?"

I seethed. This was my question whenever her navigational skills left room for improvement. "This is an indirect route," I said, trying to visualize where we might have strayed.

"Are you sure it's the right way? Where's the map?"

I winced. It was mounted, bathing my study in Old World elegance. Though my innate driving skills precluded the need for cheat sheets, I recognized the singularity of this one. It arrived in the mail in an ornately carved wooden canister. A green eye marked the Point of Percipience; a closed eye marked my house. Between them it resembled an anatomy chart of the circulatory system: roads ran parallel, crisscrossed, and wove into spirals. It seemed odd that an old map would delineate modern roads. Surely they could not have existed since time immemorial. My first inspection commenced under the nonchalant assumption that I enjoyed the liberty of choosing from amongst numerous routes. Subsequent surveys refuted this. Most of the roads did not approach it; most that did veered off. Out of hundreds, only a few had any worth. Deprived of the luxury of choice, I compiled a tiny mental list of where and when to turn.

"The map is in the bear trap of my memory," I said. "As a scholar of Euclid, I can assure you that straight lines are overrated."

"Would you please stop and ask for directions?"

"Ask for directions," I said with feigned thoughtfulness. "And afterwards I shall purchase a paper to peruse the classifieds for Eunuchs Wanted, for that is what you will have reduced me to."

"*Please*," she implored, her anxiety contagious.

"The corroboration of a third party will serve as a testament to my improvisational skills."

"You're not in a band. You're driving."

***

"It's the purple building with the domed roof, a few blocks down on the right side," the attendant said before I could open my mouth. Oil stains covered his uniform like continents on a globe and his rolled up sleeves revealed huge but flabby biceps.

"It?" I said, not used to mediums plying their trade in this line of work.

"The book party," he sighed. "I must have had fifty people stop in here and ask me about it since noon."

"Book party?"

"Yeah, look at your invitation." He retrieved a green three-by-five card from beside the register and tapped an elegant sketch of the structure with a greasy finger. "Some guy left his here."

"Utterly fascinating," I said, trying to decipher the black enamel calligraphy. "But could you tell me how to return to the interstate?"

"It figures," he said, shaking his head in defeat. He gave me directions and I asked if the party was invite only.

"You can have this one. The guy who left it hasn't been back in hours. With all the people that come and go it can't be too hard to get in."

"Who is the perpetrator?"

"The what?"

"The featured author."

He blinked.

"When did it begin?"

"I've been working here over six months and it's been going on since then."

"What manner of book party lasts that long? Few merit six seconds of celebration. Most should be inaugurated by a requiem. This one must feature a different work each night."

"You got me. But it's a strange crowd. You should see some of the people who stop in here for directions. Most of them are pretty flaky. But some of the women -- You wouldn't believe it."

"They are drawn to exhibitionists like peahens to peacocks. Whether it is a hirsute guitarist, a steroid-addled gamesman, or a pulp-excreting word-processor jockey makes no difference." He crinkled up his nose as though blinded from the light of my analysis. "You have been most helpful," I said before returning to my car.

"Lost indeed." I handed Sandy the invitation. "I wanted it to be a surprise. We have found the literary nexus of the world, a *fête* without end."

"What book is it for? The invitation doesn't mention the book or the author."

"This is a top-secret affair," I said, heading for the domed building.

"I've never seen a great novelist."

"Nor shall you, absent a time machine."

"I meant famous."

"I will catch you if you faint."

Upon entering we walked through a long limestone passage. Smooth slabs gleamed from Chinese lanterns. We emerged in the humbling vastness of a dark marble lobby. A huge window looked out on a pond at the foot of a hill covered in dandelions. Dwarfed by a statue of a zebra perched upon one leg, two men in white suits and matching visors circumnavigated the pond with the speed of a minute hand, staring intently at it. After a prelude to eternity, one pointed to the surface. His comrade ran to his side. They took turns framing it from different angles with their hands, looked at one another, and nodded. One picked up a metal pole with wire mesh on the end and scooped something out and gingerly laid it on a tray. He put the pole down and they resumed their encirclement.

Sandy tapped my shoulder. Opposite the window, seated in a folding chair, the lobby attendant faced the wall. I shrugged and walked to the door across from us, its existence only discernible from a silver knob. Like a man poised to tour Bedlam, I paused before opening it, bracing myself for encounters with MFA students, free-verse poets, English "majors" unfamiliar with Shakespeare, and worse. Sandy watched the aloof attendant. Above her, the ceiling spread to uncertain dimensions, as though something was leaking out, or, more ominously, Nothing was trickling in. She looked to me, puzzled, then to him, concerned. I jerked my head, imploring her to follow.

The smell of strawberries overwhelmed us. Lavishly attired literati crowded around three tables disappearing into the abyssal depths of a narrow room. Their whispers accrued to the hiss of a deflating tire. Unable to sneak a glimpse of what digested their attention, I assumed that a plague of novelists were diligently signing their latest exudations. We choreographed an elaborate dance through the gathering to arrive at a tiny bar in the corner. The bartender hunched over to avoid scraping his head on the ceiling. Thin brown hair plastered to one side matched his leathery complexion. Eyes dead like a shark's stared into the crowd. In the distance between his shoulders stood three patrons. Sandy gasped at the sight of a zebra pelt mounted behind him. The green clock in its center had blue Roman numerals but no hands to mark the minutes or hours.

"Excuse me," I said. "What book is this for?"

As though a hand inside it tensed to catch a ball, the bartender's face contorted. "*That book,*" he hissed like a serpent provoked, pointing to the tables.

Revelation: the people crowded around the tables were reading the book. The pages must have been spread sequentially across them. "So much for fruitful miracles in the midst of solitude," I said. "Are you selling hot dogs? Are there any cheerleaders?"

"Are you trying to make a joke, sir?" a pudgy little man beside me asked. Like most of the male literati, a Fu Man Chu beard garnished his face. Flaunting rubicund cheeks, his ponytail constrained long dark hair. A baggy paisley shirt tucked into tight jeans tucked into cowboy boots. He and the bartender vivisected me with their eyes.

"Who is the author?" I said.

The bartender shook his head in disbelief, perhaps disgust. The little man squinted at me like he had discovered a precious jewel. "Sir, the book is not finished. And it has no author. How could you not know this?"

"I am acquainted with the noxious trend of denying that books have any fixed meaning, but this must be something new. How exciting."

He stood on his tiptoes and put his mouth to my ear. "You came here thinking the book has an author?" His hand covered his mouth and his eyes extruded. "He's only joking," he told the bartender. "Drunk as a skunk. Fix me another. I'll take him outside for some air." Sandy and I followed him to the lobby. "My name is Cletus Empiricus," he announced, vigorously shaking my hand while engaged in a staring contest with Sandy's chest. I could scarcely begrudge him this enchantment. Those sweet, ripened, succulent, luscious fruits of the Orient had brought me more bliss than a *fête* of real writers could describe with a million sonnets. "You weren't joking about thinking the book has an author," he said, diverting his gaze. I shook my head. "Mr. Jablonski, the book comes from the pond."

"You mean *that* pond?"

"Correct. Do you see those men? The pond is filled with tiny letters. They search for words or phrases. Sometimes they find complete sentences. They scoop out the words and put them on a tray. When it's full they bring it inside and put it on the table. This isn't like other book parties. It celebrates the book as it's written."

"What's it about?" said Sandy.

"That depends on who you ask."

"That depends on *whom* she asks," I corrected, following the wise principle that it is never too early to establish dominion in a conversation.

"Some people are quite taken with it," he said with a shrug.

"How do you like it?" I asked.

"I was ambivalent, but I've grown to hate it," he said, as though delighted to answer the question, perhaps hoping to influence our opinions. "Can't deny it's technically well-written, teeming with interesting characters, lots of action, complex themes." He sniffed his drink and stared at the pond. One man pointed to the surface while his partner brandished the pole.

"But?" I said, severing his trance.

"But all the surface activity can't hide the hollow ground underneath it."

"Could you phrase that so someone who has not spent his life chasing the wind after an advanced English degree can comprehend it?"

"At least he declared a major," said Sandy.

"I will declare it as soon as they remove symbolic logic from the requirements. Did Socrates torture himself with those absurd squiggles?"

Cletus smiled, drank, rubbed his chin, and said, "There are so many tiny pictures you hardly notice the lack of a big one. But once you do, the tiny pictures don't interest you."

"Sandy, go fetch an English undergrad to translate."

"I know what he means, and there's something sad about it: interesting *small* things trapped in a meaningless, authorless *giant* thing."

"Exactly. That's exactly why I don't like it."

That they were on the same wavelength fascinated me. In my demarcation of the circles of benighted academic pursuits, communications occupied the lowly fifth circle, four full circles below English. Exchanges between them should have been impossible.

"The underlying hollowness compels a lot of people to either force the story into some interpretation they've cooked up, which is like trying to get an elephant into a straightjacket, or they say the pond has mysterious powers that guide the writing. That way it's always possible the meaning is hidden or not fully revealed."

"Why is that so hard to believe?" said Sandy.

"Look at it. It's a scummy little pond with millions of letters floating around in it."

"But it's writing a book," she said.

"You have to judge an author by what he, or it, writes, not by what you think they could."

"Fair enough," I said. "Aptitude is obviously irrelevant to literary matters, if not all matters. How long is the work?"

"Too long. It might be repeating itself thematically, but it's so long this is hard to verify. It just rambles on and on and on and on," he said, bobbing his head to accentuate his aversion. "One damn thing after another."

"When will it be finished?" I said.

"No one knows. Those men out there just scoop out words. They aren't proofreaders or editors. *There are no editors*. There's no one to say when the whole silly mess is over."

"But the fact that it's all being created by a pond is incredible," said Sandy.

"The regular use of alliteration, anadiplosis, and anaphora has been convincingly explained in terms of the consistent breezes stirring the water. Patterns arise."

"But the structure, the complexity of --"

"If it were my book I'd be ashamed of myself," Cletus said, throwing his head back. "I would only publish it with a pen name to make a quick buck."

"Then why do you come here?" said Sandy.

"One, the drinks are cheap. Two, the chicks." Cletus winked at me. "Don't get me wrong. Once in a while the book has its moments. Hell, once in a while it's great. It's just that overall it's nothing I'd put my name on."

"Have you ever written anything?" said Sandy.

"No. But he has," Cletus whispered, pointing at the lobby attendant.

"Why is he facing the wall?" I said.

"He's jealous."

"Who's he jealous of?" said Sandy.

"Of *whom* is he jealous," I corrected.

"He's jealous of the pond. He's the most frustrated writer who ever lived, at least that's what he'd like you to think. As the story goes, the books he's written have an underlying significance that ties everything together in the end. But his novels fall stillborn from his printer while people stand in line to read a foofaraw written by a scummy pond. That's why he sits facing the wall. He can't bare to look at it."

"A *foofaraw*? May the gods deliver me from all English majors."

"At least they don't think they're smarter than everyone," said Sandy. "Philosophy students are the worst."

"Why doesn't he pursue employment elsewhere?" I said.

"The money's probably good, and of course, the perks."

"Such as?"

"Mr. Jablonski, you've been inside the other room. They come through here, see him all despondent, ask him what's wrong. That's when it starts getting deep in here -- if you know what I mean. They bring him drinks, ask if there's anything they can do, and one thing leads to another. You know, I've thought about pulling up a chair next to him. In a sense he's one of the most successful writers of all time."

Sandy gave him a quizzical look.

"Forget all that junk you've heard about literary ambitions. It's a veneer. The brooding genius routine is an act they go through to appear mysterious and sensitive. The tormented writer shtick wreaks havoc on a woman's compassion."

"That's not true of all writers," Sandy said.

Her literary judgment devastated by a diet of "commercial fiction" (a euphemism for graceless drivel about the basest instincts unfolding in clichéd situations), she thought highly of both the perpetrators and their motives. Having had several of her favorite novels inflicted on me, I conceived a hypothesis concerning their origin: those authors must have secret ponds of their own. Such work is not the product of intelligent design, but mere randomness. The prose itself is what one would expect from letters drifting aimlessly in a pond. The numbing regularity of the themes (coming of age, the indomitable nature of the human spirit, who killed *whom*, a journey filled with conflicts, etc.) are explicable in terms of the same natural forces that create regularities like tides, eddies, and whirlpools in larger bodies of water.

"Don't be fooled," said Cletus. "The difference between what he's doing and slipping your date a knockout pill is a difference of degree. Some writers are craftier than others, but deep down they're all the same."

"Don't listen to him," said the attendant. The wall muffled any inflections his voice contained. "He doesn't understand. To write a book is to pour your soul into a canyon."

"Here he goes," said Cletus. "He's practicing one of his pickup lines. I need a drink. Come to the bar when it gets too deep in here for you." He put his hand on my shoulder. "Take a good, long look at the book. Decide for yourself." The hissing of the crowd filled the lobby before he closed the door.

The camouflage of the attendant's dark hair and jacket fostered the illusion that the wall was speaking. "An echo may ring through the canyon and the people below will look up and see who shouted. But even the clearest voice can only echo for so long. Soon it will fade, absorbed by the rocks, and the canyon will be as quiet as it was before. This is true of the greatest shouts. For most, they are lucky if their voice echoes at all or if anyone looks up."

I cleared my throat, reflected on the greatness of Pericles, and began an oration that would change his life. "Cletus and yourself may think otherwise, but over the course of conquests innumerable I have found that an air of supreme self-assuredness is the most powerful aphrodisiac. Whining about your failures may occasionally net a stray mongrel, but if you wish to mount the prize bitches you need to project confidence. Your very being must radiate strength and --"

"What the hell is wrong with you?" said Sandy.

"Disregard this conversation. I am speaking as a man to one aspiring to that status. May the gods strike me dead if my father did not say the same words to me. Perhaps the fiery rhetoric offends you, but it is necessary for inspirational purposes."

"Just stop it or I'll call Dave to come and pick me up."

"Your ex. Speaking of aspiring to a manly status. Very well. Cletus told us you are an accomplished author."

"I wrote several books," the wall said. "Their shouts were great and clear, but none of them echoed."

"Why does every shout not echo?" I asked, which seemed like the proper question. Even if his detestable strategy proved successful in practice, it was grievously wrong in principle: a man must never forge inroads to a woman's maternal instincts, only her carnal ones.

"Clarity does not entail volume," the attendant said, coming back into focus and sounding perturbed. "And a great shout does not connote a loud shout."

"Why is writing a book the saddest thing in the world?" said Sandy.

Because the foredoomed paths of solipsism, megalomania, and self-abasement intersect in the depths of Abaddon, I thought. And the injudicious use of metaphors and similes leaves the writer with irreparable brain damage.

"Where do all books end up?" the wall said as the lobby attendant faded from view. "Moldering on a shelf, packed in a box, abandoned and forgotten on a hard drive."

This routine indubitably cast him as mysterious and sensitive. But to what abysmal depths has civilization plunged when *sensitivity* is a trait willfully sought by a *man*?

"So you don't write anymore?" said Sandy, falling prey to the loathsome vice of pity, in accordance with the attendant's strategy.

"I do. But my books will not be subjected to burial on shelves or in boxes. They end up underground."

"And *underground* is a metaphor of what?" I said. Ask a writer for the time of day and you need an Enigma machine to decrypt the answer.

"It's no metaphor. I literally bury them. Six feet deep."

"No one ever reads them?" said Sandy.

"If there are no echoes you never have to adjust to the awful silence that comes when they stop."

"That's so sad," she said.

"No, it is natural."

"The Kafka gambit," I laughed. "You are aware, I hope, that he did not bury his books; he asked a friend to burn them. Clearly you are unaware that his proficiency with the ladies was not exactly --"

Sandy turned to me, only the whites of her eyes visible. An arctic breeze blew through the room. "I won't tell you again."

Piqued, I looked out the window and watched the peculiar fishermen.

"But perhaps it is only outrage that leads me to this."

"But it can take years for a writer to get recognized," Sandy said. "You should be proud that --"

"Not that kind of outrage. I'm outraged that where a book ends up is a far better place than where other things do, that even the worst book has the potential to exist longer."

"What other things?"

Go and sit on his lap, I thought. How much further can he debase himself? What final act has he planned for this play of helplessness, this self-degradation, this *sensitivity*? Will he now curl into the fetal position and weep?

After scooping several words from the pond, the men lifted a silver tray at least six feet long and four feet wide. Their cautious handling would have sufficed for an atomic bomb. The man in front held it from behind and they marched with synchronized steps. I flirted with the idea of pounding on the window to measure the depth of their concentration, but I suspected the book's fans might not view my behavior as a lighthearted prank. Cheers erupted from the next room. The attendant began to sob. Sandy pressed her lips to my ear. "Let's go read some of it."

"Of course. I'm going to fetch my notebook. Save me a place in line."

Outside, the Eternal Question blindsided me, removing the cruel shackles of Time and suspending me in a dimension of pure contemplation. A magnificent silver fortress approached. With a turn into the parking lot it revealed a black flank shining like freshly spilled India ink: black like a moonless night, black like still water reflecting a starless sky, black like French Roast coffee. I ran behind the somber but elegant exterior and waited for the owner to park.

"The 1976 Lincoln Continental Town Car."

"Good call, chief."

"It is breathtaking, sublime, imperial, resplendent …" Throwing down the impotent tools of language, I humbly adored. "Permit no one to park in the adjacent spot. I shall return with my car." And I ran across the street, thrilled and terrified at the prospect of an imminent encounter with the Eternal Question.

"That's a beauty, chief," the Lincoln man said. We surveyed the Great Ones from every conceivable angle. His sprightly steps and youthful face made his gray crew-cut seem an unreliable indicator of his age. The slender but muscular physique discernable beneath his silk blazer cast further doubt. "I think the Lincoln is a tad bigger," he said after a long analysis.

"With Cartesian certainty I know the 1976 Fleetwood is a full inch longer. Yet your observation is justified. The Lincoln appears larger."

Standing between the bows with his arms crossed, looking from ship to ship, he said, "The Caddy is more tapered. The Lincoln is more like a block, so it looks bigger."

Though reeling from the lightning of his commentary, I sustained the full brunt of its implications. "You mean the Lincoln is more rectangular?"

"I suppose you could say that. More like a brick. Why, is that important to you?"

"It is the fundamental criterion of automobile greatness."

"I don't know. You think it's that cut and dried?"

"Absolutely."

"What about the Caddies and Lincolns from the late eighties?"

"Abortions."

"Yeah, I'm not a big fan myself. But aren't they rectangular?"

After a long pause I concurred. "I suppose."

"Well, so much for your criterion. Our cars are better because they're bigger, that's all."

Appalled that the ultimate foundation of automobile judgments could itself be summoned before the high court of Reason, I lashed out in despair before dissecting his postulation. "Rectangularity not the fundamental criterion? But how did you do this? How could you drink up the Great Lakes? With what squeegee did you wipe away the horizon? Where was I when you unchained the earth from the moon? Are we not falling?"

"Take it easy, chief. No need to get all worked up."

"But consider this: Would you prefer the special Fleetwood seventy-five?"

"Way too big. But now you're shooting down both our ideas. That car's a humongous rectangle."

"Is it possible that rectangularity and size are neither sufficient nor necessary conditions of automobile perfection?" I asked fearlessly, the destination of our discourse unknown, the velocity dizzying.

"Maybe it depends on the size of the rectangle."

"Rectangularity remains the criterion, but only functions within certain parameters? You cannot have your cake and eat it."

"You know, some folks say beauty is in the eye of the beholder."

Every muscle in my body contracted. "And some folks have first cousins for parents. The sirens' call of relativism has shipwrecked our culture. Think of the consequences. The rap and hip-hob my girlfriend listens to, on par with Bruckner? Her trashy novels, on par with Lawrence Sterne?"

"You got a point, chief, but you shouldn't get so worked up."

"But I must. I am the only one who cares."

"Speaking of books, I'm going to go see how this one's progressing," he said. After we exchanged pleasantries and shook hands, he departed.

"And speaking of Bruckner." I buzzed all the windows down, programmed the stereo to play the adagio of the Sixth Symphony repeatedly, and assumed the Lotus position between the cars. The dialogue had awakened me from my dogmatic slumbers and I sought clarity and fortitude. (Oftentimes, even the most heroic effort on the Big Questions in philosophy only reveals a greater darkness beyond.) As though suspended between two vast magnets, every particle of my conscious phenomena, however dispersed or distinct, converged harmoniously on the Truth and Beauty of Rectangularity. Time became a fable.

***

Before procceding, the Reader is solicitously encouraged to obtain photographs of the exact models described above and place the Lincoln to his right and the Cadillac to his left after setting his stereo (the preferred conductor is Celibidache, not Klemperer). Some bending and stretching before attempting the Lotus position is advised. Fermented or caffeinated drinks are contraindicated, but no limit is imposed on English Ovals. (Is this movement not the greatest piece of music ever composed? Does it not capture, as though through synesthesia, the tragic grandeur of the Great Ones?)

***

"What the hell are you doing?" came an awful shriek, scattering my mental particles like confetti and severing my umbilical chord to the realm of contemplative bliss. "Where have you been?" I looked up and beheld Sandy scowling down at me. "It's the most incredible book I've ever read."

"I can imagine. You must tell me everything. I was preoccupied."

Once we returned to the main road, she began to outline it until I put *Dean Martin's Greatest Hits* on the stereo. "Can we listen to something else?"

"Certainly. The other option is Perry Como. You will choose wisely, for either choice is wise."

"Why can't I play something?"

"Because my car is not some mawkish democracy, but a monarchy where a philosopher-king endowed with the perfect fusion of wisdom and benevolence knows what is best for his subjects."

"More like a dictatorship where words words words words words ..."

Disagreements pertaining to musical selections had plagued our expedition and I feared that a revolution could sire another churlish democracy (that odious government of the rabble, by the rabble, and for the rabble will be scrutinized and exposed -- as if wise men have not already been dutifully engaged in unmasking this wretched charlatan for the last three-thousand years -- in Part VII of my annals). Driver's Choice, a policy tested in the laboratory of the wisest scientist of them all, Time, could, if one did not mind befouling himself, be established on socialist principles:

1) A person's input in a political matter should be proportionate to the impact it will have upon him.

2) Musical selection has a direct bearing on the temperament and stability of the driver, who cradles within his hands the welfare of his passengers and fellow drivers.

3) The vomitus of guttersnipes and criminals, which, to the extent one can understand it, joyously celebrates the collapse of civilization, inflames the temperament and wracks the stability of all good men.

Therefore: the driver, bearing the greatest responsibility, has the absolute right to spare himself from any horrors that could threaten his Quietude. Despite the hordes of torch-bearing ignoramuses screaming, "one person, one vote," it is only his input that matters.

"… words, words, words and why should I have to listen to things I hate?"

"O scourge of youth, dreadful night that you and *your* peers stumble through, characterized by puddle-deep convictions, vapid idealism, and, worst of all, ghastly taste in music and all things, why was I spared from your clutches? Whom shall I thank for deliverance?"

"Can't we just compromise? Let's have silence."

"*Compromise*," I gasped, so disconcerted I scarcely knew how to proceed. "Lacking the free time of Henry

Higgins I should simply ignore what you just said. Possessing the patience of Buddha, I will briefly address it. *Compromise* is the spineless essence of democracy, which, as I have stated, this car is not. Now please, regale me with a synopsis of this great book. I will reduce the volume, but not in the spirit of compromise."

While she outlined and reiterated, I brooded about the eventuality of our arrival at the Point of Percipience. The fatuous book party had provided an amusing detour, but I could not hide from the knowledge that between our destination and us lay only a stretch of road decreasing with every mile gained on the odometer. I, a lonely fisherman reeling in a behemoth from the depths of a raging sea, knew that each circle of my arm brought it closer. I envisioned a shadow beneath the boat turning the water black as oil. Before it reached the surface, I pulled out a long silver knife and cut the line. The silhouette deflated. The water returned to blue.

"Come to your senses," Reason commanded, snapping me out of this coward's fantasy. "This line cannot be cut." Then an epiphany descended. The truth of my situation, formerly obscured, exposed me to its injurious rays: I am not the one holding the reel, and the growing shadow is the hull of a ship we are approaching, having received enough slack to depart the illusion of freedom. Perhaps lobsters, as they ascend to the surface, believe they have been chosen by mysterious but benevolent forces in the heavens.

***

We entered a campsite at dusk and found a secluded spot next to a bosk of trees. In lieu of my deluxe tent with the extended porch, we made due with a pup tent lent to us by Sandy's uncle. After gathering wood I started a fire on a desolate patch of ground that had served as a home to many of them. Though edible, Sandy's stir-fry shared the gustatory defect afflicting all vegetarian cuisine: a nagging absence of meat.

The crackling of the flames eclipsed the sound of crickets and the heat forced us to retreat a few feet. Sandy leaned back on her hands and I put my head in her lap. Watching the stars, I shuddered at the patience of oblivion. They are no more eternal than breadcrumbs tossed across a dark pond. Permanence is relative. That even they must die, those cherubs who shone for billions of years in a wondrous way, should their mortality bring us comfort, a familial affinity, or despair? I visualized an alien astronomer thousands of light-years away gazing into his telescope, watching us. We should have jumped up and flailed our arms and shook our fists, for we will leave no other vestige.

"What are you thinking about?" Sandy asked after a long silence where two people in their own little worlds occupy the same one. (Is that not a magnificent definition of Love?) She played with my hair and I watched hundreds of orange serpents charmed by some wild flute only they could hear.

My stomach chastised me for its famine rations. "The cult of vegetarianism, if left unchecked, will do to our species what the Christians did to the Roman Empire," I said, more to myself than her. "Someone has to do something."

"What?"

"I mean no offense. Your intentions are honorable but hideously misguided. The human brain has slightly decreased in size during the last ten-thousand years. Was it just a coincidence that it shriveled during our species' unhealthy obsession with agriculture? I suspect that television, internets, and sundry gizmos will shrivel it to the size of a walnut by the end of the next century."

"That's not simply wrong; it's crazy."

"I speak a truth that anthropology professors fear to whisper, lest their students throw down their Hackey Sacks and brandish a rope. Our massive brains crave the heavy fuel of calorie-dense critters. The average human brain needs, at a minimum, ten ounces of meat a day. Mine can scarcely function on less than fifty."

"That's the most pathetic rationalization I've ever heard, even by your standards."

When the fire dissipated we squeezed into the tent and I remembered how dissimilar the ground is to a soft mattress. With exhaustion being the most potent tonic, I no sooner shut my eyes than the diving bell sank like a stone. And in that deep sleep my hopes dashed upon jagged rocks on the shore of an infernal vegetable-induced nightmare, impaled and left to die a pitiable death beneath the icy claws of salty waves. A perversity no less grotesque than the land of my exile tinctured all my actions and thoughts.

From extensive studies in anthropology, I recall a tribe of savages who believe that dreams are reality and our waking life is but a dream. When I first happened upon this notion I deemed it the brazen embellishment of a vainglorious anthropologist, something so delusional only Franz Boas could believe it. But after this dream I partook of their unique ambivalence and prayed they were mistaken.

As we drove along the interstate, colors and shapes revealed their hidden secrets and my thoughts flowed with the power and clarity of rapids. A green highway sign, its blank face framed by white reflectors, telepathically imparted to me the correctness of taking the next exit. Feathers rained. My initial hypothesis involved an unfortunate flock of birds crossing paths with an airplane, but soon a pink blizzard poured down on us. Shiva, god of pillow fights, danced behind a boa. Sandy giggled, dangling her feet out the window, heedless to any visibility problems.

I buzzed my window down and feathers gushed in and Sandy laughed crazily. I extended my arm to probe them but their density rendered it immobile. It seemed as though we were driving through a huge pile rather than a downpour. I accelerated, convinced of our safety.

"As long as the wheel is straight we will stay on the road," said Reason. "Vision is but one of the senses and the least reliable at that: duped by all manner of ruses and prone to infirmities."

In spite of the feathers, or perhaps because of them, an ecstatic sense of relief embraced me, as though wondrous tidings had replaced the nervously anticipated certainty of dire news. In place of exhaustion, what one might expect after an arduous journey, I found myself in a reflective mood.

"Driving to the Point of Percipience is like heating a strange liquid slowly," I said after an effortless expenditure of thought, as though inspired, as though possessed. "One does not know how it will respond. It may solidify like a brick of gold, it may evaporate in a ghostly puff of smoke, it may explode in your face, it may do nothing at all, or it may cause feathers to rain down from the heavens."

This orphic pronouncement, the perfect distillation of all we had experienced, dazzled me, but Sandy laughed and grabbed handfuls of feathers and threw them across the dash. That the mess she made did not enrage me should have provided the insight necessary to navigate my way through the slender neck of the dark bottle, if not to wakefulness then at least a condition of lucid dreaming.

Although my Fleetwood contained the largest and most powerful engine ever made, its performance under these conditions had yet to be tested. If our progress ceased, I planned on climbing out and crawling to the top of the pile. The puerile fear of being buried alive, upon which that potboiler Edgar Allen Poe based a career, did not torment me. I slipped my car into low gear to accommodate the growing resistance and the storm began to clear. "*Post hoc ergo propter hoc,*" I said, exposing the fallacy of that fallacy, accelerating through the light drizzle, hoping to make up for lost time.

A curb of alabaster appeared beside us and grew until it bisected a rainbow of pink, black, green, and gold. After we drove through a narrow gate, all the confusions and insecurities of our jigsaw journey were forgotten like they had never happened. This realization brought me closer to Sandy's giddy level.

"We should have taken a plane," I said, laughing. "We do not remember most of what happened. Wherefore the purpose of going through it?" The ludicrous desire to partake of a means of transportation as decadent and unnatural as flying clearly bespoke a vegetable-induced delirium, but it seemed quite reasonable at the time.

At the end of a winding road, a mansion with a long portico beckoned. Giant fingers probed the other side of the sky, as though it were made of Cling Wrap. The pleasing aroma of lemons greeted us long before we came to a yellow moat where blue and green flamingos strutted. We parked and approached the Point of Percipience. Three rows of portholes covered its amethyst front. Faceless eyes gazed at us through dark glass as we stood between two statues of naked elephantine men shielding their heads with their forearms. I fell to my knees and cried, "It is no mere point, but a temple. We shall enter and partake of its riches."

My effusive display of reverence did not embarrass Sandy, whose giddiness ceased. We bounced up the white Styrofoam steps as if gravity had only partial access to this sacred domain. Humbled, I approached the chrome door, hoping the correct knob would be marked.

"Let's try the bell first," said Sandy.

We waited. She pressed it again. The wall shone in the distance. The fitful jerks of the blue flamingos bespoke mechanical rather than biological entities.

"No one's answering," she said.

"It is a big place. Perhaps they cannot hear us."

"Should we try the doorknobs? Weren't you invited?"

"Yes. Try them."

We began with the one situated where a doorknob is traditionally positioned, then worked from top to bottom. She looked to me for guidance.

"Well, we tried," I said blithely. My inexorable lust for Truth had devolved to the indifference of the common philistine.

"We came all this way and you don't even care that we can't get in?"

I shrugged. "The Point of Percipience is inaccessible. Acceptance is wisdom. I can live with that. Perhaps they have a pool around back." I walked to the edge of the portico and stood between two columns. (When I look back upon this flighty reaction, so bitterly at odds with my true nature, I shudder. But in the accursed dream I cradled a puddle-deep interpretation and shunned any contamination from second thoughts or further queries.)

"Look!" Sandy shouted, *pushing* the door open. "I grabbed one of the knobs at random."

"Close it and see if any of the others work. It would be quite a revelation if all knobs open the door to wisdom."

"What if we can't open it again? Then we blew our only chance on some dumb experiment."

Although I nodded in agreement, this should not be interpreted as an acknowledgement of the superiority of practical wisdom as opposed to contemplation or thought experiments.

An icy wind blew through the door, freezing within me all insincere and frivolous things. We entered the interior of a garden shed. Cobwebs stretched across my face and I gagged from a ghastly stench. Emaciated jesters, some partially decomposed, danced aimlessly. Dingy gowns hung from narrow shoulders and broomstick limbs. I looked away, not afraid of them but for them. They made no attempt to leave and did not acknowledge our presence. I looked in vain for other doors or rooms.

We walked back on the portico and the door slammed behind us. Sandy sat on the edge and dangled her legs. "Our clothes stink," she said. "What if wisdom doesn't come off? It was stupid of you to assume that getting it would be a good thing. We should have gone to Jamaica. At least you know what you're in for."

I watched my Fleetwood glow like orange neon. A blue flamingo fell on its side but continued to move its legs, unaware of its new orientation. "It may be ironic that you cannot know beforehand of what wisdom consists, and once you have it you may loathe it and never be free of it. We should have driven to Alaska."

"No one who hasn't been on the inside would believe it was like that," she said, her voice diminishing like she was about to cry. "This stench is making me crazy." I put my arm around her but yanked it back, repulsed. She had shriveled to a third her size. A tiny red nose dotted her porcelain face and long green hair hung limply around her tiny shoulders. She fell back on the porch and a recording inside her began to weep. I covered my ears and ran, terrified that the sound would seep into my mind and dissolve it.

At my car I turned to see the obese statues dragging my little doll across the portico. They looked over their shoulders with serene indifference. "Feeling any smarter?" said one. "Don't judge a cover by its book," said the other. The doll's head cocked at a grotesque angle and her dead eyes accused me. I wanted to run to her and save her and take her back and hold her, but constrained by the evil physics of dreams I just stood there. One of the animate slabs opened the door. The other chucked the doll inside. They galumphed to their positions on the stairs and covered their faces, resuming their strange sentry duty.

I awoke and wiped tears from my eyes. After escaping from the sleeping bag and tent with Houdini-like dexterity, I stood in the cool night air. "Vegetarianism is refuted thus," I proclaimed.

On the Needlessness of an Addendum to Part VI

Whereas the arrant completeness of Part VI obviates the need for clarifications or elaborations, the Reader's captious accusation of "being forsaken" thrusts upon me the suspicion that he wants to use an addendum as he would a commercial, leaving it unattended while procuring a drink or baloney sandwich. Unlike most books, my annals are not a television program in a different format. Just as the Reader has certain expectations of his author (no doubt exceeded), his author has expectations of him: attendance is mandatory. As a magnanimous gesture, though not in the spirit of compromise, I shall permit him to ignore the remainder of this section so that he may refresh himself and prepare for Part VII.

***

If a man were called upon to compile a list of the afflictions that beset our frail species using TV commercials as his only guide, he would possibly cite constipation as foremost. Whether this reflects reality or the fathomless cynicism of advertising executives is irrelevant so long as the Truth is unveiled: no one needs the snake oil exalted in these depraved spiels.

As often as I, Petronius Jablonski, historian and philosopher, experience the sorrows of irregularity, I turn only to the soothing wrought by a triple espresso brewed from French Roast beans. Its efficacy is not in doubt. The only pertinent question is whether a man will have enough time for a vigorous stroll with his Shi Tzu before the mighty depuration descends on him with fateful imminence. On two occasions I experienced firsthand how the triple espresso is a force far greater than the will of man. On both, the insistence of an inexorable power altered our habitual walk, necessitating an emergency stop in Mr. Burzinski's bushes (and on one of those in the face of his earnest objections).

In summary: this munificent, mind-expanding gift of Nature enjoys my adoring and impassioned endorsement.

VII:
An Act of Libidinous Union is Interrupted by a Pterodactyl, I Withstand the Ravages of Tetrahydrocannabinol, Critique a Monument, Expound Upon the Perfect Government, and Reflect Upon the Night I Met Sandy but Instead Summon the Fairy Gobbler

Hieronymus sat at the table with a fork in one fist and a knife in the other, waiting for his steak and eggs. "That adorable little bird is singing again, just listen to him," my mother said.

Pressing my face against the window, I caught a glimpse of the merciless beast in our apple tree. Covered with mangy feathers crimson like blood, he jerked his head spasmodically, not unlike most rock "singers." I gave the window a few good raps and he departed, flying up to the clouds to madden the gods, permitting me to enjoy my breakfast in silence. The chirping had a definite pattern (which is not, contrary to rock "musicians," the same thing as a melody) and he repeated it interminably. The hideous tweeting carpet-bombed our helpless neighborhood each morning.

Later that wonderful day, the iron paw of Justice expedited the decession of this airborne tyrant. Our magnificent cat, Titus Andronicus, apprehended the adorable little songbird. Hieronymus tried to intercede but I admonished the child, using the episode to explicate the wisdom and justice of Nature. While the setting sun sent red plumes across the sky, our illustrious cat stood upon the feathered despot and looked to me. Seated atop our picnic table, I held out my fist and slowly pointed my thumb to the ground.

I awoke in the tent, smiling. I closed my eyes and tried to return home but the secret door had been locked until another happenstance opening dropped me through to some long forgotten locale.

Sandy crawled inside, possessed by a most pressing agenda. She disrobed and forcibly removed my clothing. Seizing my hand, she tried to pull me from the tent. I defied her guidance and feasted on the sight of her cherry-tomato nipples, their sensitivity not proportionate to their size: Mother Nature's second most wondrous use of elasticity expanded the circumference and protuberance to breathtaking proportions.

"I checked the area. There's no one around."

Preferring a banquet to fast food, I resisted. She persevered until only one of my legs remained in the tent. "Let's bring our clothes, just in --"

"We'll be right outside," she said, extracting me. "No one's going to see." And she led me to the middle of a clearing at least two-hundred yards away.

"Why don't we just go on the interstate?" I said, though the sensual overload from the cool breeze, wet grass, and sunshine registered immediately.

She grinned mischievously at me over her shoulder as she knelt down. I positioned myself behind her and we observed the redundant ritual decreed by the one mad emperor against whom there can be no uprising. O fleshly aggregate of life's bliss and purpose, beauty and filth compounded, joyous mocker of our spiritual yearnings, derider of the innocent conviction that our lives are necessary -- not the contingent by-product of hapless rutting brutes -- you lack the magnificent finality of checkmate and its snowflake variance. The only point of your game is its perpetuation.

An earthquake crumbled the crust of my mind, pulverizing the shanties that make me different from the other animals. The misery of being human abated, sweet misery. I focused on the rhythmic *squish* and looked up to distract myself and beheld a pterodactyl flying over us. A truncheon of a neck connected its sickle-like beak and head to billowing leather sails. In its talons it carried a zebra and majestically soared beyond the horizon.

"By the gods."

"Not yet," Sandy pleaded, triangular muscles cresting across her back, her head touching the ground. The distraction turned what would have been a scherzo into the Tetralogy. (Nasty, brutish, and *long* is the goal.) What permutations can determine if the different patterns of ivory drops are finite or numberless? This celebration of Nature's superfluous abundance, lacteous ropes lashed across an altar of tan skin, should it instill humility (there but for the grace of brute chance go we) or grandiosity (for each man born, a billion never exist)? We scurried back, Sandy scouting the land for voyeurs while I, my diminishing erection bouncing conspicuously, searched the heavens for reptilian predators.

Propped upon our elbows, we lay on our bellies with our heads outside the tent. I supplemented the post-coital euphoria with a cigarette and scuffled with thoughts of breakfast and flying lizards: ignoring the first, assessing the significance of the latter.

"I packed a huge joint in my bag," said Sandy.

"Save it."

"It's going to be such a nice day," she said with the mewling intonation of a pouty little girl.

"We shall return to the road immediately," I said, ousting this option with the finality of death. An extrapolation demonstrated that I would soon be besieged with signs. To attend to them I required the full acquisition of my wits.

"Let's just smoke a little bit," she said, turning on her side and laying her thigh across my back, as though such crude bait could ensnare my immutable Reason.

"And spend the rest of the day in a stupor? Save it for a night when we have a motel. The trappings of civilization have a synergistic relationship with tetrahydrocannabinol."

"Huh?"

"Hedonism is not a lifestyle for fools," I said. "Robust and systematic gratification requires punctilious planning."

"I don't see what difference it makes. This isn't about laying the metaphysical foundations of some worldview. I just want to get stoned."

***

It did, of course, make a difference. An intoxicating plant, like an intoxicating beverage, provides a splendid means of unwinding at the end of the day. In addition to aphrodisiacal properties and the enhancement of music appreciation, it accommodates reflections on the day's events while building a natural bridge to the land of Nod. It is not, however, akin to a piece of candy that one tosses into his mouth whenever the urge strikes. As always, a judicious application of the Golden Mean is called for, unless one is content to shuffle through life as a sluggard.

***

After we left the campground Mahler transformed the backseat into a leather-quilted thundercloud. With greater length than I recalled it possessing, the hood spread out in perfect alignment with the curvature of the earth; Shiva stood just out of view below the horizon. In my brittle condition I could not evade the conviction that my car was a cynosure of every eye on the interstate. I felt like a sorcerer traveling through a village of simple peasants. These ceaseless ruminations on the perceptions of others were not altogether pleasant.

"Catch a buzz?" laughed Sandy.

"Surely there exists a better description of this condition. It increases the ability to think about thinking. Regrettably I am inclined to doubt every insight it provides."

"It's not reliable like booze."

"*In vino veritas.*"

Wracked with hunger pains, we stopped at a restaurant built inside a windmill. The waitress, messenger from an olfactory heaven seen only through dark glass on swinging doors, harbinger of ecstasy, herald of things hoped for, weaver of the thread connecting prayers made to prayers answered, was she not divine? I had the Lumberjack's Stack of blueberry pancakes, a Three-Alarm Southwestern omelet, a plate of hash browns, a side order of bacon, two tofu logs I pilfered from Sandy -- almost losing fingers in the process -- and glasses of chocolate, banana, and strawberry milk. I only provide the list in full because the meal stands out as one of the fondest recollections of my odyssey. Perhaps there is significance in this. In the parking lot I affirmed the feast with a stentorian belch audible to a family eating outside McDonald's two blocks away. Sandy, enchanted with our feast, made no effort to censure me.

Light traffic facilitated progress, but my morning indulgence necessitated a Siesta. We walked across the manicured lawn of a state park toward a giant statue. In a tourist's brochure found in the restroom of a gas station, Sandy had read about some much-ballyhooed monument and insisted we see it.

"To what is this a tribute?" I said, watching two boys toss a Frisbee, reproaching myself for neglecting to pack one.

"America."

"The whole star-spangled kit and caboodle or a specific theme?"

"The pamphlet's in the car."

Hedges encircled a giant eagle with wings spread. Sandy read the inscription. "I am Ozymandias, king of kings, look on my works, ye mighty, and despair."

"Shelley was not one of the founding fathers. I do not think he was American."

"It's intimidating."

"In terms of symbolic potency this is in the same deplorable league as the Phoenix. A more apropos monument would be a replica of a waiting room where an unruly throng tears through magazines and paces a narrow floor."

"What are you talking about?"

"And instead of a doctor or dentist's name inscribed above the receptionist's desk, the word *Tyranny* would be emblazoned in red. Because that is all democracy is: the waiting room of tyranny."

"Whatever," she said, hoping to abort the simple truths growing inside me before they came forth in all their indomitable glory.

"A less abstract though equally appropriate monument would depict Washington, Franklin, Madison, and Jefferson on an elevated platform designed to resemble a cloud. Each would be covering his eyes and weeping at the melancholy spectacle depicted below: a platform strewn with feces where gargoyles shred what little remains of the ambitious constitution they helped birth. On the highest platform, also designed to resemble a cloud, Nerva, Trajan, Antonius Pious, and Marcus Aurelius would stand with their backs to the other platforms, refusing to even glance at how abysmally low mankind has fallen."

"How do you really feel? Don't hold back."

"Of course, if financial matters impose a constraint, a simple monument could consist of two weasels -- representing the beastly but indistinct political parties -- engaged in a death-struggle for the control of a balloon, which would represent the utter vacuity of the culture."

"Thank you so much for sharing that," she said. An elderly couple had interrupted their sightseeing to listen. "Without your great opinions we'd all die."

"Although, with a few alterations the current monument could be altered to something you would find edifying: a brave and mighty eagle mauling a citizen holding a bong, or a brave and mighty eagle stealing half of a man's income, which could be symbolized by --"

She seized my hand and led me away. "You're embarrassing me."

"Was I supposed to fall to my knees squealing in a fit of onanism? Am I forbidden any criticisms? Very well, we shall stick with the waiting room."

"We should finish the rest of the joint."

"No, no, no Sandy, not now. It alters the perception of time, stretching minutes like taffy. Concurrent with this, it instigates fruitless musings on the opinions of others and conjures forth a variety of worst-case scenarios."

"You never told me it makes you paranoid."

"Because it does not *make me paranoid*. It is simply an inferior choice for protracted drives. In the proper setting it is, beyond certainty, one of Mother Nature's most brilliant and gracious inventions."

"*In the proper setting*," she mocked in soprano range. "The stuff doesn't come with instructions."

"Through the use of Reason one may access Mother Nature's instructions: to be used for short cruises, the appreciation of Mahler's symphonies, playing Frisbee with your Shi Tzu, and as an aphrodisiac. These are the proper and delightful applications of Mother Nature's beneficent gift."

"Where can we hide it? The smell will give it away. Can't they seize your car if they find pot?"

"We *can* and *will* save it."

***

As I sat beneath a tree the Frisbee zipped and unzipped the sky as it flew between the two boys. My foot went down but it was poorly embedded. Sandy plied me with all manner of sophistry until Reason, battered by flimsy but multitudinous arguments, abdicated. In the land of the free we cowered like frightened rabbits to ingest a benign plant.

Sandy lay near my feet, sunning herself. A Cheshire grin covered her face. "So what is it you want? Let me guess: an emperor, just like Rome."

"One can admire what he does not fully agree with. For government, idleness is next to godliness. I dream of a libertarian emperor."

"That's a contradiction in terms," she laughed. "You can't want a libertarian government *and* an emperor."

"I am pining for both as we speak. This paradox may stand as my foremost contribution to political thought. Only the force of a wise and benevolent philosopher-king could maintain such a system."

"Then it wouldn't be libertarian, doofus."

"Need I clarify the nature of a paradox for you? It is not two Dachshunds. It is best exemplified by --"

"I know what it is," she said, obviously enjoying our discourse. The combination of tetrahydrocannabinol and sunshine invariably suffused her with the finest of moods. "You think you can just call your nonsense a paradox and that settles everything."

"What theorists fail to understand is that freedom must be enforced and that it is bitterly at odds with the collective tyrant of democracy," I said, closing my eyes and basking in the only light that shines brighter than the sun: the light of

Truth. "Indolent, cowardly, and imbecilic by nature, human beings will expand the scope of their government until it bears full responsibility for wiping their behinds. This is the deleterious repercussion of addiction to the opiate of security. Verily, a sound government cannot consist of junkies. To prevent this, to remind the populace they are not zoo animals with diligent keepers but free and responsible men, a wise and inflexible king must show the whiners no quarter."

"This is like that speech you gave in public speaking, remember?"

I squirmed at the unpleasant recollection. "Where half the deep thinkers condemned me as a fascist and the other half thought it would be cool that they would be able to take all the drugs they wanted? Another failed harvest of minds. Allan Bloom, was he not a sage, a doomsday prophet? Now, as I was saying, a benevolent force is needed to defend against the perpetual union of lazy ignoramuses."

"The professor said it was too inflammatory to be persuasive."

"That censorious fool. It was both milder and better argued than the critiques of democracy put forth by Plato and Nietzsche, not that I would expect a professor to have read either of those subversives. Now please, let me expound upon my Utopia. Should I fail to transcribe it the duty shall be entrusted to you."

"Really?"

"Come to think of it, Buzzcut Bartul is already composing a draft," I said, cheered by the thought of my friend and fellow historian. His blazing shorthand and eye for detail had proved invaluable to countless projects of mine. "Anyway, the fundamental axiom is that particles of stupidity pose no threat compared to the blunderous, nose-picking ogre of collective stupidity: democracy, in short. Particles of stupidity possess a dangerous magnetic faculty and to prevent them from clustering --"

"An emperor is needed," said Sandy.

"Exactly," I said, with the delight Socrates must have experienced in the *Meno*. "The emperor does not rule his subjects; he saves them from being ruled. No matter how the liberated zoo animals whine and plead, he will not permit them to return to their cages. Traditional libertarians hallucinate about unbounded freedom absent a powerful force barricading the zoo gate. I suffer from no such delusions."

"You know, *all* these big political ideas sound great in theory -- especially when you're stoned -- but how would you prevent a bad emperor?"

"Just as this nation once had a document specifying the limits of the government's power, we shall have a sacred decree carved in gold above a statue of a locked zoo gate. It shall specify, in no equivocal terms, that the emperor exists only to suppress democratic uprisings, ignore pleas for assistance, and shun suggestions that he forcibly meddle in the lives of his subjects. His annual State of the Diffusion speech will expound on the consummate virtue of self-determination and the unrivaled bliss of being left alone."

"Who would pay for the force that keeps people free? You couldn't tax anyone. That's anti-libertarian."

"Sandy, the philosopher concerns himself with forests, not trees. Technical details would be tweaked and adjusted as needed. The greatest leaders always gave themselves some elbow room. Remember, my vision is still in its infancy."

"Can't you think of anything going wrong with it? What's the worst that could happen?"

Contemplating this seemingly innocuous query, a hideous phantasmagoria flashed behind my eyes. To describe it was agony. "Each emperor, to accommodate the whines of his lazy, cowardly subjects, would re-interpret the sacred decree in order to expand the responsibilities of the government. Within a few generations the accumulation of these tumorous growths would metastasize into --"

"The same shitty mess we have now," Sandy said gleefully. "You're already living in your Utopia. Why aren't you happy?"

I massaged my temples. "Damn this mind-tangling weed. Once I retain my senses I shall conceive of a precisely-worded sacred decree that will both isolate and avert the cancerous growth of government."

"Dave says you're just an anarchist who doesn't like the word *anarchist*. It's totally easier to criticize all governments than to promote one or the other. It's a copout. Some sort is always necessary. Would you really want to live in chaos?"

"*Monarchist* has more of a ring to it. That an intellectual pygmy like your ex continues to exert an influence upon you is most disheartening, especially regarding the deadliest assumption ensnaring mankind. Regarding this chaos you all fear: sundry governments of the twentieth century slaughtered upwards of one-hundred-million *of their own people*. How could so-called anarchy have been any worse?"

"My dad likes that you're a conservative," she said, exhibiting the tangential, free-floating engrossment characteristic of reefer fiends. "I tried explaining that your views are actually pretty radical."

"They most certainly are not. You make it a point to tell your father I am indeed a conservative, the only true conservative. The question is what one wishes to conserve: a unique puree of polytheism, monarchy, Stoicism, and the limited government man enjoyed prior to the dawn of agriculture -- all prepared in my innovatory Blender. It is the radicals who have besmirched these venerable traditions. *New and improved* is the ultimate oxymoron."

She put her head in my lap. "Petronius, do you remember the night we met?"

My thoughts converged upon the Frisbee. It unzipped the sky and my mind drifted through. "Sandy, I remember it like it was yesterday."

***

I stood in Sheridan Park across from the supreme master of the Frisbee, Buzzcut Bartul. Squat yet graceful, his opulent lifestyle never impaired his finesse with the disk, which earned him widespread renown. A heavy rain dangled silver chords between us. As many as the Frisbee severed, the sky repaired.

"Damn this rain," he said, marching toward me in cutoff jeans and sandals, his stately midsection reverberating from his powerful steps. "Let's go in your car for a smoke."

Clouds of steam drifted off my gargantuan red Catalina as the chords lashed it. Once seated, Buzzcut helped himself to one of my Lucky Strikes. Though a tobacco aficionado, he possessed a moral terror of purchasing it.

"Let's call it a day. What time should we commence our research this evening?"

In secret defiance of geometric harmony, a round face clung to his brick-like head. He turned it from me to look out his window. "I think I'm going by Heather's tonight," he said sheepishly.

"For a night of Scrabble with a vestal virgin? You can remain celibate while engaged in our historical quest."

"Just because my girlfriend doesn't sleep around," he said, a fury displacing his quiescent nature and departing with the fickleness of a summer storm. "Sorry Petronius."

"That Tricia gratifies her lubricious needs is a fount of joy to me. One, it keeps her skills sharp. Two, the same rules apply to me. Three, how she spends her time is --"

"We've spent the last three nights working on it."

"No doubt Gibbon wrote *Decline and Fall* in three-day weeks. Dr. Harris was more than a little skeptical of our grand project. If we produce anything short of a masterwork, he, never having produced anything original or significant, will feast on Schadenfreude."

Buzzcut held his cigarette in front of his face and made small circles with it, an indicant of a conclusion rushing toward the surface.

"While our so-called peers use page-long quotes to argue for bland, harmless conclusions, we are uncovering a whole unchartered universe. We stand to become the Mason and Dixon, the Louis and --"

"Alright," he said. "Seven o'clock at Otto's."

***

The gloomy, taciturn Dr. Harris, glaring at us through his bifocals and removing them to intensify his sulphurous gaze, had stroked his unkempt beard and shook his head when we had proposed a joint independent study titled, *A History of the Cudahy Taverns: Packard Avenue*. We had returned the following day to plead our case, wielding the deadly argument that his dismissive reference to Cudahy as "some small, blue-collar abutment of Milwaukee" was no less contemptuous than describing the Temiar of Malaysia (his dissertation subject) as a group of uninteresting savages with absurd religious beliefs. A twenty-minute session of furious beard stroking had ensued, probably infested by the realization that we had actually perused his dreadful, meandering, hagiographical doorstop.

"Alright boys," he had whispered. "Three credits. Due at the end of the fall semester. I will not give you an incomplete. I will not extend the due date." After a brief but intense session of beard stroking, he had removed his bifocals and fixed us with his legendary disintegrating stare. "Don't disappoint me."

I had emerged from his office like Trajan returning from Dacia, but Buzzcut expressed reservations. Though in possession of an uncharacteristically athletic mind for a member of our generation, a congenital diffidence often restrained him from ambitions of heroic proportions. "Petronius, what if there aren't any records at city hall or the historical society?"

"Records? We are starting *ex nihilo*. The historian who relies on books is no more than a glorified plagiarist. We are poised to become the primary source to which posterity, in humble gratitude, shall turn. For this we must go to the primordial, oracular sources themselves."

***

The vintage Schlitz globe above the entrance to Otto's tavern, was it not an atlas of dreams, radiant with the light from a better world? Buzzcut did not look up from his notebook as I sat down and positioned my feet on the adjacent stool. "Bottle of Pabst," I commanded, my voice a crash of thunder. Though billions of nights had preceded this one, and billions would follow, I detected a singularity, a hand-woven weave in the strands of Fate. I beheld the label on my bottle as Edmund Hilary must have looked upon the flag he planted atop Everest. "So where do we stand, Buzzcut?"

"I think we'll need to present this thing as a horizontal tree, the trunk being the first tavern established. Branches multiply over the course of the century."

"Will we wear cute matching dresses when we present our little chart? Will we invite our mommies? Will we serve cookies?"

"We have too much data to put in a simple paper," he said, squeezing a slice of lemon over his gin and tonic.

"No doubt Boswell warned Johnson not to put too many words in his dictionary."

"Different old-timers are giving us different names and dates. We at least need a thesis."

"Please remind me, what was Suetonius' thesis? Did he use a mulberry or chestnut tree to coalesce the staggering volume of data he worked with? A great historian does not theorize; he installs a window where none existed, he provides a clear view of what has been obscured."

"Gibbon theorized."

"I am aware of that great man's shortcomings," I snapped, "all of which are more than redeemed by his pinnacling prose. Now, while we gather data unrelentingly, tonight we must address the question of whether to begin with a *prologue,* a *prolegomenon,* or a *preamble.* I contend that a *prolegomenon* is the proper choice, *prologues* being the filthy denizens of science fiction and fantasy novels. And given Harris' modest scholarship we can safely assume he has never before encountered a *prolegomenon.* The very word will strike terror into his black heart, an overture of the awe that will send him to his knees long before our addendum to our prolegomenon."

"We need to visit different bars. This well is dry. We've interviewed all the regulars."

I bristled at the gruesome inevitability of this. It was neither the patrons nor the ambience of the other taverns that offended me, but their infernal, nerve-frazzling, soul-raping, caterwauling jukeboxes. Otto's boasted CDs by Sinatra, Dean Martin, and Perry Como.

"We'll stick with the oldest buildings," Buzzcut announced, usurping my role as the commander of our voyage. "I checked with city hall. Out of the eighty-two taverns on the mile-long strip we're concerned with, only a handful were built before the First World War."

I sought Quietude with the reflection that our sudden change of method might facilitate the extraordinary evening prophesized to me. We finished our drinks and plunged into the abyss, exchanging the air-conditioned, submarine-like enclosure of Otto's for the rainforest outside. Twenty feet as the crow flies, The Stone Age beckoned.

"The name and the sixties theme is brand new," Buzzcut said, mounting a stool while I admired a laminated poster of brontosaurs sipping from a stream of beer flowing out of a giant can. Beside them, a tyrannosaurus in a tie-dyed shirt clutched a bottle in one of its scrawny forelimbs. Artificial ferns and plastic boulders segmented a hall beyond a rectangular bar, within which a cherubic girl in a cave-girl outfit serviced customers on all sides.

"You are aware that Homo sapiens did not, at any time, co-exist with dinosaurs," I said. "Furthermore, the connection between them and sixties rock music is far from transparent."

"We'll have a gin and tonic and glass of Michael Collins," said Buzzcut. "Is the owner around?"

"What's the problem?"

"The proprietor is either unaware or willfully ignorant of the fact that the Rat Pack created some of their finest music in the 1960s. Excluding them from your theme involves a most invidious distinction."

"There's no problem," said Buzzcut. "We're doing a survey." He opened his notebook and paged through it.

"On behalf of the Milwaukee Journal, my associate and I are rating the taverns of southeastern Wisconsin. Our list will adorn the front page sometime in the fall. Mr. Bartul, put down two-and-a-half stars, at least until we resolve the music issue."

"We don't have Michael Collins," said the cave girl. "How about Jack Daniels?"

"One star. Inform the owner that his neighbor, Otto, received five. Prehistoric gimmickry cannot fill the awful chasm created by a poorly furbished bar and jukebox."

"If you want a straightforward Suetonius-style narrative there's still the question of organization," Buzzcut said, barely audible above the wails of the damned seeping through the amplifier behind us.

"Transcribe this verbatim," I said, lighting a cigarette and jumping off my stool to pace behind his. The awful noise initiated a seismic shift in my critique of rock music, completely inverting the reasons why it was horrible. "Concerning the essence of rock music's awfulness: a reassessment. Contrary to my earlier condemnations, the true curse is not the appalling lack of competent singers, but the incessant repetition of phrases. Whether a distinction can be drawn between choruses and verses is disputatious but irrelevant: *some* locution is repeated ad nauseum. Far from being an artistic method, this is the bastard offspring of necessity. Were all phrases to be used no more than once, few rock songs would last longer than ten seconds."

"What's he doing?" the cave-girl asked.

"He's also a music critic," Buzzcut said.

"The upshot of this new alignment is momentous. If the primary curse was merely a function of the performers, an actual singer with the support of an actual band could, in theory, perform the songs in a manner that resembled music. This is impossible for virtually all rock songs. For example -- Buzzcut, did the perpetrators of this abomination dare to name it?"

"'She Loves You' by the Beatles."

"Now, even the Rat Pack, while reading the *lyric* off the matchbook necessary to contain it, could not salvage 'She Loves You' because it is not a song but an incessantly repeated phrase."

"This is why we never get anything done. Do you really need reasons not to like certain types of music?"

"*Et tu*, Buzzcut? Worshipping the Moloch of subjectivity? The sacrifice slaughtered on your vile altar is civilization herself."

"Vile altar? Surely some things are subjective."

"A thousand times no," I said, returning to my stool. "Were I to edit Dante's modest effort to make some improvements and updates, aside from the obvious change from mono to polytheism, the second lowest circle of hell would now be populated with the subjectivity mongers: flightless parrots condemned to eternity in a filthy cage squawking, as they did in life, 'To each his own, to each his own. No accounting for taste, no accounting for taste.' The only fitting backdrop to this nightmarish, though perfectly just punishment, would be the mind-rending wails of the Beatles."

"Who would be in the lowest circle?"

"Egalitarians."

"Of course. Isn't stuff like food subjective?"

"Truth is not an exhibitionist. Truth is a shy damsel. A man must woo the Truth, not throw up his hands with a lazy resignation of *to each his own* at the first sign of resistance." I drank the foul varnish in my glass and winced. "Now, how does my reassessment compare with last night's reflections on music?"

He flipped a few pages. "On the Greatness of Moon River? An Inquiry Concerning Mack the Knife? I don't think it contradicts them. This whole snobby music-thing of yours -- There's no virtue in being a contrarian."

"One, I am not being a contrarian; it is a matter of being right. Two, being a contrarian is, *a priori*, virtuous. Most mortals are mongoloids. Holding an opinion contrary to a majority view *ipso facto* places one closer to the bosom of Truth."

"There's a bar we need to check out called The Silver Mine. It hasn't changed hands in thirty years."

With its beige vinyl siding and white trim, it looked more like a humble home than a senescent gin mill. Only a neon light in the window revealed its quiddity. The fluid, hypnotic lilt of pedal-steel guitars and a shout from Lefty "Righty" Schlebrenski greeted us.

"Half of the stuff he tells us contradicts the other half," Buzzcut whispered.

"Nonsense. The fecund evening we spent with him at Chuck's Fourth Base could become a historical testament in its own right. Has it not occurred to you that these seeming contradictions become compatible at a deeper level? That is where a philosopher comes in. Have you not read Hegel?"

As if to purposely avoid a confrontation with his reflection, Lefty sat at the far corner of the empty bar, engaged in his eternal and mysteriously regulated game of solitaire. Beneath a Brewers baseball cap and behind Blondefade glasses, vigilant eyes swept the cards, a televised ball game, a ten-ounce glass of beer, but ignored an inch-long cigarette ash. A truculent woman beneath a red, black, and gray beehive carded us before fetching our drinks. I blanched at the harsh lighting and unpardonable absence of a foot rail while Buzzcut lit one of my cigarettes, opened his notebook, and dispensed with all formalities.

"Lefty, you told us about a popular bar called Robin's Nest in the fifties. Could you have meant The Bird's Eye in the sixties?"

Nudged between a jar of pickled eggs and a bottle of Kesslers, my reflection stared at me. He looked restless, cheated by a promise unfulfilled. I blew smoke at him, putting a little cloud between us and giving him a ghostly pallor. I must have looked like a ghost to him as well. Seneca whispered in my ear, "What man can you show me who places any value on his time, who reckons the worth of each day, who understands that he is dying daily?"

In the men's room I discovered a gem so precious I urinated on my shoes and a generous portion of the wall and floor before composing myself. Above the urinal, upon an ancient and inactive prophylactic dispenser, on a faded image of a buxom bikini-clad girl who "will love you for using ultra-ribbed," some great man had inscribed something that tells us more about ourselves than the paintings in the Lascaux Caves.

"Are you alright?" the woman asked after I returned to my stool. I put my head on the bar and laughed until I wept. Unable to transmit the revelation to Buzzcut, I pointed.

"It's nothing, ma'am," he said after an unbelievably brief inspection. "Someone wrote something on the condom machine, that's all."

"This is not only dissertation-worthy, it could earn me an entire chapter in the *Encyclopedia of Philosophy*. Transcribe it literatim." Waving away his protests, I paced behind his stool with deliberate steps, avoiding the lines between the tiles. "On the essence of humor," I said, pleased with the bold title.

"I thought you guys was writin' about bars," said Lefty.

"We cover a lot of ground," Buzzcut said testily.

"To philosophers influenced by Wittgenstein, the quest for a common feature shared by all humorous things must seem a fool's errand. Is it not amazing how one cryptic blatherskite can derail an entire tradition? I maintain that laughter is nothing more than an instinctive reaction to the misfortune of others. Misfortune is to laughter what dust is to a sneeze."

"That's called *sadism,*" Buzzcut interjected in an acerbic tone, probably in the grip of some gin-induced delusion that one more night of Scrabble would have finally thawed his ice maiden. "Lots of funny things don't involve misfortune."

"Consider my paradigm. Ponder the grim plight of the man who scratched 'this gum tastes bad' on a prophylactic dispenser. Wherefore the humor? What Aeschylus, what Sophocles could describe the torments life will divulge to him at every turn? And yet the mere thought of this poor creature chewing on a condom -- perhaps, we can dream, trying to blow a bubble -- induces laughter the way a tap on the knee provokes a kick. This is utterly inexplicable unless we grant that humor is an instinctive response. Compare this to the joy derived from *Don Quixote*, the beatings of Curly and Larry, the lamentations of Laurel and Hardy, a man slipping on a banana peel."

I turned to my audience. The beehive woman, her back to me, watched the ball game. Lefty shuffled his cards. Buzzcut lit a Lucky Strike and exhaled through his nose, an indicant of a kettle steaming within him.

"*Ohhh*, behold the sorrows of young Bartul."

"I'm getting a headache."

"Heather must be contagious."

"Hey Petey, that ain't gum in that machine," said Lefty.

"That machine's empty," the beehive woman said. "Trust me, if you guys hang around here you ain't gonna need those."

"What about a loud fart?" Buzzcut said, stopping me dead in my tracks. "Those can make you laugh your head off. Where's the misfortune?"

"Brilliant counter-example," I said, not conceding defeat but graciously acknowledging the often evasive nature of Truth. "Put that in a footnote. I shall attend to it later."

The pursuit of greener pastures sent us down the strip in search of a drinkery named Dusty's. Buzzcut postulated that its owner, an exotic dancer in the sixties, could share an oral history spanning generations. Neon-illuminated hearths lined Packard Avenue like gaudy mausoleums commemorating fallen nights and forgotten laughter, but darkness entombed each. The contrast, in synergistic conjunction with Buzzcut's sullen silence, disquieted me.

"Did you know your headache positively disproves the existence of a supreme being," I said, offering him a cigarette.

"So it's my fault?"

"Your woe is a manifestation of a general premise."

"I know," he said wearily. "The evil in the world disproves God's existence."

"That's not the argument I had in mind. Generations of maudlin numbskulls have clung to that withered tit. I have conceived an original disproof, devastating and brilliant. The fact that we are not filled with Styrofoam disproves his existence."

"What's the connection?" he asked after a long silence. Like many men, the awesome power of philosophy both fascinated and terrified him. In our relationship, I was the candle to his moth.

"Why would an all-powerful being resort to the frail, contrived gadgetry of brains and hearts and lungs and all the rest of the jerry-rigged contraptions that comprise us? With its bizarre design and myriad defects, the human body is like a car manufactured in Eastern Europe."

"What does this have to do with Styrofoam?"

"Here is the crux. Gird yourself. Perhaps you should sit down."

"I'm fine."

"A supreme being could have ordained our functions to operate with the use of a divinely charmed stuffing. This would have the added benefit of proving his existence to us. Since no degree of scientific probing could explain its enigmatic workings, we would have to accept that a great designer created us."

"So if you were God you'd make living Teddy Bears?" Buzzcut said with a snort, relieved (incorrectly) that I had not disproved the existence of his beloved phantom.

"We could look and feel the same way we do now. He is all powerful, remember? Only instead of being filled with bizarre gizmos, most of which malfunction as often as not, we would be filled with a Styrofoam-like material. The crux is actually a question of why God's designs are suspiciously akin to Rube Goldberg's and not more graceful, more *godlike*."

"Would we still eat?"

"What else would we do for breakfast, lunch, and dinner?"

"Speaking of bodily functions, let's take the alley."

We urinated behind The Bear's Lair, discussing the preferred agendum of a supreme designer until the unmistakable sound of vomitus splashing against the earth derailed our train of thought. Behind Dick & Debbie's, bracing itself with one hand against an overstuffed Dumpster of ripened garbage, an elfin girl knelt as convulsive discharges voided the bountiful contents of her stomach.

"The poor thing," I said, zipping up and stepping from the shadows for a better view. As though struggling against a gale, she rose to her feet.

"Petronius, that's the Gobbler," said Buzzcut, awestruck.

"The Gobbler?"

"Brian Waztakaluski pointed her out to me at The Pumpkin Tree. He says she entertained at Travis Olkeshevski's bachelor party."

"Let me make a conjecture. The entertainment did not involve balloon twisting."

"That's a good conjecture."

"I shall further surmise that like a plumber or electrician, she is in possession of a much sought-after skill which she exchanges for money."

"For a guy who hates theorizing you're pretty good at it."

"A true conservative can only weep when he contemplates the curse cast by prudish enthusiasts upon the very cornerstone of capitalism, the primordial exchange."

"You guys got a smoke?" she said. Waist-length hair dyed luminous framed her bony face. Scrawny arms wound their way out of an AC/DC shirt stretched over a petite but pendulous bosom. If called upon to compose an appurtenance to my earlier conjectures, I would surmise, judging from the pink pool surrounding her, that the gastric distress had been brought on by the injudicious consumption of Alabama Slammers. "This thing's harsh," she said, squinting suspiciously at her Lucky Strike.

"The only thing a regular one filters is full tobacco satisfaction," I told her, dizzy with the longing of a man waiting in Taco Bell's drive through after the bars have closed.

"You guys horny?" She blew smoke in my face and placed her hands on curvy hips wrapped by faded and frayed jeans. "You got ten bucks?"

I dragged Buzzcut to the other side of the dumpster. "Loan me twenty. I beg you."

"She's isn't very pretty."

"*Pretty*? She is positively hideous."

"Why on earth would you --"

"At a certain point, call it the Goldilocks zone, shame and revulsion become a heady pleasure. When dosed properly, repugnance and remorse are positively intoxicating. With your twenty and my fifteen and the rest of my cigarettes I shall negotiate something most men have never even heard of. When, or if she sobers up, the very recollection may send her off to join a convent. I suggest you avert your eyes and contemplate the gruesome errands Mother Nature dispatches us on," I said, slapping him on the back before drifting through the secret passage, remembering that Sandy and I had not met until the fall when Buzzcut and I were well nigh finished with our opus.

Beneath the zipped-up sky the Frisbee lay next to a picnic table where the two boys sat with their parents.

Sandy sat across from me and stretched, revealing several days of stubble under her arms. Sweat glistened on her face.

"Are you proud of yourself?"

"Very." She stood and touched her toes, flexing slender biceps and small bulbous shoulders exposed by a tank top.

"Before you disable us with any more bright ideas, we should commence our journey."

She rode my shoulders on the way to the car, steering with my head and squeezing my neck with her thighs each time I complained of back pain. The driving proceeded smoothly. My concentration, though diminished, was not congested with refuse spewed by the undertow between the conscious and subconscious. While Mary Jane gently released me from her spell, I watched fields of little golden flowers and cursed whichever evil democratic mob determined what is a weed and what is not.

Regarding the Non-Superfluence of My Remembrance of the Night When I Did Not Meet Sandy

With the insinuation that my recollection was inessential, the Reader exposes a breathtaking ignorance of the historian's task, which is not to compile thrilling highlights but to build a clear window, abstaining from judgments so the Reader may undertake his own analysis. Perhaps the significance of this remembrance lay in its insignificance; perhaps it can only be appraised when compared and contrasted with other examples semiconscious phenomena. Here the Reader is condemned to analytic liberty, for the ethics of my calling prohibit me from so much as commenting on these and innumerable other scintillating possibilities. In this respect he commands my envy. If only my hands were not shackled by the integrity of a scholar and I were free to theorize.

Had the Reader paused to contemplate the rather unsubtle point that the relevance of an event is itself a judgment, he would understand that a historian must always err on the side of inclusion, not exclusion. Note well: my remembrance is not necessarily an example of this. "Erring on the side of inclusion" is simply an expression. Like a wheelbarrow, it should not be mistaken for what it transports. (Parenthetically, the anterior point is an embryonic statement of Petronius' Wheelbarrow, which separates the literal meaning of a phrase from its actual meaning. The folly of ignoring this distinction is pandemic. In terms of momentousness, my Wheelbarrow is the lithe Artemis nudged between the Apollo and Zeus of my Blender and Shovel.)

If the time devoted to reading the additional pages pulled the Reader away from the symphony he is composing, his negotiations of world peace, or his unification of quantum mechanics and relativity theory, I apologize, but -- as I have demonstrated in excruciating detail and with patience befitting a kindergarten teacher -- I could do no other.

I suspect, but simple decency inhibits mentioning, the actual motive lurking like a lecherous little troll beneath the Reader's criticism. Could it be he is perturbed because the detail devoted to the allegedly irrelevant remembrance was not instead lavished upon the act of fleshy congress that occurred after Sandy extracted me from the tent on the earliest pages of Part VII? Is it the Reader's contention that my *raison d'être* is his titillation? Does he not have an internet?

Much like the instructions for changing a tire, descriptions of libidinous union need not exceed a few succinct sentences. For this there are four reasons. First and foremost, the human mind, of its own dynamism, creates more erotica than Southern California. What honest man can avow any conscious interval of more than twenty seconds where some bawdy phantasm did not dance across the stage of his mind? Diogenes, put down your lantern. You shall not find him. Even while one soars through the stratosphere of abstractions, Mother Nature takes great pains to swat him back to earth with intrusive thoughts of human pretzel-knots.

A case in point: during my clever but innocent metaphor involving lithe Artemis nudged between Apollo and Zeus, it took no psychic to peer into the Reader's mind. Now, why would a man turn to a great work of history for what he can procure by closing his eyes? Is this not akin to visiting Easter Island but forgoing a tour of the moai to watch Gilligan's Island?

Had the Reader greeted my remembrance of things past as a precious gift, a rare and intriguing story of two young historians taking their first bold steps towards greatness, I would have been delighted to gratify his request for an epilogue. Now, I do so grudgingly.

Buzzcut, with his voluminous notes as a secondary source and his daily dialogues with me as primary, began his watershed *Life of Jablonski* in the fall, on which he toils to this day. *A History of the Cudahy Taverns: Packard Avenue* received an A- from that green-eyed, thesis-obsessed book curator. An appeal is pending with the Chair of the department. We approached a more erudite professor with a new proposal: *A History of the South Milwaukee Taverns: Streets Beginning with the Letter M.* Germinal research is underway.

On the Persistence of My Memory

With what certitude do I recall the events of my journey? With the fixedness of *cogito ergo sum*, that 2+2=4, and the certainty of death and taxes I remember exactly and in microscopic detail what I said and thought and felt at precise moments of my odyssey and am more than a little piqued that the Reader would even raise this question. Unleash the rabid dogs of skepticism on the virility of a historian's memory? Release wild accusations of fallibility? You may as well pulverize the astronomer's telescope or burn the carpenter's bench. I may not recall how long I held this breath or that, but in reference to details of any greater import my memory is an almighty magnet that lets *nothing* fall away.

When subjected to forty hours of television each week, forty hours of an internet, and forty hours of video games, the recollective faculty, like any neglected muscle, atrophies. O the tribulations of a well-endowed man in a land of anamnestic eunuchs, befouled with the slimy excretions of rancorous minds: suspicion from his Reader, accusations of forgery and whimsical invention. An entire civilization castrates its memory yet I stand accused of embellishment.

(Not incidentally, this buttresses my critique of rock music by explaining why the face-slapping insult of interminable repetition is tolerated: the audience, its recollective faculty all but disintegrated, does not remember that the same phrase has already been screamed at them.)

The single best defense of my prodigious powers of retrospection is sublimely orbicular in nature. If my memory were poor I could not have written my annals because I would not be able to remember what to write about. Indeed, the most convincing exposition of my memory is the very existence of my narrative.

It is only a supposition, but the Reader's prejudice against circular arguments, when conjoined to a bitter awareness of his own palsied grasp of the past, could be the malefactor plying him with defamatory questions. Perchance he once awoke in the midst of a lecture to hear a nervous teacher's assistant deride "begging the question." With sleep in his eyes and drool on his chin he did not bother to ask why mathematicians are permitted to argue in circles but not philosophers.

"By what right? Are they superior to us? If your conclusion is true, why can't you use it as a premise?" he should have said, pushing the professor's lickspittle away from the podium, inciting the next generation of philosophers to storm the math department and take what is rightfully theirs.

The circular argument can be a magnificent edifice (not invariably, of course: one must assess them on a case by case basis). The only argument more unjustly maligned is the *ad hominem*, where one attacks the man making the assertion. It is the salt, pepper, and garlic of discourse. Remove it and the stew becomes inedibly bland. More importantly, if the vitriol is sufficiently exultant, one can altogether dispense with the middle man, the position.

How can we explain generations of thinkers shunning these forms of argument? If their validity were granted most philosophic problems would evaporate in puffs of smoke. Just as Einstein allegedly upended conceptions of Time entrenched for millennia, another great maverick will now overturn conceptions of what constitutes a valid argument. My demonstration is remarkably succinct, overlooked by pedants like Quine and cranks like Heidegger alike. To begin with, it is not the case that --

Losing the thread? Straying off course? My little Candide your naiveté is charming. In this age of internets, laptips, blueberries, and every other infernal impediment to Quietude, it is tempting to liken Objectivity to a snapshot taken of a certain place at a certain time. Your innocence has spared you the torments of Oedipus. As if my task were that of a baby photographer enthusing his subject to coo and snapping pictures! Reality is not akin to a cuddly infant. It is a measureless lattice that can only be safely traversed via a network of tangents. The philosopher cannot, on pain of becoming hopelessly enmeshed in a dense web of ontological goo, plunge headfirst. He must meticulously navigate the catwalks of reality spider-like, stepping from one tangent to the next.

Take heart, dear Reader, most philosophers throughout history shared your childlike faith in the straightforward, simplistic nature of reality. Lacking the fortitude to discover and probe the lattice-like structure, they became embittered and denied its Objective status altogether, blathering on about perspectives, subjectivity, and utility. Petronius' Lattice is the last bastion of Objectivity. Fortunately, it is the only one needed.

When to disengage one tangent and traverse a new one? Which of an infinite number to take? A demonstration is worth a thousand descriptions. Heretofore I began with the strand of memory atrophy and went to the strand of unjustly maligned arguments. Just as I was about to demonstrate the validity of circular and *ad hominem* arguments, I raced over the strand of introducing my Lattice. Now, I shall double back along a strand to quell yet another of the Reader's hobgoblins: his suspicion that my political convictions are unorthodox, which swelled to dangerous proportions when he read the portion of Part VII where I critiqued a monument and expounded upon the perfect government. I fear that unless this boogeyman is dispersed, our progress will grind to a trickle.

(Given the prior sentence, I could have opted for the strand of mixed metaphors, but seeing as I traversed it posterior to Part III, I shall instead proceed along the strand of comforting the Reader.)

Now, in the political climate of our time there exists one axiom known to every schoolboy and beast in the field: a man's political opinions are not merely viruses spread by ideologues on campus and media rabble rousers. And they are tangibly more than a tribal tendency to bifurcate all things into Us vs. Them. *They constitute the essence of a man's soul.* When his body and mind pass away, his political convictions will shine on like the spectacular remnants of brilliant stars. How can the Reader trust what he reads in my annals unless he is fully assured that unclean spirits do not possess the writer? To alleviate his trepidation I shall demonstrate the smooth orbit of our ideological satellites. Then he may proceed free of the nauseating suspicion that he is in the presence of one of Them.

Like any astute man with eyes warily fixed on the events of the day, the Reader holds his maxims and theories close to heart. And even if those wary eyes rarely move beyond the television and two internet sites for news of the world, these convictions are no less vital, no less cherished. Unquestionably he agrees that our nation is experiencing minor disturbances. The perpetual motion machine of democracy (or "constitutional republic" or whatever we're calling it this week) requires perpetual tuning. Little wonder the engine knocks and grinds and belches greens clouds of noxious vapors. Assuredly the Reader entertains a theory explaining its disrepair. With the unfaltering conviction that we think with one mind on this matter, I will leave it to him to transcribe our brilliant diagnosis.

The Primary Cause of our Nation's Difficulties

(Not to Include the Possibility that the Original Design is Hideously Amiss)

A List of Culprits, Scapegoats, and Malign Forces Responsible for the Divine Breath of Freedom Reeking of Halitosis

I would wager my very life that the Reader, like any aspiring mechanic, knows how to tune the grand engine of government and declaims his expertise as often as the subject arises (or after he has enjoyed the requisite number of thought-provoking beverages, whichever comes first). Certain of our coterminous ideas, I shall take Zeus for a walk while he commits our grand vision to paper. If only the clever but misguided Tocqueville could have enjoyed the fellowship of a coauthor.

The Secret Recipe for New & Improved Liberty and Justice

(Now with Equality, Fraternity, and Nine Essential Nutrients and Minerals)

His heart unburdened by fears of impure doctrines, my little Robespierre may now safely turn the page in the tender presence of one of his own.

VIII:
We are Joined by Hitchhikers, I Expound Upon the Significance of the Bubblegum Slayer, We Join the Rainbow Gardeners, Sandy Dissolves my Prodigious Hang-Up, I Debunk a Puerile Legend, Introduce My Unnumbered Sensation, and Dream the Worst Dream of All Time

Hands of dread choked me at the sight of the gaudy bohemians. "The Brethren of the Free Spirit marches on."

"I swear to God if you don't give them a ride you'll get carpel tunnel syndrome from jerking off," said Sandy.

They scurried to the car. Like mustard gas wafting over trenches, the stench of patchouli seeped from the backseat.

Sandy kneeled on her seat to face them. "Where you guys going?"

"The two shows in Colorado," said Steve, introducing himself and his friend Kelly. "We're doin' the tour."

"Phish fans," I said. "O sweet release of death."

"Quit it," said Sandy.

"Phish? Dude, where've you been?" said Steve, as though I had been keeping track of the various musical circuses enticing juveniles.

"This is an awesome car," said Kelly.

I adjusted my mirror and discovered that the garish rags and paisley bandana could not completely hide the fact that she was rather fetching. "Do you like it? It is a Fleetwood."

"I love the voodoo doll."

"After we stop for gas, you and Sandy will have to switch places. You probably can't tell from there, but it has a tag around its leg. If it is ever removed the icon will come alive and run amok."

"Please watch the road," said Sandy.

"Do you have any other tunes?" said Steve.

"I have a vast selection," I said, turning the *Missa Solemnis* up a notch. Condemned to give him a ride, I'd be damned if I'd miss the violin solo at the end of the Sanctus. "Please, regale me with tales of your travels."

As they chronicled "set lists" and compared the acoustics of various amphitheatres, Reason reminded me that the poor girl's dissolute lifestyle was not entirely her fault. Just as Goethe's wretched *Sorrows of Young Werther* once inspired droves of youngsters to shoot themselves, Jack Kerouac's insipid and shameful glorification of hitchhiking possessed this sweet thing to wander the countryside in search of thrills or highs or what-have-yous. The two of them represented a living testament to the importance of literary influences. Books are our peers. If formative years are squandered with delinquent thugs, the outcome is all too predictable. Once Sandy joined Steve to rhapsodize about the latest jam bands, I planned on introducing Kelly to the towering peer of John Cleland.

"You guys ever hitchhike?" said Steve, lighting the first of several hundred pipes of marijuana.

"I suspect the sight of my shotgun, .44, and machete would deter most cars from stopping. And I would not dream of entering a stranger's car without them."

"Aw c'mon. It's as safe as any other type of transportation."

"You are whistling in the graveyard," I told him. "The problem with hitchhiking is its presupposition of a hilariously optimistic assessment of human nature. You put yourself and little Kelly at the mercy of strangers, ignoring or denying the inherent savagery of the human spirit."

"I think most folks are pretty decent. We haven't had too many problems."

"Wishful thinking will not change our blueprint. We were designed to reproduce and slaughter one another. The rest is window dressing. A wise man, upon reflecting on this simple truth, will arm himself to the teeth and trust no one, certainly no stranger."

"Here we go," said Sandy. "Petronius has this goofy theory that the reason everyone is interested in evil men, like serial killers and dictators, is because they would if they could. They're pissed that life has cheated them."

"Dude, that's fucked up," opined Steve.

"Totally," said Kelly.

"And *that* is not my theory at all. It is more of a free-floating observation regarding our obsession with bloodthirstiness."

"Oh, that's cool," said Steve.

"I have not made it yet," I said, beginning to feel a deep empathy with Dr. Doolittle. "Tell me five things about the Bubblegum Killer."

"He put a piece of gum on each of his victims," said Sandy. "But only the police and him knew what flavor. That's how they caught him."

"He was always chewing gum because he was a tweeker," said Kelly. "He's kinda cute."

"Gross," said Sandy.

"Why else did all those girls let him into their dorms?"

"He's the dude who had all the victims who looked like his ex-girlfriend," said Steve.

"Was she a busty Asian?" I asked.

"Like all serial killers he worked as a security guard," said Sandy.

"Which does not mean all watchmen are serial killers," I said.

"He just got married in prison," said Steve.

And for the next fifteen minutes they painted a remarkably clear portrait of a creature with a fifth grade education who spent his cowardly life murdering defenseless women in cold blood, including such minutiae as his unusual relationship with his mother, his favorite baseball team, his bizarre antics in court, his surprising discovery of religion, and the "kinda deep" poetry he had composed in jail. Apprehended four years earlier, he cast a giant's shadow over popular "culture." A man could not walk past a bookstore without seeing a new title in the window offering a different angle on this sphinx. Documentaries and even a motion picture had been devoted to him. In a better world, a small group would have turned out to see him broken on a wheel. And no man would ever speak his name again.

"He'll probably get another trial because he was on meth when he committed his crimes and the defense never talked about diminished capacity or --"

"Very good," I said, unable to stand it any longer. "That was far more than five things. What sweet nostalgia. Tell me five things about Buddha."

After an awkward pause, Steve, feigning confidence, said, "He found the path to enlightenment."

"The path had five gates?" said Sandy, turning away, appropriately ashamed.

"It had eight gates," said Steve.

"It was an eightfold path," I said.

"He's the savior of the Buddhists," said poor little Kelly.

"For shame. You know more about a serial killer than the Buddha? Please explain."

"I really don't know much about that culture," said Kelly.

"So much for multiculturalism. Very well, five things about Plato."

"He wrote *The Republic*," said Sandy.

"He hung out with Socrates," said Steve.

"He was black," said Kelly.

"He was Polish," I said. "Tell me one thing about Holbein."

"Classic composer?" said Steve.

"Poet," said Kelly.

"Astonishing. Fishwraps like the *Mona Lisa* are worshipped while his masterwork is obscure. This little episode speaks volumes about human nature. A clearer window to it does not exist. A psychologist needs to look no further for a frightful glimpse of our blueprint and a hitchhiker should ponder it every time a car slows down."

"Your're pissin' all over my buzz," said Steve. "What's your point with all this?"

"Even those of you who deny the inherent savagery of man know more about the crimes of monsters than the teachings of sages."

"This is one of his annoying head games," said Sandy. "Just because we know about something doesn't mean we stew over it. It means we're interested, that's all."

"That is the whole point of my exposition," I said in despair. "I want to know *why* you are interested. I am not insinuating that we are all potential murderers, especially not you, Kelly. I am asking why humans are endlessly fascinated by them as opposed to the oracles and --"

"What-*ever,*" said Sandy, indicating that our gaze into this particular abyss had come to an end. "You don't practice any of the stuff you preach, Buddha boy. What kind of Buddhist owns guns? And all the booze. They aren't supposed to drink. I don't think Stoics are either."

"I have pureed the teachings from a multitude of sources."

"If you really believe that humans are savages, why did you stop for us?" said Kelly.

Forgetting Sandy's role in my decision, I explained the strategic superiority of pessimism. "I may have stopped but

I expected the worst. Now that you haven't slaughtered us, my joy is palpable. This would not have happened with a shallow optimistic outlook on the world, given which I would have taken your benign nature for granted."

"Hey, are you guys in a hurry?" said Steve.

"A hurry? What's that?" said Sandy. "This thing's never driven over forty-five. What'd you have in mind?"

"The Rainbow Gardeners have a campground about twenty miles east of here. We've hung out with them before."

Sandy clutched my arm. "They're supposed to be totally cool. Please."

"Party with the totally cool Rainbow Gardeners?"

"They're nudists," said Kelly.

The golden rays of a dream fulfilled perforated the shadows of an interminable night. "I need to be entirely clear on this point," I said after a long pause. "No one will be wearing any clothing."

"Right," said Steve.

I buzzed up my window and buried the gas pedal. After years of reading about these hallowed celebrations from ancient sources I was finally going to attend one. "At what time does the Bacchanalia commence? Will the *orgia* have rites of initiation for newcomers? What is the male to female ratio?"

"Dude, it's not like that."

"Not like what?"

"It's not sexual. It's natural."

"Is that some kind of koan? No one is wearing any clothing, correct?"

"Right. They like to hang out in the nude."

"And this gathering is attended by members of both sexes."

"Yeah, but it's not sexual."

"It is natural but not erotic. What is the sound of one hand clapping? Natural but not erotic. What did my face look like before I was born?" The koan withheld its secrets.

"It just feels really free," said Kelly. "You're thinking about Roman orgies."

"Correct. That is precisely what I am thinking about."

"That's a stereotype. Society has this hang-up; the Rainbow Gardeners don't."

"It is not a *hang-up*. As a conservative I am committed to the restoration and preservation of man's noblest traditions. Removing the erotic element from an orgy is no less perverse than staging an all-you-can-eat buffet without a vomitorium."

"You're really creepin' me out today," said Sandy.

"It's not meant to be an orgy," said Kelly.

"And therein lies the tragedy. Radicals have destroyed civilization to the extent that when a man attempts to conserve a decent tradition, *he* is the one considered radical.

Who is the host or founding father? Perhaps with a heartfelt oration I can convince him of the correctness, the primordial integrity of --"

"Dude, there's no leader. It's not a cult or nothing," said Steve.

"You mean a group, of its own free will, in the absence of a charter or spokesman, has decided to engage in festive acts of non-erotic nudity?"

"I suppose you could say that."

"Did they gather one day and proclaim, 'Let us all remove our clothing and refrain from erotic undertakings.' Do they wave a flag with a round triangle?"

"They've risen above society's narrow-mindedness," said Kelly.

"Risen? Perhaps my critique of culture is ignoring a bigger picture. Is our species devolving? What would my great namesake, Gaius Petronius, Nero's tutor and adviser say? Would he not cover his eyes?"

"Maybe you should wait until you see it before rippin' on it," said Steve.

***

"If you don't quit staring at Kelly's tits I'm gonna smack you," said Sandy as I paced behind a shrub. All around us naked people of various ages swam, sunbathed, lounged, barbecued, and snoozed. While the non-erotic quality of the gathering defied comprehension like a drawing by Escher, there were notable exceptions: a group of young ladies played volleyball not far from where we parked. The laws of physics governing the undulations, did they not provide evidence that this is, if not the best of all possible worlds, a worthy candidate?

"It's because you're not used to being naked," Kelly had told me before taking a hike with Steve.

Lamenting the absence of an *orgia*, I had tried explaining there was a more traditional explanation.

"Did that thing go down yet?" Sandy said, trying and not succeeding in her attempt to appear natural. The main problem involved the positioning of her arms. Across the chest they made her appear apprehensive. Dangling at the sides did not feel right, as though hands were meant to be placed in pockets.

"I do not think it is going down anytime soon," I said. Like some giant divining rod near Niagara Falls, a part of me was pulled toward the volleyball game. Although the proportions of this obeliscal symbol of power and life, this conduit of bliss, this meaty connector of present and future, are of supreme importance, beyond a certain degree it can become a burden, a veritable millstone.

"No one gets a hard-on at a nudist colony."

"Is that one of their dogmas? Is that in their manifesto? That has the delicious stupidity of *bourgeoisie oppression of the proletariat*. Apparently I have not transcended this particular *hang-up*. Not to worry, for it is natural, not sexual or erotic." I stepped from behind the shrub and stood next to Sandy with arms outstretched. "Much like the emperor with no clothes, I shall go unnoticed. The oblivious Rainbow Gardeners will attribute the condition to humidity, the barometric pressure, or some other phenomenon. I wonder if they have alternative explanations for pregnancy, such as tidal patterns or moon phases."

"Oh hell. Get behind the bush. We can't walk around yet."

Realizing there was only one certain means of diminishing my prodigious hang-up, I plunged headfirst into the center of the storm. "Did you see Kelly's awesome little tattoo? It's a butterfly."

"You hate tattoos on women. How many times have you told me it looks tacky? That's the lamest hypocrisy and you words words words words words words words …"

And in less than a minute I emerged from the shrub with flaccid innocence and we commenced our promenade. An article in *Scientific American* once declared peripheral vision to be illusory. That article was wrong.

"Behold the ravages of gravity," I said, squeezing Sandy's hand as an elderly man jumped to catch a boomerang.

"Is that going to happen to you?"

"Verily, gravity is a heartless scourge."

"I don't know if I like this place."

"Traditions are not created willy-nilly," I said, staring at cloud formations while testing my fledgling peripheral powers on a bronzed woman with barely discernible tan lines lathering herself with buttery lotion. "They arise via a long and rigorous process of selection. To shun a tradition perfected by the Greeks and Romans in favor of this nonsense is no less calumnious than the destruction of the nuclear family."

"I'm not saying I'd prefer group sex. I'm just agreeing there's something freaky about this."

I tested the icy water of a lake and looked away from two male manatees splashing after a football. "*Group sex* is not an encompassing summary of the tradition. Heavy petting amidst feasting and imbibing is perhaps a better description, which, you must admit, is infinitely preferable to wandering about in some Garden of asexual Eden. Clothing is another of mankind's hallowed traditions. Contrary to these silly people, it is not a hang-up. One of its purposes is specifically erotic in nature: Who wants to receive an unwrapped present? In addition to protecting us from the elements, it inflames the imagination in a way that a dangling scrotum or sagging bosom does not. This hatred of tradition plagues us in such a multitude of forms a man scarcely knows where to begin a critique. A pattern emerges: arrogant little know-it-alls toss aside centuries of established wisdom with catastrophic results. Consider the revolutions in France, Russia, and America, the catastrophic 1960s, the substitution of polytheism with monotheism, women shaving their pubic region. I am not referring to Kelly. These women are hippies and they're doing it. From whence does this urge to desecrate Nature's beauty arise."

"It's a porn thing."

"Of course. Standards in our republic are decreed by pornographer kings. Please find me some hemlock."

"Hey you two," Kelly yelled to us. "This guy knows where we can find drum trees."

She stood beside an RV with Steve and a cinnamon man with no tan lines. A scraggly gray beard dipped below his sternum. Gandhi was muscle-bound by comparison. He watched Sandy approach from behind mirrored sunglasses.

"Again lament the depredation of gravity," I whispered to Sandy. "Swing low sweet chariot."

"Knock it off," she said, suppressing a giggling jag, a conniption that once initiated had a slow rate of entropy and could not be prematurely terminated.

Steve introduced us to Clicky, who had been with the Rainbow Gardeners when they were called Sunshine Farmers. "The magic drum trees of azure," he said in a slow drawl, leaning on a walking stick topped by a brass skull. "There's a grove not too far from here. You know anything about them? Gourds dangle from the branches and beat against the trunk. Squirrels get knocked out or killed trying to eat them. The Native Americans thought the ones that succeeded were sacred."

Sandy and Kelly stood with arms crossed, enthralled. To debar a return from my hang-up, I avoided the sight of Kelly, looking away from the smooth, impossibly narrow entrance to heaven, which was not obscured by any dark mediums. To dispel dreamscapes of them rubbing whipped cream on each other and feeding me strawberries, I initiated a dialogue. "The wind blows the gourds against the trunk. They make a drumming sound when they hit. If that constitutes magic the magician should stick with card tricks."

"How can normal gourds whack a squirrel on the head?" said Clicky.

"The sheer number of both ensures that *some* will be bonked. This was probably an early form of gambling. Archaeologists should dig for a terracotta Bingo parlor. You are not suggesting the trees aim at them."

"The indigenous people believed they did. I doubt if you're any wiser, son. No offense."

"None taken. But you must acknowledge the ludicrous nature of the traditional story."

"It comes to us from thousands of years of their wisdom. You think you can just throw all that away?"

Sandy flashed a wicked grin, as though *all* traditions were somehow equal.

"It is explained by a drug in the seeds, which deranged the squirrels and their audience," I said. "No man has greater sympathy for tradition than I, but a line has to be drawn."

"How do you draw it? And where? And says who? You never seen them with your own eyes, have you?" He took a step forward. His scrotum swung in the breeze like a pendulum. "You just read about them in books, maybe seen a PBS special. It ain't the same. I've hid in the brush and watched for hours, watched the gourds beat faster as the squirrels approached. I've seen squirrels knocked on the head twenty times get right back up and try it again. The ones that don't get eaten by wolves."

"The trees are purple?" said Sandy.

"They don't have a name for this color," Clicky said. "The settlers called them *azure*, but that's just fancy talk."

I yawned. "Because of their proximity to water a cerulean faculty has been selected for by evolution. Their relationship with squirrels is a classic example of symbiosis. The squirrels spread the seeds in the gourds. The trees enhance the squirrel gene pool by eliminating all but the best and brightest squirrels."

With the predictability of integers Steve said, "What if a human eats the seeds?"

"You don't wanna do that, son."

"Is it bad?" said Kelly.

"No, it's good, but it's too good," said Clicky. "It don't do the same thing to people that it does to squirrels. It was part of a sacred ceremony."

"Edwin Schwankmeyer documented their psychoactive properties over a century ago," I said, smiling at a young lady walking past. Below her pierced naval, four tiny tattoos depicted an animated sequence of dancing bears. The first bear, red, stood with feet planted. The second bear, green, lifted one leg. The third --

"Why don't you take a picture," said Sandy.

"Schwankmeyer, in his watershed *Seedling Papers,* compared the affective properties to nutmeg."

"What's that like?" said Steve.

"If a totalitarian regime permits its sale at grocery stores how fun can it be?"

"The indigenous people believed that spirits lived underground," Clicky told his captive audience. "The same spirits that pushed their crops up through the soil also controlled the branches of the drum trees. They called them the fingers of the gods."

"How could gods live underground? Were they moles? Who would revere such preposterous beings?" I prepared to demonstrate the metaphysical absurdity of this when the aroma of grilled food called to me. While they plied the directions to the secret grove from Clicky, I attempted to establish a tab with a man barbecuing Tofu shish kebob. The futility of my generous offers to pay him birthed a revelation: the Rainbow Gardeners' banishment of all pockets was merely an attempt to subvert the tradition of capitalism.

***

Enervated by cannabis, Sandy left the three of us seated around the fire and entered our tent shortly after nightfall. Kelly and Steve smoked *more* marijuana as we listened to the sound of fingers tapping. We planned on visiting the nearby grove in the morning when there would be fewer scavenging predators.

"Dude, I don't care what you say. There is something far-out about those trees."

"I would be the last to dispute the far-outness," I said. "It is a question of the fundamental explanation for it. Just because they are not fingers of the gods does not mean they are boring. Must everything have an outlandish tale to explain it? What is the Grand Canyon, the vagina of the gods? This anthropomorphic tendency is the bane of science."

While my crass denouncement initiated a giggling jag in the reefer fiends, an owl perched in the uppermost branches of a pine. Its amber eyes glowered down at us. Steve reclined on his side and I added a thickset log to the fire, hoping the crackling would serve as a protective cushion of white noise to the menacing drums, which were not commensurate with the wind.

"You gonna eat the seeds?" Kelly asked Steve.

"I don't know. Clicky said the men from the tribe would see who could climb the trunk and get them."

"How did they avoid being thrashed by the gourds?" I asked, watching Kelly's blues eyes search the tongues of flame, as her foremothers did for thousands of generations. (Though she looked decidedly better without her clothes, this in no way detracts from my general critique of nudism.)

"That was part of the ceremony," said Steve. "It was a rite of passage. You weren't a man until you climbed the trunk and picked a gourd and ate the seeds. Different injuries meant different things. The ones who lost an eye were brave, but the ones who lost both were considered visionaries because the tree gave them sight-with-no-sight."

"I shudder to think what befell the ones who used a pole to knock them down," I said.

"Are you gonna try the seedlings, Petronius?" said Kelly.

"Barge into an alien culture and exhume an extinct tradition for the sake of catching a buzz? It may have been a sacred rite of passage for them. To us it is a bizarre, masochistic curio. Though I did enjoy bungee jumping once."

"Man, Sandy's got her hands full," said Steve. "Why do you have to knock everything?"

"Your reverence for their tradition is misplaced. If a man is raised to honor certain beliefs, it is unlikely that he will question them. Consequently, we should feel sympathy for those at the beck and call of ruthless mores. We should not humor or emulate them."

"Why is that tradition worse than any other?" said Steve.

"*That* is the question," I said, jumping to my feet. "Since both Reason and emotion can lead men astray, the steadfast rudder of *tradition* is not to be shunned thoughtlessly. Ideas tested and perfected in the great laboratory of Time deserve precedence."

"Yeah, and you're pissin' all over theirs," said Steve.

"The questions of consummate importance are how to select from competing traditions and when Reason should override tradition," I explained. Steve, Kelly and the owl sat spellbound as I elucidated Petronius' Criteria for Tradition Selection and Rejection (which shall be disambiguated later, when it will not forestall the spellbinding sequence of events that follows).

***

At the cue of Steve's snores, Kelly moved closer to me. "I've been thinking about what you said this morning,"

I surveyed the armada of profundities that had left my port during the day but could not find an obvious flagship. "And what was that?"

"About how everyone would kill if they knew they could get away with it," she said, misstating Sandy's misunderstanding of my simple exposition. "I think you're right."

While I massaged the bridge of my nose, Reason reminded me that the day is the time for refutations and the night is the time for other things. A man might just as well juggle squid than philosophize with reefer fiends. They not only won't comprehend his scintillating analyses; they won't remember his corrections. He is condemned to begin *de novo* every few sentences. "Have you ever thought about it?" I said.

She threw her hair back and stared into the fire. Orange phantoms possessed her eyes. "Just between us?"

"Well of course, a secret," I said, clasping her hand.

"One night I was watching Steve sleep. We'd had a fight. I don't know why I thought of this. It just popped in there."

"You are not responsible for your thoughts," I said, touching her shoulder.

"What if they're evil?"

"Thoughts are neither good nor evil. Only actions can be evil. What thought, that you could not help having, popped into your head through no fault of your own?"

(If the Reader wishes to look down his gin-blossomed nose at me for espousing half-baked doctrines I do not even hold for the purpose of relieving a priapism inflicted by a thoughtless little tart who spent the better part of the day parading around in the buff, I challenge him to recall some of his own pickup lines and compare them. The very thought makes me wince: "Gee, you sure are beautiful. Are you a model? No, really, I think I seen you in the Sears catalogue.")

"I thought, just for a second, that if something happened to him no one would know. We met on the tour in St. Louis. It's not like anyone knows we're going out. I'd just head home." She smiled. Like the ripples on a stream, her dimples tugged my mighty divining rod.

"Know one would know but you," I said. "Was it the ability to get away with it that thrilled you, like when you shoplifted when you were little?"

"Maybe."

"Or was it because you would have a tremendous secret trapped inside, one you could never -- no matter how intense the need -- share with anyone else?"

"I don't know. I didn't think about it very long."

"No one would have seen it but you."

"No one would have seen it but me."

I tried to discern the pattern of Sandy's snores in the tent. The ominous drumming, in conjunction with Steve's raucous gurgles, gave me little confidence regarding the depth of her unconsciousness. I surmised that my window was narrow and closing fast.

"Why do you think about this stuff?"

"It is a subspecies of a general observation. Having a secret you want to share but cannot is, by turns, maddening and exhilarating. The border between misery and ecstasy is porous."

"What are you saying? This is why people do bad things, to have a secret?"

"It opens a private world inside that no other soul can enter, both Eden and Elba."

She stared at me. I kissed her.

"Petronius! *Don't.*"

"No one is seeing this but us."

"Is that what the thrill comes from? Or is it from not getting caught?"

"Both, but adequately describing the circles of this *Paradiso* would require a poet, the likes of which has not been seen for centuries." Her misgiving gave way to silent endorsement. Shadows danced on the pebbled dirt beside her head like jealous specters and the magnetic force deep within the earth pulled me into her again and again and again.

O the ecstasy of the Unnumbered Petronius Sensation: *the joy of getting away with something.* Often it is only experienced in flashes, moments of overconfidence when one is unconcerned with apprehension. Its intensity is usually but not necessarily proportionate to the severity of the offense. If Sandy had awakened, nothing short of military intervention would have spared me from her wrath. (And what would the drive home have been like? The testimony of Hippocrates would not have sufficed to persuade her that Satyriasis is an affliction, not a freely chosen state.) How cruel of Nature to place the sweetest fruit on such dangerous branches.

***

I squeezed into the coffin-sized tent only to discover Sandy on my side. I squirmed restlessly until I found myself walking down the street toward her parents' house. The fact that I was not driving gave me the requisite insight to avoid another nightmare. But why was I headed *there*? Who dreams about his girlfriend? The whole point is the attainment of what we do not have.

The screen door slammed behind me and I heard splashes in the tub. An epiphany struck. The cuckoo clock clucked "Ode to Joy" and I removed my clothes in the hallway and entered the bathroom where dozens of candles illuminated in hideous detail Sandy's ex reclining in bubbly water in a pose intended to appear seductive. I fell back and clutched the doorframe.

"Jablonski," he yelled, sitting up so abruptly the water doused most of the candles. "What are you doing here? You gonna steal Sandy from me again? You're a class act, a real class act."

"What are you doing in a dream of mine?" I had to send him on his way before the wonderful part could commence. "Where is Sandy's sister?"

"I thought you dropped that algebra class," he said, wrapping himself in a towel. "Then you show up for the final exam to cheat off my girlfriend and ask her out."

"Your girlfriend's inability to bridle her animal passions was *your* problem. Please excuse my unfamiliarity with the dating code alluded to. Was I supposed to wait until you filed an Official Declaration of Separation with the Repository of Dating Intelligence, then fill out a permission slip in triplicate? I cannot believe you are still brooding over this. There are approximately three billion of them -- two or three of whom might even endure your shortcomings if sufficiently inebriated. Who else is in this dream?"

He barged out and I entered the bath and turned the hot water to a trickle and waited for the good part to begin. And waited, and waited, and ...

I awoke in the tent and rubbed my eyes. "That Viennese charlatan would say my unconscious is having a recession," I said. Exclamations from outside summoned me. Sandy, Steve, and little Kelly sat around a fire.

"It was the coolest dream I've ever had," said Sandy. "It was *so* trippy. I was walking across a frozen pond on a summer night. All these weird colors and shapes glowed beneath the ice but I couldn't tell what they were. I couldn't see clearly through the surface no matter --"

"Oh by the gods," I cried. "You had *my* dream. That is the dream *I* was supposed to have. You slept on the wrong side and he sent it to the wrong person."

Sandy's mouth fell open. "He? Sent?"

Bringing characteristic clarity to the situation, Steve said, "Dude, what the fuck?"

"What else happened?" I said.

"There was this giant fish on the shore. He was flashing like a stoplight and he was crying for help. I felt sorry for him and I tried to help him get back in the --"

"That was obviously a distraction, a red herring. How much clearer could it have been? The importance of that dream was beneath the surface."

They stared at me. The fire crackled. A bird cried for its mother. I lit a cigarette with a burning twig and tried salvaging what I could from my stolen dream. "What was under the ice?"

"I couldn't tell. It was like swirling mist. Some of the shapes were huge. Just as I was about to make them out they moved away."

"Did you put your face to the ice? Was any attempt made to break it? Was there a tool nearby, perhaps a shovel?"

"Dude, your freakin' me out," said Steve.

"Did you have any dreams last night?" said Kelly.

"As a matter of fact, I did. I had Sandy's dream. While she ignored a valley of jewels to help a red herring, I made awkward small talk with her cretinous ex-boyfriend. The candles surrounding the bathtub were such a romantic touch. Do you have this dream often, Sandy?"

She burst into laughter. "You and Dave took a bath?"

"No, I offered him some desperately needed advice. Now, did you attempt to break the surface?"

"Please stop this. I can understand that you're all freaked out because you took a bath with Dave, but that's no reason --"

"No bath was taken."

"Dude, it's cool," said Steve.

"It's nothing to be ashamed of," said Kelly. "All men have fantasies like that."

"The hell we do. How did the dream end?"

"A voice called me. No, it was a bunch of voices speaking at once."

"That is called a chorus. What did it tell you?"

"I walked toward these zebras. I think they were the chorus. Then the poor fish started crying and I ran back to him and I couldn't hear the voices anymore."

"Incredible. The herring distracted you twice."

***

"He gets too excited sometimes," I heard Sandy say while I stared at tire tracks in the dirt where we'd parked. The drums had dissipated to periodic thumps.

"It's cool," said Steve. "No big deal."

"He has a lot of ideas that don't make sense the first time you hear them, but then after a while you realize that --"

"He seems real smart," said Kelly. "Maybe he's --"

"Maybe that dream freaked him out," said Steve.

"We'll get our stuff together and hopefully stop for breakfast before we see the trees," Sandy said. "I'm starving."

"That's really cool of you guys and all, but you're not heading anywhere near Red Rocks and the sooner, you know, we hook up with someone else doin' the tour --"

"He's fine," said Sandy. "There's nothing wrong with him."

"We always hitch like this," said Kelly. "You gotta look for a ride goin' the whole way."

Sandy walked from the campsite and joined me by my car, waiting until my eyes met hers. "You're scaring me. Do you have any idea what you sound like? Are you okay? This is all because you're homophobic, right?"

"I am aware this sounds a tad whimsical, but you must trust me. The precise explanation cannot be revealed until --"

"Whimsical? You yelled at me for stealing your fucking dream. You're totally freaking me out."

"Steve has made that point eloquently. Apparently you're all *freaked out*. Duly noted. Now, what must I do to *un-freak* or *de-freak* you?

"Stop talking *crazy*," she pleaded. "This is the way your dad sounded before he --"

I raised my hand but instead turned and slapped the roof of my car. "What Cato did, and Addison approved, cannot be wrong."

"I'm sorry. I didn't mean to bring it up. But you're scaring the shit out of me."

"Tell those two lampreys it is time to find another host. We need to be on our way."

***

The horrific music I permitted Sandy to listen to served as a fitting backdrop to my grave queries. Clearly, that was my dream. In the same way our bungling mailman delivers my copy of *Chess Life* to Mr. Burzinski by mistake, my dream was sent to Sandy. This hypothesis, though colorful, is perfectly rational. My mind is functioning normally.

But what on earth does *normal* mean? Normal for whom? The rest of the drooling nebbishes stumbling across this dismal planet? To think normally in that fashion I would need to be contemplating the significance of the Bubblegum Killer's poetry or reading a vampire novel.

My thoughts are in concord with the way they usually are. They are *normal* in that sense.

But if your thoughts are the measure by which you judge your thoughts and you need your thoughts to conduct the measurement …

Can a ruler measure itself to see if it is twelve inches long?

IX:
The Ripened Fruits of the Mind

If only Memory could be cleaned out like an attic, the important and treasured items restored and preserved, the rest discarded like the junk they are. How often must unmarked boxes fall off the shelves and bury us in knickknacks, few of which were worth anything when we first encountered them.

While Sandy devoured a breakfast of blueberry pancakes, mighty tremors shook the cluttered storage in my mind, dislodging a cobwebbed memento of the day before our departure.

***

I paused before entering the ashen building to fortify myself with meditations on the insignificance of my Sociology seminar in the greater order of things. "A million years hence, no one will know of this day's existence," I said cheerfully, watching the bustle between summer classes.

As always, I toiled to penetrate the topsoil of my studies, heading straight for bedrock, thereby enriching the learning experience for my professors and fellow students alike. Alas, my preoccupation with the Chosen Chariot and the impending journey constrained my labors, leaving me stranded in the limbo of mediocrity with the rest of the ciphers.

Two fellow pariahs joined me outside, also consigned to the smokers' colony by a collapsing civilization that bestows eminence upon life extension but not the pursuit of Truth, for which tobacco is an absolute necessity. (Have we not modeled our "culture" on the vain, greedy, and shallow Croesus, king of Lydia, who, when he asked Solon, the lawgiver of Athens, to name the most fortunate man, was horrified to hear examples of ordinary men dying noble deaths, not rich men living long lives? All things in moderation, dear Reader, *especially* life.)

Mysterious but not secretive, both girls were members of an exotic coven whose presence at school grew with each semester. They dressed entirely in black with matching hair, lips, and nails. Buzzcut entertained the ludicrous theory that they were nothing more than meretricious art students obsessed with vampire lore. As I fell spellbound against the wall, paralyzed by their macabre charms, I understood that his sneer masked the terror of a man confronted by powers far beyond his ken. Their dark allure presented me with the antithesis of Sandy's wholesome beauty. Paying my discourteous inquisitiveness no heed, they seduced me with their indifference.

I tore myself away and ascended the steps to the third floor, contemplating an ominous yet delightful vision of a torch-lit catacomb filled with the dark priestesses and the rest of their brood. Surely they do not hold their gatherings in the library. Fleeing enslavement and failing to suppress a part of me that yearned for it, I hurried down a long white corridor and stood before a heavy wooden door, bristling at the prospect of being engaged in dialogues whose subject matter had not been mastered.

In a gesture of respect, not a posture of submission, I bowed my head and entered. The white speckles on the dark floor instigated soothing thoughts of the innumerable other galaxies and the consequent extraneousness of our Milky Way. As expected, silence permeated the room, the professor's prohibitive measure against tardiness. I studied the nebulous swirls in the grain of the table's surface, seeking consolation through reflections upon the enormity of time leading up to this moment and the eternity that would follow.

Silence persisted. Having attained Quietude, I looked up. My fellow scholars sat around the table, but their heads had been replaced with giant blueberries. Faceless, they differed in size and ripeness. The leaves varied in length and style. As though performing a magic trick, the professor gesticulated wildly, punctuating silent words.

My hand trembled before it explored the familiar topography of my face. I ran my fingers through my hair for further confirmation while my eyes darted around the table, finally settling on the student across from me. I identified Angie, who often sought my counsel after class, by the generous contours of her bosom. What would it taste like if I kissed her? I wondered.

Feeling exceptionally visible, as though consisting of five dimensions rather than three, I opened my notebook with feigned nonchalance and glanced at the student on my left. Only slightly smaller than a healthy pumpkin and more purple than blue, with any careless handling his head would have exploded. The leaves were styled to stand straight. Due to the pungency of his cologne, I could not ascertain if he or any of the students smelled like blueberries.

With tumultuous thoughts yearning to coalesce, I sat back and pretended to take notes, hoping to ward off the professor's attention. Patches of gibberish emerged and evolved.

This is what happens when each prodigal branch of inquiry leaves the mansion of philosophy: big blueberry heads.
Perhaps I need more sleep.

Maybe Dr. Ferguson was right. But those ghastly potions extinguish the fire of genius and, far worse, reduce the number of my conquests to that of a normal man. Call her in two weeks if ripened heads remain.

Ripe fruity heads?

THE FRUIT OF THE MIND IS RIPE!!!

The significance invaded the territory of my mind. It was the sign spoken of by the Horned One, heralding the beginning of my journey. With thoughts in harmonious convergence, I looked up. With the transitory configuration of a cloud, my enlightenment dispersed. The professor's motionless blueberry faced me, her hands dead on the table. Surrounded by a gallery of expressionless orbs, I had no idea what they sought. My episodic attendance left few clues of what we had been discussing in class. I had to say *something*. I would not cower from any intellectual provocation. I cleared my throat and reflected on the greatness of Cicero.

"It has occurred to me," I said, my voice a crash of thunder preceding the lightning of my analysis, "that the problem we have been discussing will parry all resolutions until we contend with a metaphysical difficulty undergirding all sociological investigations. The problem is that sociology, like most disciplines, has been erected upon a cockeyed foundation. As a consequence, it stumbles away from the truth with every step it takes. After re-aligning the base, we may confidently proceed, prepared to explore the new horizons it shows us. The issue in question is modernity's debasement of polytheism. This grand truth has been replaced with a most baneful tale: the crass reductionism of monotheism."

I paused to catch my breath. I had no idea what we had been discussing but that scarcely mattered. This gambit had been successful in other classes. When faced with a discussion beneath me, I would declare the issue insoluble without the beacon of polytheism, thereby deflecting the focus from some ephemeral blathering to a question of eternal proportions.

"As you know, monotheism is the preposterous doctrine that only one god exists. The main argument for this absurdity is based upon an analogy, which I will demonstrate points directly to the existence of *numerous* gods. If I took the class to the parking lot to behold the august beauty of my Fleetwood, only madness could compel us to believe that its miraculous inter-workings are the result of chance. Bumper to bumper it bespeaks a wise and powerful designer. Can the same conclusion fail to overwhelm us when we examine our world, with its slightly greater beauty and complicated machinations?"

I paused and looked around the table, making blueberry contact with my audience. The juicy spheres sat motionless, enraptured by my presentation. I had no doubt the rest of the semester would be spent building upon this immutable foundation. I pretended to check my notes, a pause for dramatic effect. Then, with history's preeminent delusion squarely in my crosshairs, I pulled the trigger.

"But this argument is specious. My Fleetwood did not have a *single* designer; it had many. One group labored to perfect the five hundred cubic-inch engine. Another, learned in the sublime teachings of Euclid, toiled to produce the perfectly rectangular body. Another worked to establish the proper thickness of leather lining the interior. Now, when we behold our world with its many parts and layers, how can we propose that only one designer is responsible? Our very analogy suggests -- nay, demands -- the opposite."

Breathless, I paused. How is it possible that eloquence and profundity can join in such perfect concord? I wondered. Can abstruse philosophic ideas be expressed with any greater lucidity? A look of tranquil satisfaction spread across my face. Perhaps pride could be discerned, but not arrogance.

"Furthermore, monotheists ascribe to their deity the moral attribute of benevolence. Even the most cursory glance at our analogy reveals the fatuity of this. When we examine my Fleetwood, the idea of a wise and good designer implants itself in our minds. But look, I beseech you, at the Cadillacs created after 1977. What remains of our judgment as we curse these monstrosities? In the same fashion, how can the horrors embedded in the fabric of the world proceed from the hands of a single, benevolent deity? The conclusion is obvious. *Numerous* gods exist, some good, others mischievous. I suspect most are as inept and indifferent as any of you. The exalted truth of polytheism, well-known to the ancients, I now bequeath to this seminar."

I looked up, prepared as a statesman of Truth to humbly accept the gratitude of my fellow scholars for their newfound satori. All the student blueberries were bent over the table as though embarrassed on my behalf. Seeking vindication I turned to the professor. She scribbled in her notes and slowly shook her blueberry: *no, no, no.*

The room spun in a kaleidoscope of rage and disbelief. Like an activities director on a ship of fools, the professor wrote an assignment on the board. A gate deep within me opened. Fury escaped; pity entered. I departed before the end of class, abandoning them to their folly. I ran down the long white corridor and took the steps down three at a time like gravity was making an example of me. Outside I leaned against the wall and lit an Oval and waited for my dark priestesses, prepared to submit to whatever vile rites they commanded.

Concerning the Reader's Puerile Criticism of My Thunder Metaphor in Part IX

Yes, dear Reader, I have "noticed" how lightning is prior to thunder. I am not confined to my study (as though one could be confined to an oasis). On occasions innumerable Zeus and I have stood in the backyard and marveled at nature's impetuous fury. The defense of my thunder metaphor will be binary. The second part is an appeal to common sense; the first shall allude to no less a giant than David Hume. (The appeal to authority is another unjustly maligned argument. A man who has been pulled over and fails to mention that his uncle is the mayor is a fool.)

Now, when I wrote, "my voice a crash of thunder preceding the lightning of my analysis," I implied nothing about a causal relationship between the two. To state "X is prior to Y" is not to insist that X *caused* Y.

Assuming we stoop to a less austere conception of causality: Did the Reader not consider the possibility that in the metaphorical storm, a flash of lightning (which was not mentioned) occurred *before* the thunder of my voice (which began the sequence)? Am I prohibited from mentioning any series of events unless I provide a list in full? May I not focus on a mere slice of a sequence, graciously expecting the Reader to rouse his dormant imagination? Verily, his penchant for literality would bring to my annals the cadence and fiery rhetoric of an Applebee's menu.

Parenthetically, if the Reader thinks he can casually peruse my annals while his lady friend is in the room he is as grievously mistaken as I am appalled. The very sight makes me shudder. In censorious pursuit of brilliant metaphors he lackadaisically flips the pages. "Honey, what's on the other channel?" he asks his "lady friend" (or whichever euphemism is preferred). "Are we all outta Boone's Farm? Aha. This metaphor don't look right."

Note well: my annals are not a pipe organ in a pizzeria. Now send her home. It is only through the gate of solitude that the Reader can enter my enchanted kingdom.

X:
We Stay at an Inn, I Introduce my Seventh Sensation, Behold Pitiful Armadillos, Dream of a Great Orange Train, and Encounter a Vicious Meat Puppet

Furious clouds tumbled across the sky like boulders down a mountain and smokestacks of lightning turned the buildings on the horizon into tombstones. I should have been looking forward to a peaceful night of indulgence but my trepidation only swelled as we approached the inn.

"Are you sure this is it?" said Sandy.

We expected a single level of twenty rooms marked by a neon NO VACANCY with at least three letters burned out. Instead we discovered brick rotundas flanking a glass dome and a sign bathed in golden lights. The brass front desk, reflecting a plush green carpet, gleamed like an emerald. Sandy tracked the scent of chlorine while I went to check in. The clerk who finally deigned to appear eyed my drenched condition with revulsion, as though I had purposely collided with each of the raindrops to provoke his aquaphobia. I waited for a proper, servile greeting but received none. "Yes, you may help me," I said, laying my wet arms on the desk and shaking my head like Zeus after a bath.

With a series of distinct movements, each separated from the next by a miniscule but perceivable hesitation, the insolent clerk produced a massive tome from beneath the desk and sifted through its onion-skinned pages. Perhaps he wanted his slicked back hair to convey refinement, to earmark him as a survivor from a better time. It dissented with a multitude of subversive ideas. He may have sought an intellectual bearing from his granny glasses. They disobliged, casting the sinister air of a deranged scientist or frenzied Wall Street investor. "You'll be in the east tower, fifth floor," he said, removing a key from one of many golden hooks behind him. "Has Mrs. Jablonski arrived yet?"

I laughed until I wept. "Never say never. Madness can strike a man down when he least suspects it."

"They say the worst part is not knowing it's already happened."

"Where is the pool?"

"We have a deep one. We have a shallow one."

"Is the small one a Jacuzzi?"

"You're not afraid of deep water, are you?"

I dropped the key and took a step forward. He tried to grin, making his thin lips disappear. "They're around the corner. Enjoy your swim."

The poorly-lit dome consisted of concave bubbles. A stained glass rendering of a Georges Méliès sun filled the center. Dark clouds swirled above and fractures of lightning illuminated palm trees, ferns, and a Tiki bar. Sandy stood beside the hot tub with one sandal in her hand, dipping her foot and watching the fountain change from blue and green to red and yellow. I walked across two shuffleboard courts and stood beside her.

"The water's so warm."

"That loathsome creature manning the desk probably accounts for the modest rate."

"Why is he loathsome?"

"Why is the Big Dipper shaped like a big dipper? Some things just *are*. We should wear pillowcases during any acts of fleshly union if we wish to remain anonymous."

"You think he'll be watching?"

"Or preserving it for posterity."

"With hidden cameras?"

"Sadly, the days of commemorating erotic acts on fresco murals are behind us." I walked to the pool and stopped a safe distance from the edge. Like a big hand silencing a scream, the insidious water stymied the lights, making the depth unknown.

"Let's dump our stuff in the room and go for a swim," Sandy said, heading for the exit. I followed her, taking furtive glances at the black hole.

The bouquet of a clean motel room, is it not similar to the illusory freshness of spring or the dawn of a new generation? How many prior occupants had rutted their night upon this stage, ordering room service before being heard from no more? Yet it seemed as though it had been prepared only for our enjoyment.

Unlike the majority of artwork one is condemned to view when staying at an inn, the picture on the wall was neither abstract nor vile in any fashion. It depicted the shadowy image of a train, the first few cars of which headed down a track at night. Behind them only shapes could be discerned, as though the train took on form as it emerged, joining reality on the tenebrous track between Nothing and Something, a journey for which all things have a two-way ticket.

We purchased two lemonades at the Tiki bar and billed them to the room. Three adolescent boys sat at a table covered with thousands of puzzle pieces. An ashtray and pack of cigarettes balanced precariously on one corner. The luminous fissures above erased their shadowy profiles, revealing faces animated by enthusiasm, or, more precisely, faces wracked with the edgy tenaciousness of dreamers setting out on a fool's errand. The miserable lighting made their success inconceivable. Ignoring us, they worked with an intensity juveniles usually reserve for idleness. The one who eventually bothered to look up seemed to resent our very presence.

"And what will this be a picture of?" I asked.

"We don't know," he said. A neon polygraph line filled the sky, illuminating his defiant green eyes as they contemplated the fractal pattern on Sandy's bikini. "The box it came in has no pictures."

"How many pieces?"

"We don't know that either," another said, not bothering to raise his head, as though such questions placed us beyond the confines of sensible interaction.

"Permit me to make a conjecture. You are anticipating a picture involving supermodels."

"We really don't know what it is, mister."

"But surely its eventual form is not a matter of indifference to you? After hours of painstaking toil, will you not be disappointed if it turns out to be a basket of kittens or a group of shirtless firemen?"

"Don't you think they'll be able to figure that out long before they're finished?" said Sandy.

"Why would you solve a puzzle if you already know what it looks like?" said one.

"Why bother if you do not? What if the result disturbs you? Oftentimes a man is better off with the little pieces."

Sandy nudged me in the ribs. Another explosion shattered the sky. The first boy looked up, his eyes smoldering. I grinned, silently mocking his futile endeavor and savoring the sweet nectar of his failure long before he failed.

(This beatific sensation, Schadenfreude *before the fact*, the pleasure derived from the *expectation* of another's failure or misfortune, clearly deserves a name of its own. I hereby designate it the Seventh Petronius Sensation. Note: the occurrence of failure or misfortune must be probable. Mere fantasies of them are in a separate category to be disambiguated and titled when it will not interrupt the mellifluous cadence of my narrative.)

We walked past the dead pool to the hot tub where the dancing waters bloomed like giant orchids in some primeval jungle. Sandy entered the bubbling cauldron and moaned. The hot water induced euphoria and I urinated instantly (this bliss, too, will be titled later). Resting my elbows on the ledge, I looked up at the concave barrier protecting us from the darkness above.

"Is it safe to be swimming? When there's lightning aren't you supposed to stay out of the water?"

"We should definitely avoid the big pool," I said.

"Why? What makes this one safer?"

"Oliver's Principle of Voltaic Minutia," I said after a long but fecund pause. "If lightning must choose between a large body of water and a tiny one, it always selects the former."

Sandy rose, peeked her head about the fountain as though checking for predators, and walked through the waterfall. Cocking her head to the side, biting her lower lip, and playing with her bikini to reveal flashes of what I had implored her not to shave, she stood before me.

"Do you have a principled objection to doing this in private? It cannot be instinctive. Our ancestors sought safe places when mating."

Her serene gaze nullified my apprehensions. The protean flowers bloomed behind the rise and fall of her shoulders and her wet hair slapped against my face. The water created the illusion of super-human strength as I effortlessly bounced her on my lap with a simple motion of my forearms, accelerating the flower eclipses.

"*Would you be quiet,*" I said. "Do you want those ne'er-do-wells running over here to watch? The depth of your depravity is unfathomable."

We finished our drinks and watched the surface water scramble to avoid the melting flower drops from above. When we returned to the room we fell asleep moments after touching the bed. I awoke rested and buoyant, assured that my dreamless sojourn in the abyss had balanced all my humors. Sandy lay beside me with her arm across my chest, blowing in my ear. A cross between dolphin talk and a muffled vacuum cleaner, her snores were more endearing than annoying. I limboed out from under her arm and headed to the window, pleased at how well the curtains kept the prying sunlight at bay. I opened them ready to face the bright new ... *darkness*?

I bumped the glass with my forehead, hoping to fix the sun the way one might reprimand a reluctant appliance with a few good taps. Certain that sleep would parry all threats of capture, I worried about the stupefied mess I might be in when it came time to leave: characterized by the hideous sum of grogginess, irritability, and despair.

I was a voyeur when it came to sleep, never having experienced much but painfully mindful that others did it effortlessly and with considerable pleasure all the time. I leaned against the headboard enthralled and watched the ecstatic look on Sandy's face. Like any voyeur, I was envious, even bitter. Unlike other voyeurs, I experienced no vicarious pleasure.

With dashed hopes of fleeing this unique anguish, I picked up the phone. My mother was quite the night owl and I had not checked on Zeus since the afternoon. It rang at least fifty times while I found an interesting documentary on the television. The show began with a group of armadillos in the desert.

"I was in the bathroom, Petronius."

"I was concerned. Tell me of Zeus."

Initially the armadillos huddled together, but as the sun molested them they waddled away, with the exception of a green one who curled up in a ball.

"Zeus is fine. Where are you?"

"How were his walks?"

"He doesn't need walks. He runs around in the yard."

"Mother, after each meal he needs a counterclockwise walk around the block followed by a vigorous belly-rub. These are not luxuries."

A gold armadillo took off at a good pace, kicking up sand as it raced up and over the mounds like a tank. The narrator indicated that it headed north. A blue one headed in the opposite direction, taking the utmost care with each step.

"He needs a walk so that he may check his pee mail," I said.

"His what?"

"When a dog urinates on a tree or hydrant it is like posting a personal ad: Handsome male Shi Tzu seeks female for sniffing, maybe more. An original theory of mine is that this is also a means of creative expression. Zeus is probably the canine equivalent of Li Bai. By withholding walks you are not only removing him from society, you are censoring him."

An armadillo with a crystal shell headed east, neither slow nor fast. A white one began heading west but soon trudged north, unaware or unconcerned by its rudderless bearings.

"Okay, we'll start tomorrow. Now when are you coming home?"

"Followed by belly-rubs? A morning belly-rub is to Zeus what a Bloody Mary is to a man. The fate of the entire day is contingent upon it. It is the hinge of the door through which --"

"Okay, okay. Did you train him to bark at Mr. Burzinski? Today in the backyard he --"

"*Train him*? The native genius of the Shi Tzu senses a heart of darkness and responds accordingly. If that statist oaf so much as speaks to either of you, remind him of my high esteem for the second amendment, not that I need the government's permission."

The camera zoomed in to show the lot of the white armadillo. Its underside looked like burnt scrambled eggs. Three huge vultures landed and began ripping chunks of meat from the sun-scorched belly.

"And there is no need to train a Shi Tzu. One learns from its Buddha-nature. They were bred by Tibetan Buddhists, you know."

"Hieronymus trained him to bark whenever he sings *Figaro*. It's the cutest thing I've ever seen."

"How much were you drinking while pregnant with him? That was when Quaaludes were widely prescribed, wasn't it?"

"He says that dog is too smart not to know any tricks."

A little head and four legs stuck out from under a green shell like five lumps of coal. Two vultures landed.

"Intelligence is an intrinsic good, not something to be utilized for tricks. Barking in response to a yodeling idiot, for instance. The dignity, the nobility of the wise Shi Tzu is derogated by such shenanigans."

A vulture landed on the blue armadillo and flapped its wings for balance. The monstrous bird let out a hideous screech and the poor creature twisted up its head to behold its fate.

"Now what's this place you're going to? Hieronymus wanted to know."

"The Point of Percipience. It is not completely unlike the Cadillac Ranch. I will call tomorrow. Remember, counterclockwise walks, then belly-rubs, and no more tricks."

A circle of vultures created a halo around the angry sun. When the crystal-shelled armadillo stopped and tucked its head and legs into a ball, they descended. After encountering initial resistance, their resolve appeared to fade. But this impression arose from an underestimation of their patience. They were stepping back to let the wrath of the sun work its black magic. Their cunning soon proved fruitful.

The steadfast gold armadillo plowed through the sand, periodically pausing to rest. The cowardly vultures swung low, preparing to reap the harvest of exhaustion. It adjourned and resumed the desperate voyage no less than ten times before collapsing.

"What manner of brutal spectacle is this?" I said, heading to the bathroom, disappointed that even PBS would resort to such tactics to entice viewers. Not that I blanched from the sight: only a dunce could be blind to the crimson tint of Nature's teeth and claws. The much-ballyhooed natural world is an abattoir, yet minions of simpletons revere it as some kindly, doting matron.

When I returned the show appeared to be winding down. Trails lead up to four little suits of armor, none of which had traveled very far despite their considerable efforts. As the camera revealed more of the desert, no significant distance separated the progress of the gold armadillo and the green one that had never left the starting position. The wind smoothed out the footprints and soon erased the shells. The camera flew across the desert, over the endless saffron mounds and the countless journeys they concealed.

Taunted by the stingy god of sleep, I decided to return to the hot tub, its proximity to the Tiki bar not ancillary to my plan: this deity is not impervious to incentives. Cringing from my cold swimsuit and deliberately stepping from daisy to daisy on the plush carpet, I headed to the elevator, relishing the generic aroma of the motel's corridor: associated with joyous festivities no less than the taste of Champagne.

The insolent clerk had abandoned his post. I envisioned him performing some gruesome experiment in a dimly lit chamber hidden within a maze of recesses behind the desk. In the dome, the painted face of the sun looked down as though weary. Only the outlines of palm trees and ferns were visible, misted by an eerie glow emanating from the seltzer water of the hot tub. The pulsating orchids were no longer in bloom and the meager light in the pool had been vanquished, leaving a huge hole in the jungle. Despairing at the sight of the closed bar, I realized I would have to enter the kingdom of sleep as an honest man rather than storming the gate.

Embers hovered in the air not far from me and I took cover behind a fern. As my eyes adapted to the darkness, three men with long silver hair and beards materialized around a table, frantically sorting something on its surface.

"Enough of this stupid puzzle," one said. "The pieces don't fit and the picture looks like *nothing*. Enough of it already," he cried, sweeping his hands across whatever mocked his efforts. His comrades flinched but made no attempt to restrain him. He stood, shook his fists at the indifferent sun, and dove into the black hole. Curiously, he made no splash.

Not wishing to share the dome with such eccentrics, I wandered through the empty lobby and into the warm moisture of the protracted night. My car faced away from the building in the last row of parking spaces. Across the street, trees with branches wriggling like sea anemones veiled the forbidding shadows of monstrous buildings, a reminder of our proximity to a large city. When I sat on the curb, my car became a train with no foreseeable end. I leaned on the grass and propped myself up with my elbows, disclosing the chrome wrapped around one of the taillights. "There is the caboose," I said. "There is the silver caboose on the end of the great orange train that is as long as forever."

My eyelids fought valiantly against the stealth force of gravity, their first dozen skirmishes ending in blurry stalemates, their eventual defeat not marked by any formal terms of surrender. A zebra-striped bar fell and a bell clanged and the ground bounced me like a child on his father's knee and a whistle screamed and the waxy light of a shooting star preceded an orange blur. Free from the intrusive and dubious measurement of clocks, the train -- its gaseous appearance a function of its speed, its luminosity inexplicable -- whizzed past for hours or days or weeks or none of these. Floating distressingly close and suspended from the ground by the vibrations, I stretched every muscle to reach the sea anemones but the milky tubes pulled away each time my fingers approached.

As the train decelerated, cars with a silky consistency appeared. "After" a void of what the officious calibrations of a clock would have decreed to be a very, very, very long time, the silver bullet caboose arrived. A bright light within illuminated two thin vertical windows on the back. The pink slits vanished and the concrete received me.

I sat up and rubbed my eyes, affected by a most pleasing stupor. I could have slept there but in a final sortie against gravity I rose and headed to the inn. The silence of the night kept the approaching dawn a secret.

Like a trapdoor spider waiting to spring, the clerk lurked behind his desk. "You prefer our parking lot to your bed?" he called with venom in his whiny voice. "You should have said so when you checked in. I could have given you a discount. There's a dumpster round back you might want to try."

"You miscreant," I said, charging the desk. While seizing his throat I noticed tiny wires connecting to every portion of his anatomy, controlling his every motion. Many were attached to the top of his head, of course intended to signify the contingent nature of his thoughts (even the thought that he is free). The obscene production had the ingenuity of a grade school science-fair exhibit.

"And this tawdry spectacle is intended to influence my profound and final analysis of free will," I said in soliloquy. "Just show me someone covered with wires and *vwalla*, I become a determinist. For *this* I exchanged my Bonneville? I presume this puerile sign is intended to demonstrate how a man's actions are caused by things ultimately beyond his control, how they're nothing more than the last dominos in a long chain. O the banality."

(The Reader must excuse my outburst, but the gimcrack display desecrated something hallowed. The preciousness of free will can be summarized thus: it vouchsafes to me full responsibility for my greatness. How may I mock the inferiority of others if I am not accountable for my qualities? Why, if free will were a phantom I could scarcely look upon some ignorant wretch and joyously assert, "There but for the assiduous application of free will go I." One of the two greatest joys a man takes in himself would be poisoned.)

"Do we choose the thoughts that cause our actions?" the meat-puppet asked, his mouth opening but not moving in accompaniment to his words. "If so, do we *choose* to choose those thoughts? If so, do we *choose* to choose to choose them? If so, do we --"

"Yes. Most assuredly. The bigotry against infinite regresses has left us defenseless. Most problems in philosophy admit of no solution without it, the *ad hominem*, and the circular argument."

Chuckling, he returned to his lair. Weary, I wandered back to our room and removed my shirt and trunks and climbed into bed and wrapped myself around Sandy's warm naked body. My last thoughts before hobbling wounded across the bridge to Nod resembled a prayer of thanks. Grateful for the gift of sleep, I blessed the arbitrary, callous, and deranged source that meagerly doled it out, the way prisoners freed after years in the Gulag thanked comrade Stalin. A dream about marionettes riding a train with no conductor curdled my sleep.

Preparations for Part XI

Books have different prerequisites, conditions essential for the reader's derivation of all they have to offer. For most, the ability to read three-letter words and concentrate for up to five minutes at a time is sufficient. Other books, their authors seeking rehabilitation for shoulder chips suffered at creative writing programs, presuppose a tolerance for pyrotechnic narrative styles camouflaging vacuous content. Heretofore my annals have asked for no more than legerity, but now a state of heightened awareness is requested. Just as the foreman would never send his worker down a goldmine with a plastic spoon, I will not let the Reader enter Part XI without the tools needed to retrieve its precious nuggets.

***

The Reader closes my annals and looks over his shoulder. He turns off the lights and walks to the window. A cloud floats in front of the moon. He contemplates the cold vastness of space. In his heart of hearts he asks, "But who will know if I comply with the prerequisites?" With the malevolent hubris of

Leopold and Loeb he asks, "What is to prevent me from ignoring them? Surely I can get away with it."

***

Prevent? *Get away with*? And what became of Leopold and Loeb? Dear Reader, there is no perfect crime. Compliance with my prerequisites is a matter of honor, an intellectual duty, the dereliction of which is a species of the genus theft: the Reader is robbing himself of a sumptuous banquet prepared on his behalf, and he is spurning my friendship to embrace the corpse of sloth. He may just as well throw my annals across the room and pick up his banjo, for our travels together are at an end.

Before making an irredeemable decision, he should take a moment to compose and refresh himself by returning to the addendum to Part VI.

***

An original hypothesis of mine posits a connection between the mind and body, from which it follows that to prepare the former, the Reader must first attune the latter. To recreate the discombobulation I experienced during the events described in Part XI, he must abstain from food, sleep, and all drinks save caffeinated ones for a period of three days. Then, while pacing a path of no more than ten feet and no less than five, he should begin Part XI on a street corner congested with traffic.

Thirty minutes prior to driving to the busy intersection, he should prepare the following recipe and bring it with him in a thermos. Note: this is only a crude approximation of the drink described.

Twelve ounces frozen strawberries in syrup, partially thawed; eight ounces light rum; three scoops of ice. Combine strawberries, rum, and ice in blender and blend smooth. Do not drink or even taste. Await further instructions.

XI:
My Fleetwood is Transformed Into a Tavern, I Receive a Rebuke from Agents of the Venerable Horned One of the Lake, Consume Several Strawberry Zebras, and Introduce My Special Potation Theory

Following an uneventful day on the road I succumbed to a devastating infirmity. Clutched by talons unseen, I lost the will to drive. A perverse and alien longing stirred within me, a desire to park and take a walk. Desperately I searched my heart for the root of this malignancy, but the pernicious force constricted its grasp and the ensuing restlessness impeded all reflections. In my pitiable state, unadorned conversation would have served as a soothing balm, but my little Burmese cat was busy attaining her mandatory minimum of sixteen hours.

Signs, gas stations, even trees had long since fled the forsaken road. Despite a starry panorama, I felt confined, as though driving through a big but cluttered closet. Unable to make a musical selection, I drove in silence, a victim of the same irresolution as the starving donkey who could not choose which of two apples to eat. I glanced in the rearview mirror while lighting an Oval and a pair of bleary eyes stared back.

They were not mine.

My heart misfired and I seized the wheel with both hands. Electricity surged up my spine, tautening even the muscles of my forehead. I held my foot over the brake and prepared to pound down as hard as I could, my modus operandi being that the sudden destabilization would favor me as it would not take me by surprise.

While different scenarios raced through my mind like rats in a maze, the voice of Reason demurred through an adrenaline-charged amplifier. "What if he has a gun? He'll be furious at you after a panic stop. What if he shoots you? Then he'll be alone with Sandy, *and your car.*

I pulled my foot away from the brake and fought to keep it steady on the gas. My heart, having survived the initial shock, pumped so hard my shoulders twitched. I struggled to conceal my disordered breathing, not wanting the intruder to know I was aware of his presence or, if it were too late for subterfuge, not wishing to disclose the rancor his parasitic hitchhiking provoked.

I tried to pry my fingers off the wheel and recline, to paint the classic portrait of the driver in repose, but I could not maintain the illusion for more than seconds at a time. I stretched my eyes as far as they could move without my head accompanying them. Sandy remained asleep, curled up in a ball that would make a gymnast flinch.

"Whatever you do, do not look in the mirror," Reason's sonorous voice commanded. "He does not know you know or he would have said something. No matter what, keep your eyes away from the thing. Do not, whatever you do, look back …"

In the mirror, the eyes glaring back were close enough to be from someone seated next to me. Asphyxiation debarred screaming.

"Stay focused. All thoughts, all energies must converge upon driving," Reason said in a tremulous falsetto. "Look straight ahead and concentrate. Do not look back again. Remember that the door to Quietude is always open to a man who has developed his mind in the weight room of philosophy. It is not the menacing stowaway in your backseat who troubles you, but the opinions and principles you form of him. He too is a citizen of the universe, a fellow actor in the gaudy burlesque of life. Breathe. Take little breaths until you can take normal ones. Oxygen is your friend. Keep your eyes on the road. Do not look …"

In the mirror, the white lights in dark craters were close enough to be my own. Panic struggled with confusion for control of my helm. I listened for his breathing but heard nothing. My nostrils prowled for his scent but caught only a faint whiff of strawberries. The wheel, which normally resembled a slender ring of marble, felt like a rubber hose engorged with hot water. Tiny shards of salt covered its pliable surface.

"No!" hollered Reason with some semblance of authority before I could look up. "Stare at Shiva. You cannot stop until you are near some remnant of civilization."

My beloved hood ornament, discovered in an antique store and soldered onto my car downstream of Mr. Burzinski's befuddled stare, waved her four arms as though casting a spell and reached above her head to pull down a red, white, and blue-striped screen, which she hid behind. A slender silver pipe protruded beneath it and grew to a height of two feet, creating a Pabst Blue Ribbon tapper.

The eyes in the mirror retreated, exposing temples stampeded by crows' feet, pouches two shades darker than pitch, a Neanderthal brow, and an absurdly messy crop of dark hair. My mind flipped through its disarrayed archive of people I knew by face but not by name until I recognized the ogre-like barkeep who served me the night of my dizzy-spell.

"Enjoying the view?" he said.

"What are you doing here?" I said, before pulling my fingers away from the giant steaming pretzel that had been my wheel. By gingerly tapping the edges, I kept my car on course. With the presumption that the barkeep possessed a privileged understanding of the situation, I turned to confront him.

Amidst all the commotion I scarcely noticed his absence. The backseat receded and expanded while a mushroom with a green and rectangular cap sprouted on the floor and grew to enormous proportions. Balls of different colored fungi grew on its flat surface. Through my sunroof, a shaded light descended, suspended from a bronze chain.

"But my car does not have a sunroof," I cried.

The car veered and I turned to straighten it, burning my fingers again in the process. Three tappers now stood where the mighty Shiva once reigned. Given my predilection for simple elegance, I found the new arrangement ostentatious.

My seat moved forward and I knocked the pretzel aside. It narrowly missed my lap as it fell to the floor. When my elbows rested on the dash, Reason declared that we ought to pull over before the situation became unmanageable. I concurred, but my feet could no longer reach the brake.

Inch by glorious inch the hood receded. Five tappers passed through the misty shroud of the windshield. Below it, glass buds sprouted from a ghostly garden and grew into bottles. Fury supplanted bewilderment. I could, in Stoic magnanimity, acquiesce to the new hood ornaments. With the aid of Petronius' Shovel, I could countenance the presence of an unkempt barkeep in my rearview mirror, but not a small car. Too bereaved to speak, I watched the accelerated crystal growth of the reading lamps create Endless Knot lanterns.

Above two bottles of Stolichnaya and a stocky bottle of Chivas Regal, my reflection stared back wide-eyed and ashen. Next to him sat a little man sporting a Fu Man Chu beard and a condescending smile. Hovering behind the tappers, the rearview mirror grew to the size of a door and the barkeep strode through. A tight Hawaiian shirt wrapped his oil-barrel chest and beach ball abdomen.

With trembling hands I extracted a cigarette from a fresh box resting near my elbow. A slender flame appeared inches from my face.

"Was the pretzel too hot?" the barkeep asked, leaning on the other side of the dash. My authentic voodoo doll, quintuple his original size, perched atop a cash register.

"Do you have any pickled eggs?" I said.

"Of course. You need a drink, don't you?"

I spun around on my stool for a quick appraisal. A long but cozy room led to the bar. On one wall, a rabbit's head with a rack of antlers loomed above an oil painting of Edward Gibbon. Mounted on the opposite side, two hammerhead sharks, one white, one black, formed a Yin-Yang circle around a portrait of Arthur Schopenhauer by Robert Crumb. The walls, bright orange, combined with the amber wood on the ceiling and the glow from neon signs to convey the impression that the sun had snagged on something while setting, perhaps to suggest it was always five o' clock here.

"You do remember me," said my fellow patron. Silver dragons covered his silk shirt. "Cletus Empiricus, from the book party."

"This tavern is not permanent, is it? My Fleetwood will be returned to its original form?"

"This tavern is transitory. Your car is fine."

"Oh, and Sandy, is she --"

"All things will be returned to their original forms." He picked up a mayonnaise jar and finished its red slush. The gargantuan drink looked ridiculous in his tiny hand. "Another Strawberry Zebra," he told the barkeep.

"And how is the book proceeding?"

"Mr. Jablonski, for reasons of alphabetical precedence I'm going to dispatch matters of business before matters of pleasure. The Horned One is perplexed by you."

"You two work for the Horned One?"

"That's not the best way to characterize our relationship. We don't punch a clock, if that's what you mean to imply. We don't have a 401K plan."

"Is there a company picnic?"

They sipped and glared at me. I put my empty glass on the bar. The barkeep hesitated, then attended to it, keeping his steely eyes on me.

"Very well," I said, summoning my courage with a dig of my trustworthy Shovel. "What is the nature of his perplexity?"

"You were sent on a solemn voyage, a consecrated quest. The Horned One didn't send you on spring break."

Given that my conduct had been exemplary in every way, I recognized this vile denunciation as a test and decided to play along, to humor them. "Is there something in particular I am missing?"

"Let's just say you're putting yourself in positions where it would be easy to overlook things."

"Like that deeply enigmatic tunnel, that unfathomable meat puppet," I blurted, unable to contain myself. "Those had the subtlety of dynamite, the depth of puddles."

They took synchronized sips from their Strawberry Zebras and observed me as they would a zoological specimen. The red rings around their lips made them look like macabre transvestites. Enunciating each syllable, Cletus said, "Have you considered the possibility that neither of those signs were revelatory?"

"Those were red herrings? So the tunnel's over-the-top, *Plan 9 from Outer Space* awfulness was a *reductio ad absurdum* of atheism. You mean ... *Theism's* the right position? You could have simply mailed me *The Enneads*."

"I can't endorse or reject any interpretation."

"How do I know, with any degree of certainty, what is or is not important?"

"Mr. Jablonski, the Horned One didn't mince words with you."

"How do I even know if something is or is not a sign?"

"Different answers to that question will give you different groups of signs to sort through. Different groups of signs, once sorted and unveiled, will provide different messages. Perhaps the answer to that question is in the signs. Perhaps not."

"Perhaps we could skip the rest: the Horned One returns my Bonneville, permits me to keep my Fleetwood, and we call it even."

"Mr. Jablonski, that's the fatigue talking. The signs and the answers to questions about them are cloaked in the thickest robes of obscurity. They aren't freebies."

"Do they mean the same thing individually as they do in a larger context?"

"Perhaps some only have meaning in a bigger picture; others, individually. Maybe there are several contexts and the signs mean different things in each."

"As a Stoic, I am committed to reducing everything to its elementary components and meditating upon them with the humility befitting a mortal. The Horned One may rest assured that hubris will not be my downfall."

Cletus Empiricus smiled, making his eyes all but disappear as two little stars replaced them. "Don't worry Mr. Jablonski. Your downfall will not be from hubris."

The barkeep approached to replenish my drink but I covered it with my hand. "I would prefer to try what you gentlemen are having."

"A Strawberry Zebra?" he said, furrowing his brow.

"Is it classified otherwise? Many drinks, perhaps the majority, have more than one moniker."

"By no other name," he said solemnly.

"And the ingredients are ...?"

"That's a secret, Mr. Jablonski. He shouldn't even be fixing them out in the open where you can watch."

"What is the appeal?"

The barkeep grinned and leaned over the bar, not stopping until his face was inches from mine. "They are the stuff that dreams are made of."

"One of the ingredients in particular, or does the combination mimic the essence?"

"Yes," they said.

"Good dreams, bad dreams, or is it a coin toss?"

"Would you like one or not?" said the barkeep.

"By all means," I said, afraid of losing my opportunity.

The barkeep filled a blender with ice and stood in front of the concoction to ensure its sacred ingredients would not be seen by my heathen eyes. On first glance it looked more like red cotton candy than slush. Upon a closer inspection it appeared to be a red cloud confined to a glass.

***

At this point the Reader must find a quiet park bench and begin sipping the contents of his thermos while awaiting further instructions.

***

I put my lips to the edge and a portion of the vapor seeped into my mouth. Though it made no contact with my tongue, it had the Real Presence, that distinctive and divine sensation conspicuously absent in those preposterous non-alcoholic beverages. The flavor of strawberries, though undeniable, did not overwhelm, which was most peculiar since their aroma could be discerned from across the room. Cletus and the bartender watched in silence, their pupils reflecting neon splashes from the signs in the window.

"Most impressive, and I am not a man who is tempted by drinks containing ice or fruit," I said, licking my lips to remove a ghostly residue. "Not to imply that this contains either."

"It's not like other drinks," Cletus assured me.

***

At this point, the Reader should finish the remainder of his thermos while reading the next paragraph. Before reading the paragraph posterior to it, he should wait forty-five minutes.

***

Infused with a mystic property, Strawberry Zebras vacated the glass in favor of my mouth. I scarcely opened it a sliver and most of the arcane contents snuck in regardless of any efforts to restrain the flow. After only seven of them I found myself delightfully disabled, savoring the crux of Petronius' Special Potation Theory: fermented drinks alter a philosopher's outlook from dyed-in-the-wool misanthropy to near misanthropy. (The Reader will remember my General Potation Theory from Part V. My Special Theory shall be expounded upon when it will not disrupt the euphony of my narrative.)

"Now, what lesson have I missed that I need to know?" I said, dispensing with mundane chatter in the hope of prying the Cliff Notes from Cletus.

"Mr. Jablonski, surely you don't think a simple summary is possible. That's the Zebras talking. Once you've caught your second wind you need to carefully meditate on all you've seen."

"Can you give me a hint? How do I know if my interpretations are correct? Is there a final exam?"

"You want to know if you're on the right track?"

I nodded, pleased that my persistence bore fruit, but disappointed that he had not confirmed the existence of a test. After all, even in the unlikely event of an A- I would still obtain the correct answers afterward.

"Follow me," he said and jumped off his stool. I followed him outside. We were in the middle of nowhere, standing outside a stately orange manor in a vast field.

"*Pssst*. Over here," he called, hiding beneath the window. Our heads went up like periscopes. The oblivious barkeep whistled while he wiped the bar with a big black rag.

"Do you see the stools we were sitting on?" Cletus asked.

"Yes."

"Now who's on them?"

"No one."

"Do you remember all that we said, all the words we spoke?"

"The most important ones. I am a historian."

"Do you see them in there now?"

"No."

"Where are they?"

"What on earth are you talking about?" Not even my inebriation could compensate for the insufficiencies of this underwhelming revelation. I felt like an adolescent who sneaks into an R-rated movie only to discover it contains no nudity.

"What's left, Mr. Jablonski? What's left of the rise and fall of the evening, of that whole little epoch?" The barkeep put our glasses in the sink. When he picked up our ashtray Cletus grabbed my shoulder. "Look. That's what remains."

The ashtray contained a pile of debris. The barkeep dumped it out and put it back empty. Empty as though it had always been that way.

"Did you see that?" said Cletus.

Eyeing him with a world-weary disdain normally reserved for panhandlers and used-car salesmen, I nodded.

"Then you're on the right track. And remember, all the nights to come will be like that too." He walked away into the grass.

"And now? What is the next sign? Are you going to pick your nose?"

He stopped but did not turn around.

"So the Horned One is running low on funds. How does a sea god run out of money, especially with family members running hot cars?"

"*Mr. Jablonski*," Cletus sighed with characteristic exasperation. "There's no need for insults. Your car was just transformed into a tavern. Or had you forgotten?"

"So *that's* all there is?"

"Of course that's not *all there is*. But without that you're lost. You should sleep on it. That tree over there looks awfully cozy. Don't worry about the bugs. They're not too bad in these parts."

"Tree? Where's my Fleetwood?"

"Mr. Jablonski you're exhausted. I'm sure you'll wake up with a fresh perspective. You can't drive in your condition."

"Is my car safe? Will it be returned?"

"Yes Mr. Jablonski, yes."

"And Sandy? Is she --"

"You'll see them both in the morning. Goodnight Mr. Jablonski." As he merged with the night, the dragons on his shirt became glowworms and slithered away. I stumbled to the tree and everything began to spin.

The Essential and Non-Negotiable Preparations for Part XII

I can see it all so clearly: the Reader's reluctance to prepare for Part XII stems from an irrational reaction to the tragic, vexatious nature of life. Yearning for permanence and something of transcendent importance in a world that seems specifically designed to frustrate these longings, he, with an impulsivity born of despair, arrives at an extreme and cantankerous position.

"If nothing is eternal or of ultimate importance, then nothing matters. The universe itself shall fade away, so why prepare for Part XII? Why not skim through it as I would anything else?"

But here an invidious distinction is drawn. If nothing matters, *why not* prepare for Part XII? The Reader's plunge into nihilism has left him with no grounds to reject *any* requests. A sadistic author could now command him to court and marry an ugly cousin. And how can he refuse? Not even the hedonist's pleasure principle will rescue him.

"You do not *feel* like it?" the wicked writer says, laughing demonically. "Of what significance are your feelings if the universe itself shall vanish? In the cold night of eternity your preferences and desires have all the importance of microscopic particles on specks of dust. Now go, call Ethel or Bertha and declare your vile intentions."

Perhaps the Reader should take a moment to acknowledge that the world is not as tragic and vexatious as he thought, for he finds himself in the gentle hands of a benevolent author whose only concern is his welfare.

***

With the predictability of the seasons, he clings to hedonism, the last refuge of the philosophaster, and declines any "elaborate preparations" on the grounds that he would derive more pleasure without them. Dear Reader, this road is steep and anfractuous. Do not equate hedonism with staggering down the path of least resistance. Sometimes the greatest pleasure requires the greatest expenditure of effort. Oftentimes it demands no small degree of planning and analysis.

The conscientious hedonist must assess the costs as opposed to the benefits of his intended course of behavior beneath the dim light of the pleasure principle. As applied to our present situation, begin with the question, "What is the nature of the pleasure I will derive by forsaking the prerequisites?" Then proceed through the following list of gratifications from common to sublime until a match is found.

"Will it be akin to the humdrum contentment gained from culinary indulgence?"

Not even this.

"Will it compare with the mirth of driving through a curbside puddle beside a crowded bus stop?" the Reader asks hopefully.

As remote as alpha to omega.

"Will it approach the esoteric delight of clogging the toilet at work?"

Scarcely.

"What type of pleasure will be gained?" the Reader asks in resignation, despondent from the calculus required for robust and consistent hedonism.

None whatsoever. The lethargy of the sluggard is not pleasure, but a pathologic condition. In supreme opposition to this effete state stands the delectation of preparing for and indulging in Part XII. The hedonist's scale is not merely tipped in its favor, but buckled by its immeasurable, unquantifiable bliss. The pleasure involved may very well surpass all prior joys and cast a pall upon all joys to come.

To extract the fruit from this most gravid part of my annals, the Reader must take between one-hundred and three-hundred micrograms of lysergic acid diethylamide on a sunny summer day after a good night of sleep and a hearty breakfast. Part XII involves an altered state of consciousness (Petronius' Ninth Sensation) that can only be approximated in this manner. Note and note well: *the following parameters are mandatory:*

- A steadfast friend must accompany the Reader throughout the day (concubines can prove especially enchanting on such occasions).

- The lysergic acid diethylamide must be consumed in a pastoral setting (a quiet park will do splendidly).

- Two hours after it is ingested, Part XII must be *read to* the Reader, not by him.

- The remainder of the day should be devoted to readings of other portions of my annals, Frisbee, and the music of Ludwig van Beethoven. It is no exaggeration to state that until the Reader has listened to Beethoven in this condition he has not lived at all. Anterior to this point, he has been trapped in a dingy, grimy garage. This dovetails with my watershed contribution, not to philosophy so much as to Life herself.

Petronius' Garage is analogous to Plato's much-ballyhooed Cave in some peripheral respects. The difference is in his appalling lack of specificity: How exactly -- not in terms of mellifluous abstractions -- does a man leave the Cave and enter the sunlight above? To leave the cobwebs and oil stains of Petronius' Garage and enter the paradise of a sunny park he need only listen to Beethoven's Sixth Symphony posterior to the ingestion of lysergic acid diethylamide. If what he experiences is not "enlightenment" then that word has no meaning and should be encased in lead and dropped into the sea. What the Reader erroneously thought of as life will be revealed as a wretched crawl across a filthy concrete floor while confined beneath a greasy monolith of steel.

Unlike my Garage, an absurd and contemptible situation arises with other systems of enlightenment, salvation, and sundry sham vantages. The aspirant invariably wonders, "Do I really have it?" -- a certain indicant he has been duped. Petronius' Garage is unprecedented in this regard. Concurrent with listening to Beethoven's Sixth, posterior to his ingestion of lysergic acid diethylamide, the aspirant will scarcely be second-guessing himself. On the contrary.

Unlike Plato's Cave, my Garage is no mere allegory but grounded firmly in experience. One fateful afternoon, after ingesting a yellow blotter hit emblazoned with a red lightning bolt, I made the grievous decision to change my oil while waiting for Sandy and Buzzcut to arrive. The effects descended with frightening celerity, expanding the straightforward operation to Homeric dimensions. The procedure is normally encapsulated by a handful of distinct steps. Cursed with the eyes of Zeno, I perceived new steps between each of the traditional steps and more steps between each of the new steps. While I rolled about in filth and cursed, steps multiplied like Irish serpents. Then a gentle summer breeze swirled through the garage: the first notes of Beethoven's Sixth. It repeated, more pronounced as Sandy pulled into the drive. I bounded to her car and collapsed in the backseat. At my behest, she drove through Sheridan Park and Grant Park and Wilson Park until I heard the entire piece. Words run aground on this shore. Like fish thrashing on the beach, they are forever barred from the land beyond. The First Petronius Sensation burns with a longing that parries all attempts at gratification. Consequently, we shall continue with the mandatory parameters:

- Though false starts are possible, acts of fleshly congress can be uniquely rewarding.

- Tetrahydrocannabinol and fermented or caffeinated drinks are contraindicated.

- If television is unavoidable, motion pictures featuring the Marx Brothers are recommended.

- Insomnia is a distinct possibility. Again, the answer to most queries regarding lysergic acid diethylamide is Beethoven. The compatibility of other symphonies can be determined with Petronius' Second Theorem: S/3 (for the layman, symphonies divisible by 3).

XII:
I See the Sun For the First Time

In the beginning there was warmth. Evanescent sparkles dappled a muddy pond behind my eyes until I opened them. Between my shoes, tiny beings propelled by a mysterious dynamism transported granules in their mouths. Above me, at the behest of an invisible but perceptible force, a branch of green ovals quivered.

That my perceptions were detached and convoluted did not register in the mysterious theatre inside my head. To the contrary, its sooty windows had been removed, ceding access to alien forms that failed to correspond with their previous nicknames.

The petals, too small and sparsely allocated to offer any cover, permitted the light to warm me. My inability to connect them with their name constricted my stomach. I looked up and beheld a hovering molten ball, impossibly bright, tethered by a chain unseen. Claws of panic burrowed through me as I tried to find the appropriate label to affix. When I rubbed my eyes, white sparkles haloed a yellow circle on a brown screen. An effortless and uncontrollable process connected this to the fiery sphere, but the covert internal operation only fomented my disquietude.

"The sun," I finally said. "That's what it's called."

After a moment of serenity an ominous realization assaulted me. "But I have no idea what the sun *is*. As many times as I've seen it or heard the name I've never thought to ask."

This is scarcely unnatural. The frequency of a man's observation of X is proportionate to his disinclination to ask, "What is X?" Petronius' Third Theorem: $x > f(x)$

A man becomes accustomed to things. Long before adulthood, any sense of wonder or curiosity is buried. A thick layer descends, stultifying him, protecting him. A foundation of things intrinsically unfathomable becomes presupposed, humdrum, taken for granted, the standard by which other things are deemed "odd" or "normal."

In my brittle state I managed to compose a dossier of the monstrous blazing ball. "It has flares; it is 46,500,000 times as far as my house is from The Bear's Lair; it has malignant spots; we revolve around it and it revolves around something else."

This was no help. *I was not sure what I wanted to know.* It was as though the name and everything I had ever heard or read about it had been blown away, leaving me without words or symbols or stories to hide behind. The countless times I had seen and felt it had been peeled off, revealing its raw essence as something beyond strange, beyond terrifying: features I had never noticed yet they had always been there.

I looked at my car, hoping to beguile the dire spell with cheerful distractions. I recalled the night it flew through the air, the Rat Pack tunes that brought me fortitude, the horrible faces, and the penetrating meditations that revealed the illusory nature of my "strange" circumstances. These reflections prompted a premature glance toward the volcanic hole above.

"What if it starts leaking? One drop will burn you to cinders. Run for cover," howled the primal scream of Instinct.

"Gradual exposure, you fool," I said, returning my fragmented thoughts and singed eyes to my Fleetwood. "You know, gliding through the fog in an orange Cadillac while gruesome faces materialize is not one whit stranger than seeing the sun," I said, channeling the distant but resonant voice of Reason. "The latter is every whit as weird and incomprehensible, only we see it all the time and a thick callus of familiarity grows around it, covering its strangeness, protecting us from questions that can never be answered, *from questions that cannot even be sensibly asked*. A man never thinks of it as bizarre or frightening, and certainly not as something in need of any explanation.

Why, were I to fly around in my car day in and day out, a callus would eventually form around that too."

Such wisdom bestowed an oasis of Quietude. I scooped a handful of dirt and squeezed it in my fist, marveling at its inconsistency. Most of it fell through my fingers and dispersed in the breeze in little clouds. What remained covered my palm, filling the tributaries with powder. Upon closer inspection, what had first appeared solid, then gaseous, revealed itself to be composed of individual grains. I closed my fist and scraped them across my palm.

"What is this stuff?" I said, wiping my hands of the alien substance in disgust and fear. The surface it came from spread out beneath me in all directions, covered by green reeds. I pounded the ground in amazement before dismay descended. "And I have no idea what this is. All I have is some noise I am supposed to make when I come in contact with it, a name to call it."

The ground no longer felt right, not firm and stable, but soft and mutable the way one would expect trillions of particles to feel. I jerked my hands away as though I had touched a snake. "It's everywhere. We spend our entire lives upon it. Some pull their food from it. We cover our dead with it. *And we do not know what it is.*"

I leaned against the tree, unprotected by the word-shield "sun" from the orbed pyre above, undefended against the bizarre particles beneath me by the word-shields "earth," "ground," and "dirt." Once composed of iron, they had been replaced with glass.

"What is all this stuff?" I cried. But the question made no sense and there could be no satisfactory answer. It was but a groan of dismay at the absolute strangeness of things that are not supposed to be strange.

Even I, Petronius Jablonski, with my erudition and eloquence, am unable to summon the befitting terminology to legibly impart the frantic examination I undertook. The impenetrable veil of familiarity, our steadfast protector, was raised, and the Reader must pardon me if my descriptions of that dreadful sight are less than crystalline. Verily, the First Petronius Sensation is a cruel scourge, demanding the afflicted writer share what can not be shared.

I reined in my thoughts and demanded answers, hoping that by negating the cause I could negate the effect. "How did this happen to me?"

The rejoinder overcame me like a fever. "It was those vile Banana Giraffes. No, what were they? Cantaloupe Antelopes? Molasses Elephants? Pineapple Rhinos? Whatever they were, those things bruise a man's soul. Nausea and dizzy-spells are one thing: insignificant in comparison to the treasures reaped during a night spent irrigating oneself. *This,* however, is not."

Certain that conventional therapies would prove ineffectual, I channeled the ever-soothing voice of Reason to pontificate on the virtue of fortitude. "Time heals all wounds. Consider the hangovers of Vespasian: Where are they now? Time is the only unfailing defense, your staunchest ally, the boat that shall deliver you across this Styx."

A thought split my head like an axe, mortally wounding my invisible mentor: *What is Time?* The currency of this word-shield is universal, but when one peers behind it what does he see? The abstruse gibbering of a patent clerk? The bafflegab of a seminarian from Heidelberg? *Nothing at all?*

I closed my eyes, hiding from rattling questions, focusing on the operations of the mysterious theatre, preparing to find and follow a familiar path. "If there is any place to turn for comfort, it is within," I said. (In accord with one prominent theory that posits the existence of "walls" preventing some parts of the mind from directly communicating with others, soliloquies are necessary to ensure that all sectors receive information of unique importance. Correspondingly, interior monologues are the only reliable means of hiding sensitive information from untrustworthy agents. For the pursuit of Quietude, I have found it beneficial to have all hands on deck, whereas secret plans and fantasies are best kept behind non-verbal doors). "After all, does not Quietude spring from a man's rational faculty? When he goes deep within, is that not his true home, the only refuge from the savage spears thrust by the bloodthirsty hordes of Fate? Certainly."

Confident my brutal sojourn was at an end, that I had finally found a road out of the alien badlands, I embarked down sacred but well-trod paths. My reflections began in earnest but thickets covered the ground, causing me to stumble and lose my way. I found myself alone in a dark forest where creatures with shining eyes growled and squealed and laughed and whispered. As my thoughts assailed me I cried, "What in the world are these things?"

The dark forest within was as odd as the blaze above or the grains below and I despaired of finding solace. "Everything is strange, fundamentally unfathomable, alien and obscure. And there is nothing to cling to for diversion once the familiarity is stripped. Only this is hidden from us. Born into the strangeness, a very part of it, few of us are ever confronted by it. Mother Nature protects her children from explicit sights the same way human parents do. Perhaps this is for the best. Such a glimpse conveys no obvious benefits and is debilitating while it lasts. Anyone unfortunate enough to see it on a regular basis could never go about his business. His life would come to a halt while he groped along like an infant asking, 'What is it?' The word-shields covering things do not explain them."

Convinced that the unknown without was the lesser of two terrors, I opened my eyes. The molten ball seemed brighter and in a slightly different locale. The question of how this happened sliced me like a sickle, as did the question of how I could ask the question, as did the question of what is a question.

Hoping to break the spell, I looked at my feet. They knocked together, then the right one bobbed on its heel. The question of how I accomplished this sent me reeling. Like a man who walks the same path for decades and one day discovers that its steps and variegated rock formations are the fossilized remains of monstrous beasts, I squirmed from the sudden realization of something obvious yet not obvious: I hadn't the foggiest idea how my body functioned, how I willed it this way or that.

All this time the tiny beings had continued their errands, ignoring the blaze above and the strangeness of the grains they carried in their strange little mouths to build their strange little castles. They worked in their garden, arranging each inexplicable particle and scurrying off for more.

"Thus they live," I said with more than a trace of envy. "And they work like this until they die, blissfully free from ever knowing how weird everything is, including them. Lucky little bugs," I told them. "You were not drinking Pineapple Possums last night and you have no idea how strange --"

"Who the fuck are you talking to?" asked a voice, a sweet *familiar* voice. Beneath a familiar face, a familiar lithe body walked toward me through the grass.

"I may have discovered a new species of ant," I said. "Buzzcut is a budding endocrinologist. This will delight him."

I did not care if she pressed the issue. The relief I felt was as soothing as the combined negative results of all the do-it-yourself pregnancy tests she had ever taken. (Also, a man should never feel ashamed of gratifying himself with his own conversation. Frequently his company is superior to that of others. Should he therefore shun his own scintillating discourse at the behest of imbecilic mores? This of course equally pertains to singing, dancing, and other forms of gratification.)

"*Entomologist*, doofus. Where the hell are we?"

Panic slithered up my back. Where indeed? In the solar system, but where is that? In the universe, but *what* is that?

"Cease this folly and gird yourself," Reason commanded, closing the valve on this septic flow. Though the worst of the hangover had passed, I resolved to remain alert for relapses.

"I don't remember us pulling in here. I must have slept like a rock. Petronius, are you okay?"

No longer estranged from that which is most familiar, as my spiritual mentor, Heraclitus, once phrased it, I welcomed back my old friends: the ground, the sky, my feet, my thoughts.

"Seriously. Are you okay?"

"What do you last remember before waking up?" I said.

"Driving. Why?"

"Just curious. After experiencing some troubles concentrating I had to pull over."

"How far from the road are we?"

"Somewhere between a quarter mile and twenty."

"It's good that you drive when you're exhausted," she said, patting my knee.

"Nonsense. Driving is controlled by the most primitive part of the brain, the last to succumb to fatigue."

"The reptilian part?"

"Of course."

"Why can't lizards drive?"

"In theory, a Komodo dragon could, probably better than you, but such an experiment is patently unethical insofar as it would subject that regal creature to the potential indignities of an automobile accident."

"How much farther is this place?"

"How much *further* is this place. We are closer now than we were yesterday and much closer than we were three days ago."

"We've had a nice time. Maybe we should head home. You know, just hang out. Hey, let's get that whirlpool suite again. We'll chill out for a while. Just me and you."

Her eyes had the emotional depth and breadth of Elisabeth Schwarzkopf's voice. While she spoke of going home, they cross-examined me but absent any search for guilt, as though they did not want to find what they sought.

"You don't know where we are, do you?" Her eyes indicated she already knew the answer and it terrified her.

"It was dark when we pulled in."

"Do you know where we're going?" Her eyes begged me to say yes.

"Of course," I said, trying to sound offended or at least surprised.

"The new owner of your Bonneville said this is a cool place to check out, right?"

I winced, hoping to nip this inquiry in the bud. "Very cool indeed. And we can *hang out* or *chill out* or *space out* once we leave."

"But what is it? A campground? A theme park?"

"Mr. Horn's descriptions could best be described as ambiguous, but exactitude is not essential. Much like life itself, the final destination is irrelevant. Preeminent is a luxurious and agreeable ride." I stood, stretched, and forfended a swell of vertigo. I took her hand and pulled her up.

"You know you can tell me anything. You know that, don't you? There'd be no shame in admitting you're having problems -- if you were."

"Speak for yourself. And may the gods consign this whole foul epoch and those perverse transvaluations straight to the underworld." I headed to my car and examined it for any residual tavernesque features. At the helm I checked the wheel for shards of salt and ensured that all buttons controlling my throne functioned. Shiva stood on the horizon. I smiled. My car started without a sound and mastered the severe topography. I drove past the familiar tree and haphazardly made my way to a road that took us to the highway.

While the reptilian functionaries of my brain dealt with traffic-related details, I could not refrain from meditations concerning the incongruity between what a reasonable man could expect and what had in fact happened. On an odyssey where I watched a pterodactyl clutching a zebra and beheld a town of ghosts (among countless other curiosities), the strangest part of all was the morning I saw the sun and the earth and thought my thoughts. The road twisted into a corkscrew. I put on my shades and lowered the visor.

XIII:
We are Vexed by Incomprehensible Signs, I Expound Upon the Origin of the Shi Tzu; and Introduce my Tenth, Eleventh and Twelfth Sensations

"You know what else was fascinating about the pond's book?" said Sandy, somehow laboring under the misapprehension that after hours of her painstaking reiteration I still cared. Had I been driving any other car I would have jumped out the window and taken my chances with the pavement. The only thing worse than reading contemporary fiction is hearing an enthusiast gush over it. In the former case a man can simply hurl the book in the trash and gladden his heart with real literature from the eighteenth century. In the latter case, after the calamity of feigning interest he may have to brave a lingering storm.

"The narrative arc. It reminded me of --"

"Narrative arc," I cried in agony. "My kingdom for bourbon. Please use your cell phone to call my house. Request from my mother a complete account of Zeus' adventures today. Remember them with the same death grip in which you clutched every semicolon from the pond's book, then relay the story to me."

"Why don't I just hit the number and give you the phone?"

"Because it is an infernal device."

"That's a rather odd view for you," she said, digging through her purse.

"The telephone is Quietude's greatest foe. Proust did not care for them either. They remind me of the delightful story of the wise Chinese emperor and the flying machine. The inventor breathlessly told him about it, apparently believing all progress is good. The emperor, realizing the vile contraption's potential for evil, had him put to death and the machine destroyed. If only Bell had stood before me with his nefarious device." I smiled, stretched my arm to tap my fingers on the side-view mirror, and watched the trees rushing past in front of the moon.

"Mrs. Jablonski? Hey, it's me …We're good … No, he's being mostly nice. How's puppy Zeus?"

***

During Sandy's interminable disquisition on the book, I managed to make major progress on my revolutionary thesis regarding the genesis of the Shi Tzu. I empathize but disagree with the Reader's pragmatic reaction.

"Scholar, of what import is their origin? One can scarcely accommodate the joy and gratitude their company invokes, much less murky historical references. If the phylogenic tree bore any resemblance to reality, man and Shi Tzu would stand coequal, far above monkeys and dolphins. The dog may be our best friend, but the Shi Tzu is our allegiant peer. What more needs to be said?"

Dear Reader, knowledge of Shi Tzu history is an intrinsic good and thanks to my fruitful meditations is murky no more. According to the traditional legend, Tibetan Buddhist monks bred them to resemble lions. Folklore alleged that the Buddha traveled with a little dog who could transform itself into one. This is suspect for six reasons. First, Buddha was a great philosopher, perhaps the first rigorous empiricist; he was not a wizard. The urge to deify great philosophers can be very strong, but Hume and Schopenhauer should be the first choices. (It is not impossible that one day legends about Zeus and I will abound, starting innocently as factual accounts of our daily wanderings through Pulaski Park and growing into wild tales of his metamorphosis to a great cosmic yak.)

Second and most importantly, the Shi Tzu does not look anything like a lion. How to account for the discrepancy between the traditional legend and the contemporary reality? I here offer four plausible accounts. The most tenable was conceived during Sandy's exposition, the deliriant properties of which rendered me more prolific than an oracle.

It is conceivable that the monks began with sincere intentions of breeding lion dogs, which they presented as oblations to the Chinese emperor (perhaps the great man who destroyed the flying machine). The folklore surrounding magic pups probably intrigued him. Different sects of monks, not unlike car dealers hoping to allure customers, vied for his favor.

As we all know, craftsmanship leaves when the bottom line enters. Breeding became sloppy. At least one sect of monks lost its tenuous grasp of teleology. When quantity replaced quality, as it invariably does, they produced a batch of dogs not only distinct from, but superior to the lion dogs of their competitors.

"But how could such dogs be presented to the emperor?" the Reader asks.

Beyond certainty, the following conversation occurred (in Mandarin, of course).

"These dogs you present to me, they look not like lions," the emperor says, stroking his long wispy beard as he scrutinizes two puppies playing at his feet.

The nervous monk, dreading this response all the way from his mountainous village and through the palace strewn with Shi Tzu poo, experiences the first in a series of life-saving inspirations. "No, your highness," he says with a deep bow. The palace eunuchs inhale in unison. "These two are not lion dogs."

"*They are not?*" the emperor asks in justified horror. To defile the breed is a crime against the emperor, the Buddha, and a harbinger of certain doom.

"They are yak dogs, highness," the monk says. With head still bowed he sees the feet of the guards approach the throne. "Highness, the yak has true Buddha-nature and is the persevering friend of man."

Eunuchs and guards stand immobile but their eyes bounce wildly, seeking attestation from one another. Within the context of another religion, such talk would be deemed blasphemous.

"And the lion?" says the emperor. The creases across his forehead bode ill for all three visitors.

"The lion is holy, highness," the monk says, trying to ignore white sparkles twinkling around the hem of his red robe. They subside with deep breaths. "But he spends his days in indolence, sleeping and fornicating. He is not the friend of man; he eats man. The yak spends his life humbly lessening backbreaking toil. And like the Buddha, the yak causes no sentient being to suffer. The lion, despite his holiness, inflicts terrible suffering on sentient creatures every day of his life."

"How is it I have never heard this teaching?" says the emperor.

"Highness, teachings are so many that a thousand monks in a thousand years could not learn them all."

One of the little yaks pees on the emperor's foot. The monk closes his eyes. He opens them at the sound of gasps. The emperor is on his knees, delicately petting the puppies. "Go, wise monk, bring me more yak dogs."

***

"What the hell is that thing?"

The elaborately lit billboard reminded me of the opening night of an outlandish Broadway spectacle, except nothing accompanied it. The metallic surface, swept by floodlights, had the glare of reflectors on a bike. Abstruse markings insinuated grave importance -- at least to Sandy.

"Slow down," she said. "What does that mean?"

"Cliff ahead?"

"I don't remember anything like that from driver's ed."

"And I would? Did Poseidon study oceanography? Tell me of Zeus."

"Puppy Zeus is fine," she said, kneeling on her seat to watch the garish menace to traffic fade from view. "Your mom took him for a walk today."

"Did he defecate?"

"*Yes*. Twice. She said she didn't have a bag to pick up the second one but she's going to send Hieronymus to get it tomorrow."

"Where did the second defecation occur?"

"Seriously?"

"Call again and ask to speak with Hieronymus. If the second defecation occurred on Mr. Burzinski's property, tell him he is not to touch it."

"*Hieronymus* and *Petronius*: that's too funny."

"As opposed to an adjective describing the nature of a beach. Yes, how funny of my father to name his sons after a great artist and writer rather than something innovatory like John, Mike, Dave, or Steve."

***

During Sandy's relentless synopsis of the book, after I brilliantly resolved the question of why the Shi Tzu retains a name meaning "lion dog" even after it was recognized as a yak dog, a fascinating argument, compelled by the subject of teleology, seized my attention:

The Impossibility of Creating Anything From Scratch

1) Before X can be created, there must exist the idea of X. For example, the monks who bred lion dogs had paintings to work with, a clear conceptual goal.

2) To have an idea of X, X or something similar must exist
   in some form. Ideas, be they of lions or anything else,
   do not arise from thin air.

Therefore: Nothing could be created out of the blue, from scratch, or *ex nihilo*, as the monotheists maintain.

Notice how harmoniously this argument blends with polytheism. The gods did not create; they prodded, nursed, and sculpted the crude materials already present. Notice the important corollary: they had no idea what they would eventually wind up with. The artifacts of nature are as accidental as most pregnancies.

Perhaps this simple refutation of monotheistic creation accounts seems banal to the Reader. I mention it only because of my delight at encountering it during an analysis of the origin of the Shi Tzu and the alchemy-like nature of teleology.

"And where did all these gods come from?" the precocious Reader asks. "Aren't you ignoring Occam's Razor, the preference for the simplest explanation?"

Ignoring it? Nay, I am discarding his rusty, dull blade in the trash where it belongs. The befuddling nature of Reality commands the most complex theory at all times. Accordingly, the gods evolved from lesser gods whose ultimate origin was a supernatural stew. This primordial soup was created by an earlier group of deities who were wiped out by a metaphysical meteorite. They too arose from prior gods, and so on, and so forth, down through the canyons of eternity.

What, does an infinite regress offend your little mind? How about the speed of light? Are you alright with that or is it impossible because it aggrieves your intellect? If the Reader wishes to overcome his childlike obsession with dramatic beginnings, plausible stories, and tidy endings with distinct morals, I suggest he abstain from motion pictures, which the universe is not.

***

"Your mom wants to know if you trained Zeus to go on your neighbor's lawn. She says the second time it looked like he was forcing it."

"Trained?" I chuckled. "The native genius of the Shi Tzu intuits the appropriate receptacle for fecal debris. Inform my mother that with a counterclockwise walk he would not have needed to strain himself a second time."

Another ominous billboard loomed as I came out of a turn, more formidable by virtue of markings greater in density and extravagance.

"Please pull over," said Sandy. "Mrs. Jablonski, I'm sure he'll call tomorrow. Yeah, I noticed that too," she whispered, glancing at me and looking away.

Obliging her trepidation, I parked on the shoulder, fortified myself with an Oval, and watched the confounding billboard glimmer from the floodlights. Two swept in horizontal strokes, one vertically.

"Maybe it's an advertisement for something," said Sandy.

I mused, then pronounced judgment. "No. The intellectual deficit of advertisers is best likened to a black hole from which no creative or intelligent light can escape. This exhibits trace evidence of planning."

"Maybe it only applies to truckers or locals."

"*That* would have *never* occurred to me," I said after an agonizing pause. (Spellbinding aphasia from the eye-crossing stupidity of what one has just heard is Petronius' Tenth Sensation. In its throes, a victim goes through four distinct stages: denial, anger, despair, and then back to anger.)

"Why?"

"Because my subconscious filters such ideas, keeping them a safe distance from my intellect. Do you think the highway planners anticipated a steady stream of psychics, or did they believe that drivers are born knowing what this gobbledygook signifies?"

"Please stop at the next gas station. Find out what's going on."

"And register my withering contempt," I said, checking my mirror before brushing my toe across the pedal to instantaneously attain the speed limit. "The only signs on a long dark road are unintelligible. Who would be foolish or cruel enough to invest so much energy in something that only serves to confuse and distract? Oh, did Zeus receive a belly rub?"

"Yes, and your mom kept the classical station on for him. He spent the day looking out the window or watching Hieronymus' piranhas."

"He probably spent the day in contemplation of what kind of man-child keeps carnivorous fish for pets. Did he finish both meals?"

"Look, an exit," Sandy said like a castaway spotting a seagull.

The rest area pavilion resembled a flying saucer. I approached a driver foraging through his trunk while Sandy headed inside.

"Did you happen to see two rather unusual billboards on the way here?"

"I'm going the opposite direction, buddy," he said, not looking away from the boxes he was arranging. "But I know what you're talkin' about."

"Is something the matter with the road?"

"Not as far as I know."

"Then what message are those signs supposed to convey?"

"I drive through here threes times a week for my job. I hear a lot of things about them. They say different things to different people. Some folks even fight each other over what they mean."

"If you were in the least concerned with the welfare of your fellow man you would assume the noble responsibility of burning them down. As a frequent traveler through these parts you are undoubtedly familiar with the terrain. Purchase a can of gasoline one night, hide your car on a back road, and you know the rest. Your selfless act will benefit generations of travelers with fretful copilots and prevent credulous fools from fighting over meaningless signs."

He stepped back. His appearance seemed contrived to convince clients that he cared for naught but his product, to fill their minds with the conclusion that anyone whose contours and wrappings concerned him to such a scanty extent must have his eyes fixed on another beautiful horizon.

"Do you deny their unsettling effect on woman? I attest it from firsthand experience."

"Buddy, just because everyone don't agree on what they say don't mean they should be ignored. Those signs are important to a lot of folks."

"But if no one can agree on what they say how do you know they are important? If they are, why weren't they written clearly, so all could understand them?"

"Hey, I didn't say no one agrees about what they mean. There's different groups who think they mean one thing and other groups that think they mean something else. Some folks have even been killed over disagreements. But that ain't no reason to burn them down."

"You have left the larger questions unanswered," I said. "How do you know what the message *is* if no consensus exists on its interpretation? And why was it not written with a clarity enabling everyone to --"

"Let me give you some advice. Most folks think it's impolite to talk about them in public. You might wanna consider that."

On the way to the saucer I encountered a couple sharing a cigarette on a picnic table. The girl's hand-woven anklets stirred a pleasant query regarding the tactile experience of clutching them during a particular act of libidinous union. To alleviate the caponizing effect of her nose, lip, and eye rings, I recalled Benjamin Franklin's wise observation that all cats feel the same in the dark.

"Could either of you tell me what the two hideous billboards down the highway refer to?"

"They're art," the man said from behind a frightening array of face décor. Conspicuous in their absence were the lip plates worn by the Kayapo. The green splotch on his bicep demonstrated how even the lowly art of tattooing has declined.

"Art." I reeled from the Tenth Sensation. "And you know this how?"

"What else could they be?" said the girl, exposing, of course, a metal bulb on her tongue that stirred an earnest query regarding another pleasant tactile experience. The tattoo on her lower back did not need to be seen. I intuited it.

"Am I to understand that in your estimation a sufficient condition for an object's categorization as art is that no competing justification for its existence is forthcoming? How lofty. Incomprehensibility is the essence of art. That would explain most of what we see, hear, and read these days."

"Maybe they mean something but no one knows what," the man offered half-heartedly.

"Then they *mean* nothing at all. Something only has meaning if there is someone there to understand it," I said, devising an expository thought-experiment with a glance at the pavilion. "Imagine a UFO flying over a city and dropping thousands of unintelligible pamphlets."

"Just because we can't understand something doesn't mean it's meaningless," the girl said.

Exasperated, I wondered if Socrates encountered discussants hermetic to reason. Plato probably "misplaced" the fruitless dialogues. No doubt the finest ones shine from the whitewash of an adoring pupil. If only Boswell had been his contemporary, or mine.

Like children stricken with gigantism, my thoughts grew too fast for words to fit them, but it was essential that the couple understand. "Consider a tangential topic: the incomprehensible ravings of Nostradamus and other cryptic prognosticators. When something is open to innumerable interpretations, none of which command precedence, we can safely deride it as meaningless by virtue of its arrant ambiguity."

"Wasn't he trying to disguise his message?" said the girl.

"When no one can agree on the interpretation of something it ceases to be a message!" I told the imbecilic couple.

"I guess," the man said, staring at me, his jaw agape. "Hey, you asked us if we knew. We don't. Why are you yellin' at us?"

"Clearly, the meaning of a message is determined by the intention of the sender, the means by which he sends it, and the recipient's ability to understand it. What would you say about me if I wanted to warn you not to eat a certain type of berry because it is poisonous, but to achieve this I sent a card that says, 'Slippery when wet' written backwards in Sanskrit with half the letters in invisible ink and the paper torn to pieces? And no, the subterfuge of *potential meaning* is not a solution."

"What the hell are you talking about?" said the girl, giggling, her eyes wide.

"Honey, don't," the man whispered. He led her to the pavilion while keeping his eyes fixed on me.

Was I out of line? I wondered. I knew what I meant. But what if no one else does?

Sandy headed for the car. "Nothing to fear," I said.

"That's not what I heard. The janitor said something's wrong with the road ahead. There's a special way we need to go."

"Very well. At least we settled this unpleasant account."

"But he didn't say what was wrong or where."

"How crystalline. Though unable to interpret the signs, he knows what they refer to. We shall leave the area before *we* succumb to this bucolic madness."

"There's a gas station next to here."

"Is that a test? Yes, I still recognize that the term *gas station* refers to that structure. My cognitive circuit breakers have yet to be thrown by the malady afflicting the locals."

"Please stop and ask."

"It would be so much easier, and in keeping with local customs, if we form our own crackpot theory and argue with anyone who disagrees."

"*Please.*"

***

A white tendril wound its way from black crust in a coffee pot, filling the station with an acrid gas. The younger attendant stood at the register and clicked a pen with the incessancy of a cricket. The elder sat at a table chest-deep in receipts, typing a calculator without watching his fingers. Above them a fluorescent light produced a disorienting strobe effect. Like a judgment of Solomon taken literally, the radio, tuned between stations, played snatches of different songs.

"Those two billboards down the road, what do they mean?" I asked with a nauseating congeniality that Sandy would have recognized as sardonic.

The younger stopped clicking his pen and turned to the elder who ceased his calculations and sat back in his chair. Their profiles could have been bookends.

"Those signs have been here longer than I have," said the elder.

"I will be sure to put that in my diary. What do they mean?"

The elder came to the counter and removed a pen from his shirt pocket and began a duet with the younger. The only differences between them were a few strands of hair and twenty pounds. Both sets of eyes looked out from the same cold gray room.

"A whole lot of work has been put into them, to maintain them," the elder said.

"Now, as a driver who has gazed upon them but not understood them, who longs to rectify this ignorance, what should I know now that I did not know before?"

Cicadas sang. Sulphuric gas seeped from the glass volcano. The Sons of the Pioneers morphed into Karen Carpenter and back. A malign presence filled the gray room, warming cold eyes with the flame of suspicion. "What makes you think you're supposed to know anything?" the elder said.

"Why put a billboard next to a road unless you want the drivers who pass it to learn something, to receive its message, to bathe in its --"

"Wait a second. You think the billboards were put next to the road?"

"I did not say that."

"The hell you didn't," the younger said.

"Which do you believe: Were the signs built next to the road or was the road built next to the signs? You believe one or the other. Now which one is it?" The elder cross-examined me while the younger reached under the counter.

"Sir, I simply had some questions. Now I have several more pertaining to eugenics, but I need no help with those. You have been most helpful."

"Around here we believe the road was built next to the signs. You got that?"

"What did they say?" said Sandy.

"As best I can tell, generations of bewildered troglodytes have been preserving the useless, annoying beacons because they deem them *authoritative*. What they fail to understand is how a vague message undermines the *authority* of the sender. We shall proceed as though they do not exist. For all practical purposes, to all enlightened drivers, such is the case."

***

Having quieted my restive passenger, I slouched until my eyes were well below the dash. An elementary extrapolation revealed the straight road would tolerate this indulgence. I put my hands by my sides and looked through the uppermost quarter of the windshield. Blobs like the foam on root beer stood between the drab sublunary region and the twinkling lights of the empyreal. While my peripheral vision acknowledged the beam of light leading the car and the mangy silhouettes rushing past, the sky absorbed my attention, admonishing me for neglecting a breathtaking panorama in favor of a hood ornament.

A discombobulating sensation overtook me, insisting to my cowed senses that *we* stood still while the plane connected to the dark shapes moved beneath us. This was not merely an amusing hitchhiker picked up by my lonely intellect. *I felt it.* The earth spun beneath the car, which was suspended by invisible wires. "So which one is truly moving?" I whispered, wondering if anyone else had experienced this curious spell, hereby baptized Petronius' Eleventh Sensation, which may have some interesting entailments.

Rotating green and purple lights in the sublunary zone exorcised the disorienting hex, forcing me to sit up and take the wheel. A billboard approached, more outrageous than either of its brothers. I looked upon the tight little ball Sandy had curled into, realized a similar opportunity would never arise, and prepared to savor the Twelfth Petronius Sensation: the experience of a pleasure that cannot be adequately described to another. I sucked my finger and gently placed it in her ear.

"What the fuck," she yelped, clutching her head and nearly falling off the seat. "What the fuck is wrong with --"

"Look. Another one."

As she wiped her ear out with her shirt, the hideous billboard absorbed the wrath that would, under normal circumstances, have been discharged upon me. "This one has to be important. Look at the flashing lights."

"Ostentation and vulgarity neither entail nor bespeak importance," I said, not bothering to glance at the display. "And what manner of beast sends an important message in such a fashion that no two people can agree on its interpretation. These crass exhibitions speak volumes about the ignominious nature of their sender, but have nothing to say to us."

"I hadn't thought of it that way," she said, as though my obviously correct stance were novel.

"If a man has an important message, a message crucial to the well-being of others, and he does not divulge it in a manner that all relevant parties may comprehend, his conduct is beneath all contempt."

She knelt on her seat to watch the meretricious billboard's departure. "Most people would keep trying to interpret it."

"Most people are fools," I told her, and turned my attention to the composition of a historical narrative regarding the arrival of Shi Tzu in the New World.

On the Felicitous Absence of Part XIV

As with most of the profane graffiti adorning the restroom wall of common sense, the allegation that the number thirteen is accursed is not simply erroneous, but prejudiced and dangerous insofar as distracts attention from *the* baneful number: fourteen. The following is a distillation of my critique of this noxious numeral.

Compare the relatively bland thirteenth century with the nightmarish fourteenth. Need I continue my analysis? What event in the thirteenth compares with the Black Death? What event in history? My purview does not, of course, include the decline and fall of the dinosaurs. (Although their demise, given the nature of integers, occurred fourteen years anterior to, and fourteen years posterior from, two other years.)

In August of 1814, a tornado interrupted Britain's heroic siege of Washington, making the wrong call for the wrong side like some referee from hell. (On the wrong side of History, am I? Thank the gods! I urge the incredulous

Reader to reconsider his opposition to George III. How was this decent man worse than the many murderous and tyrannical thugs elected by American mobs?)

The war that began in 1914 was mankind's worst cataclysm since the fall of Rome. The litmus test of a man's political spirit is the contempt in which he holds Woodrow Wilson, the twentieth century's patient zero of democracy, who outlined *Fourteen* Points as his grand solution to the Great Stalemate he needlessly and disastrously spoiled by dragging our nation into the war. This phantasmagoric vision filled every little thug on the playground of Europe with delusions of grandeur, inspiring them to become bullies in the glorious name of "self-determination." Verily, the sleep of monarchy breeds monsters.

In a fourteen-day span in October of 1962 the world tottered precipitously on the brink of nuclear destruction. Compare the sheer magnitude of this crisis with that of the Black Death. The number fourteen is involved in catastrophes or near-misses so vast in scope that humanity's very survival is contingent upon their resolution.

A historian may not, on pain of breaking his vow to Objectivity, silence the testimony of his senses. These earnest witnesses deserve their moment on the stand, where the court of Reason may rule on the merit of their statements. My fourteenth year, blackened by the infliction of algebra, condemned me to months of agony while refuting the infernal alchemy. In a different key, during the antecedent year I lost my innocence.

And the number thirteen? Wherefore its vilification? The twelfth disciple of a Roman mystery cult betrayed the founder: 12+1=13. This singularly overrated, interminably squawked-about hubbub destroyed the Great Empire and waged intellectual genocide against Reason for two millennia, but with its besmirchment of a blameless integer it has crossed a line.

Consistent with their rationality, the cult's practitioners arrived at the exact opposite of the correct conclusion regarding the luckiness of thirteen. To the extent that I am capable of unraveling their snarled and refractory beliefs, the betrayal led to a sacrifice that saved mankind from the primordial curse suffered by the first two humans when a talking snake beguiled them to eat a forbidden apple. According to this "logic," thirteen should be *the* lucky number.

Now, how can anyone who listens to talking snakes be held culpable for his actions? Is not a man who entertains their counsel a candidate for the insanity defense? And who would want to eat an apple? (Yes, dear Reader, I am familiar with the case of David Berkowitz but it does not apply here. He fabricated the story about receiving instructions from his neighbor's dog whereas Adam did no such thing.)

Hopefully I have dispersed the menacing clouds looming over this innocent integer. Why, I would rather stay on the thirteenth floor of 1313 Thirteenth Street listening to Mozart's Thirteenth Symphony than compose part XIV of my own annals. The Reader may breathe a sigh of relief as he turns to the Preparations for Part XV.

Preparations for Part XV

As he approaches the summit of my annals, the Reader is encouraged to reflect on the cautions observed by Sir Edmund Hilary before he conquered Mt. Everest. He did not knock on Tensing Norgay's door one morning and ask him if he had any plans. In the same manner, upon entering the Death Zone at 26,300 feet, he did not declare, "The rest is gravy. See you at the bottom."

As the Reader's faithful Sherpa I have never permitted my humility and deference to hinder stern cautions about the jagged terrain and deadly crevasses. Now, as he enters that perilous zone where the oxygen is thin, my words may sound grave and insistent, but it is only because I so desperately want him to reach the glorious summit.

***

The Reader closes my annals and paces his room, knocking over empty bottles, kicking cans of Spam and Sterno. "I doubt this is like climbin' a mountain," he says, ignoring the inspirational nature of my comparison. "I don't need to prepare for no ascent."

***

The Reader should not deceive himself. It is not mere skepticism that causes him to balk at preparations. A virtue when not exceeding incautious doses, skepticism is naught but a high standard for accepting beliefs. If left uncurbed, however, this virtue transmogrifies into leering, jaded mockery. Once upon a time, the good skeptic checked each belief's resume, partitioning them into those worthy of assent and those unworthy. Now a bitter cynic derides everything as fraudulent, expecting the worst and invariably finding it.

And if the Reader's condition persists? Surely he does not think it represents a quiescent demeanor? The perpetual suspicion of cynicism is but a way-station to paranoia. That enemy will fire no warning shots across the bow. Absent a reversal of this grim progression, the Reader will be chest-deep in recursive theories involving extraterrestrials, CIA agents, and international bankers. On this Möbius treadmill he may run for the rest of his days.

Perhaps it is too late. Does he think I am involved? When not studying my annals does he wrap it in foil, zip it in a leather satchel, lock it in an attaché case, and bury it in his backyard?

What elaborate rituals and redundant cautions does he undertake to shield the penetrating gaze emanating from my throne of darkness? And what other macabre secrets lie beneath the oft-disturbed surface of his backyard?

The Reader's delusional haste is a symptom of the thin air he climbs in, and I, his modest Sherpa, do not take offense. To recuperate and acclimatize for the summit, he is to draw a hot bubble bath in the evening. The soothingness of the opium he consumes must occur slightly after his immersion in the water but concurrent with the beginning of the fourth movement of Mahler's Ninth Symphony. This altered state is only a crude approximation of the curious one I experienced in Part XV (Petronius' Thirteenth Sensation), but approximations are superior to contradistinctions.

If the Reader, aflame with the cantankerousness of paranoia, wishes to dispute this point, he may, on the following evening, peruse any of the offal from the bestseller list in an icy bath concurrent with the cacophony of rap and after the ingestion of an emetic. This experiment will, in addition, cement a point I have labored all my life to prove. Even in the glum dusk of civilization there remains an Objective difference between abominable things and great things. Contra Buzzcut, contra Sandy, contra everyone, the difference is not a function of arrogance, but of Truth.

XV:
I Experience the Rapture of a Knife-Edge, Introduce Petronius Time Types I and II, and Demonstrate to Sandy the Consummate Importance of the Difference Between Denotation and Connotation

Along a road flanked by squat and gnarled trees the sun splashed my face with steady bursts of warmth. The incense of freshly cut grass emptied my head of everything but the endless orange prairie of my hood. I brushed my toe across the accelerator and melted the peripheral landscape like solids in a clear plastic blender. For the only time on our expedition -- indeed, one of the only suchlike intervals in my life -- my mind suspended its analysis, ruminations, remembrances, and even its production of erotica. How counterintuitive, especially upon reflection, that this constituted one of the most gratifying moments of the journey. How curious that a period devoid of rational delineation dyed my memory with such pleasing hues.

The present, formerly a watchtower from which I surveyed the grisly battlefield of the past while nebulous but threatening shapes amassed on the horizon of the future, became a meadow flanked by walls of gold, beyond which the terrain was of no concern, as though Reason had been cloistering me from my surroundings and informing me via outdated and arcane journals. Was I awakening from a nightmare of abstractions, like a man escaping a shadowy underworld? Unperturbed by the approaching Point of Percipience, unsure how to assess the revelations I had allegedly been subjected to, I drove. All crude fixations had been blown away like dust off a mirror. And how the mirror shone!

"Perhaps the knife edge of Now is what truly matters," my heart said. "Technically speaking, it is all there is. The rest is fantasy or hearsay. The present, this flickering candle carried down a dark switchback, casting its measly glow on no one knows what, away from one abyss and toward another, what makes it seem unreal like a night between two days, one illumed by the terrible clarity of hindsight, the other distorted by the hallucinatory glare of dreams and expectations?"

***

Late in the afternoon the unique clarity disappeared as mysteriously as it arose, though I must stress that the reunion with my friends, Reason and Reflection, was not in any way unpleasant. A dismal gray quilt smothered the earth. Even the wildest imagination would have been unable to find faces or shapes in the filthy clouds. I yearned for the euthanasia of night, the peace of oblivion.

At dusk we departed the interstate and mounted the final road, a series of declivitous hills. During a flash of time at the top of each, I expected us to drop off the edge and fall into nothing. The thought of my headlights idly illuminating empty space as we fell enchanted me. In the absence of a fixed point of reference, would we even be falling?

(In the anterior paragraph, "flash" designates an interval not objectively longer than the same period experienced by a third party engaged in something numbingly mundane but felt by me as lasting longer due to its extraordinary nature. Tentatively, this shall be designated as Petronius Time Type I. The taffy-like stretch that absolute time undergoes whilst a man is under the influence of tetrahydrocannabinol is Petronius Time Type II. To forfend a disruption of the balletic grace of my chronicle, Types III through XVI shall be elucidated in an excursus.)

My odometer vindicated my calculation that it would perform the big roll before our arrival. The numbers would soon read 00000. I shook Sandy's shoulder. "Look. It's going to flip. What should we listen to? Something reflective? Something triumphant? Something melancholy?"

"I can't believe you woke me up for this. Don't you sleep anymore?"

"It is not what they denote; it is what they connote."

She watched me, uncomprehending, scarcely sensate.

"They denote a distance traveled, the same distance traveled by millions of cars. What they connote is their special significance to me." It was essential that she understand the gravitas of what was about to occur. "When it was 85,000 we were in Grant Park with Buzzcut and Heather and he lost his keys and we had to find them before the sun set."

"Is this that memory thing? The one where you can remember all the cards in a shuffled deck?"

"That is Simonides' trick; anyone can do it. This is important. At 90,000 we were on our way back from the bed and breakfast in Door County where we played Scrabble with the couple from Toronto who insisted on using a dictionary but we still bested them. You cheated with *cryptonite* and they never caught it. Remember when we all tried to find a word that rhymes with *armpit*?"

"Please pull over. I'm going to drive. Just for a while."

"Do not be absurd. You have never driven my car."

"Okay, then we're going to park. You need a nap."

"Around 95,000 I heard the third movement of Beethoven's Fifteenth String Quartet for the first time and you said it was depressing and I demonstrated how the greatest music, of necessity, is sad music, except for the instances when it's not." My thoughts were not fitting the tiny words at all, squeezing out like toothpaste while I searched in vain for more commodious containers.

"At 98,000 we were parked on the hill across from the airport and that cop interrupted our consensual act with his flashlight. And the numbers go up and up and reach the pinnacle, the apex, the culmination, soaring all the way, to zero," I said, suddenly sad and frightened. "That is what everything returns to."

Sandy started to cry. She finally understood the difference between connotation and denotation.

XVI:
The Panting Wall of Gloom

Scabs of crabgrass covered the gray plane and clouds weighted down by their own filthy bulk descended. Sandy stared out her window while I contemplated the plausibility of various explanations. Darkness like a wave appeared on the horizon. My obstinate foot decelerated until only a heroic determination kept it from the brake.

"What the fuck is that thing?" said Sandy.

"Do you know any sea chanteys? An eye patch and parrot would compliment the salty dialect, as would the occasional tale of creatures from the deep."

"I'm serious. What is that?"

"It appears to be a wall." A silver line vertically divided it. The map gave no explicit instructions about what to do upon arriving. The road ended where the Point of Percipience began.

"Oh my God. Look at it."

"Please remember that the earth is round. This is not the edge. Sailors were the first to recognize this. A sea chantey please."

"Why is it moving?"

My glib façade would henceforth demand the versatility and dedication of a Shakespearean actor. Massive bubbles formed and receded on the surface. It appeared to be gasping for breath, suffocating in a netherworld plush with crabgrass. I stopped the car. "How interesting."

"What is this place?" Sandy said coldly.

"Mr. Horn declared it the eleventh wonder of the world. No doubt the interior is even more impressive."

"We're not driving through that thing."

I put my head out the window and looked up. Squalid clouds slid over the top, conveying the illusion of the bastion collapsing, drowning us in a sea of shadows. The road went through the silver passage but the other side appeared hazy. I prepared to drive through before it changed forms to block the entrance or digest us as we passed.

Sandy bludgeoned me with her eyes. She looked older, haggard and confused, quite possibly on the brim of savagery, preparing to pounce. Her look demanded an explanation while simultaneously insisting that none would suffice. Its only precedent involved a misunderstanding when she discovered panties beneath the seat that did not belong to her.

"Permit me to put this in perspective. You were awestruck by a giant eagle, but for this magnificent optical illusion you have naught but scorn and apprehension."

Feigning exasperation, I consulted with my voodoo doll. "What would Henry Higgins do?"

"Optical illusion?"

"Well of course. The refraction of the bubbles is predicated on ..." I awaited salvation from my steadfast muse. "... a convoluted prism. The *ignis fatuus* is the oldest trick in the book. Plotinus wrote about them in his *Seventh Ennead.* This one is unique only by virtue of its size."

"Whatever," she said with halfhearted ascent, grabbing the door and armrest.

As we passed through the narrow passage I noticed the odometer continued to read 00000. It must have been stuck.

How the Reader May Halt the Foredoomed Voyage of Time to Prolong His Enjoyment of My Annals

Curse this prescience. It is not a gift, but an affliction. I see the future so clearly and it breaks my heart. The Reader finishes my annals and wipes tears from his eyes. "My only complaint is that it had to end," he sobs. Clutching his chest he cries, "Verily, it melted the frozen lake within."

There, there, dear Reader, dear friend. Would that we could avert our heart-rending adieu. By means of Petronius' Box we can at least forestall this sorrow. Perchance the advertent Reader has observed how events fall into three broad categories: those that have happened, those that are happening, and those that have not but shall. (I am aware that subdivisions could be added. For our purpose we need only concern ourselves with the three listed.)

No doubt the Reader, perspicacious to a fault, has grown to loathe the cheap gimcrack of time travel resorted to by every hack not excreting thrillers. Nevertheless, does he not, midst his unrequited longings for permanence, secretly bemoan the reckless pace at which the palpable present dissolves irreversibly into the gloaming fairy tale of the past? His curiosity at the beck and call of his heart's deepest longings, no doubt he wonders what it would be like to experience life in the absence of Time, to step from the temerarious train and sit at the park bench of permanence. By means of Petronius' Box he shall.

In Part XVII is a box of Ps. Presently it represents the Reader's future. When he happens upon my Box it will represent his present. If he simply glanced at it and continued reading it would fade into the past.

Now, if he comes upon my Box and does not continue but stares fixedly, he *ipso facto* steps out of Time. He leaves the ill-destined ride and enters a state whispered of by mystics.

Be forewarned: my Box is not a toy, but an entrance to another dimension, a gift lovingly bequeathed to a friend, and, as will be demonstrated, far more formidable than Plato's much-ballyhooed Ring of Gyges.

"But why not place your miraculous Box here?" the Reader cries. "Petronius, I can't wait another moment for your Box."

Dear Reader, so that it can represent the future it must be at least a few pages away. As a fellow itinerant on the meandrous road of life, I empathize with this enthusiasm, but as a historian I have conditioned myself to enjoy the gratitude of posterity. Just as light from long dead stars continues to shine, the full radiance of my genius will not reach its audience in my lifetime. Consider all who shall delight in my annals a thousand years hence. How will I enjoy the generations of ovations if not via the anticipation of them? (Not incidentally, reveling in the adoration of posterity is the Seventeenth Petronius Sensation.) The Reader, to allay his yearning for my Box, should contemplate the sublime rewards of delayed gratification. Soon he will be liberated from that wicked taskmaster, that crazed and merciless tyrant, Time.

XVII:
The Introduction of My Nineteenth Sensation and Petronius' Box

"The philosopher-king changes a wheel," I said, throwing the jack beside the tire and bracing myself, not against the indignity, but the torrent of reflections on the ill-timed occurrence. Out of several million miles driven in my lifetime, this was, beyond certainty, the single most inauspicious moment for a flat. My concern: the inauspiciousness could embitter and enrage me, inducing a reckless maneuver that would exponentially increase the inauspiciousness (stripping the tire iron on one of the lug nuts, for example).

This precarious position I hereby baptize the Nineteenth Petronius Sensation. It refers to inauspicious situations where the threat of far greater inauspiciousness lurks like a sniper. Heretofore, the calamitous and expansive nature of inauspiciousness has been ignored or downplayed. My Nineteenth Sensation shall serve as a warning of this looming cliff. It is the slipperiest slope, the mortal enemy of auspiciousness. A man no sooner lowers his guard to curse it when it increases a thousand-fold.

"This place creeps me out," said Sandy, surveying the desolation behind the panting wall of gloom. Hideous trees with branches like broken fingers obscenely clasped in prayer lined the mazy road, begging for mercy and receiving none from the void above. The dusty plain, cured of its crabgrass rash, stretched out with no horizons as though the earth did not curve beneath this forbidding land. "Is there another optical illusion here?"

"It would seem so," I said, testing the tire iron for signs of weakness, the first in a series of prophylactic measures against the expansion of the Nineteenth Sensation. The landscape's varying shades of gray radiated a peculiar and irritating luminosity akin to tarnished chrome reflecting the sun. A cloudless day would have necessitated a welding mask.

"Petronius, this'll kill you. Check it out."

"It is the abject simplicity of changing a tire that renders it so mind-bogglingly complicated. Please, silence."

"We're no more than a few minutes' walk from where we drove in."

"The road was a trifle serpentine."

"A trifle? How many hours were we driving? What, are we going to stay on it forever?"

"Nothing lasts forever."

"I could call triple A, but I don't think they'd ever find this place."

"If you must emasculate me, please apply chloroform, ether, or preferably nitrous oxide. Although …" I paused, engrossed in a thought that I placed on probation until its true import could be discerned. I stood next to her, squinting from the glare. "Anyone could find this place. The roads are neither hidden nor dangerous. Yet we are either alone or two of very few who have discovered it."

"Who the hell would want to come here?" she said, rubbing her arms to scrape off the goose bumps. "I don't know if you've ever made this connection, but popular places are usually fun places. This place sucks. Why do I feel like I'm freezing? Why is everything shining when it's cloudy?"

"When you leave Cudahy you bid civilization adieu. You may wait in the car."

"Really?"

"Truly. But do not bounce around or leave once the operation is in progress."

She entered the backseat.

***

PPPPPPPPPPPPPPPPPPPP
PPPPPPPPPPPPPPPPPPPP
PPPPPPPPPPPPPPPPPPPP
PPPPPPPPPPPPPPPPPPPP
PPPPPPPPPPPPPPPPPPPP
PPPPPPPPPPPPPPPPPPPP

***

I positioned the jack before remembering that the lug nuts must be removed first, a harrowing escape from the tar pit of the Nineteenth Sensation. "Why is everything shining when it is cloudy?" I asked myself.

On the Superiority of Petronius' Box to Plato's Much-Ballyhooed Ring

Alas, the Reader has left the Nirvana of my Box to return to Heraclitus' stream. If only it were a stream. Nay, Time is a waterfall splashing down on jagged rocks. The destruction of all condemned to that plunge is sealed.

The Reader prepares to turn back the page, to return to the haven of my Box. "I shall hide from the cruel executioner. Time will not look for me there. Sanctuary, Petronius' Box, sanctuary."

But it is too late. My Box permitted him to step out of time, not travel backwards in it. Surely he is not confusing my annals with some odious sci-fi trilogy. Perhaps in the addendum, appurtenance, excursus, postscript, supplement, or adjunct to my annals I will include another. Hopefully, with the bittersweet taste of my Box fresh in his mouth, he will not take such precious asylum for granted again.

The Reader's desperation is understandable. The expanding universe of Time diminishes all men, shrinking them until they vanish. Given its infinitude and our insignificance, do we even exist now? Before and After, are they not the fanged jaws of an insatiable beast grinding us into nothing? Consider my cruel plight: though my nineteen sensations will one day be as familiar as anger, boredom, joy, and the rest, people will refer to them by number but with no reference to the tireless scholar who discovered and catalogued them. A vainglorious man would flail his fists at the heavens, galled by the generations who shall never pay their onerous debt of gratitude, but the philanthropist is paid in full by the satisfaction he takes from expanding mankind's modest conceptual frontiers.

Now, to the task at hand. Plato's brother, Glaucon, told a story about a ring that turned the wearer invisible. This was in pursuit of a question so obvious it scarcely merits stating: Do men behave themselves of their own accord or due to the observation of others? In the story, an invisible shepherd proceeds on an admirable course. Generations of philosophasters have held forth on the issues raised by this magic ring, all of them overlooking something fundamental, something conclusively resolved by my Box: a man capable of freezing Time could violate moral norms with immeasurably greater ease and comfort than an invisible man. In this respect, Plato's Ring is the Pinto to the Fleetwood of Petronius' Box.

The importance of my demonstration precludes a synopsis. Hopefully the lucidity and poise of my oration will cloak its volume. First, an invisible man, unlike a man operating outside of time, is not immune to the self-defense of his prey or even his own capture. If we raise the question of --

I bleed! A dagger in my back. Et tu "dear" Reader?

O Petronius, how could you tempt the Reader with your Box, a box more embryonic with calamities than Pandora's. He stated his obsession, pointing to the object of his frothing mania as early as Part I, yet you trusted him. Verily, the vice of faith will be your ruin.

And what hath he wrought? Rather than detached observation in a timeless dimension, instead of savoring the Eden of permanence, the Reader, to use his own schoolyard dialect, "used Petronius' Box to get his hands on Sandy's."

Frozen in time in the backseat she was as defenseless as a fawn. The subjugation of a non-consenting, *non-animated* partner is ineffable in its degeneracy. I hereby command the Reader to proceed forthwith to his liquor cabinet, pour a glass of whiskey, and throw it in his face. I challenge him to a duel.

The Prearranged Terms of Our Duel

In a manly society, the duel is the only certain means of keeping uncouth tongues and avaricious fingers in check. No gentleman refuses this call, only a poltroon. The non-negotiable conditions are as follows.

At dawn, the Reader will arrive at a pastoral valley with a velvet-lined mahogany box containing one .50 caliber pistol loaded with one bullet. A third and neutral party shall bring my annals in a rectangular sedan and place it on a post no more than one meter in height. The Reader is to take two-hundred and fourteen paces from the post, turn, and fire one shot.

If he misses, he is to put one bullet in the chamber, spin it, point the pistol at his foot, and fire. Should Fortune smile upon him, he may take one step, aim at my annals, and pull the trigger. If he misses or if there be no shot fired, he is to again turn the gun on his foot. In this fashion we shall find Justice. As a final gesture of magnanimity, he may postpone the duel until after he has read Part VXIII and my majestic epilogue.

Note well: if he misses my annals a fourteenth time he loses, thereby fully and unconditionally conceding his vileness and perversion. A duel is no game of rock-paper-scissors, but adjudication by the court of Fate. The man who walks away with a bullet hole can safely conclude that Her Honor has ruled against him. Perhaps the low watermark of our "culture" is the illegality of this appeal to otherworldly justice.

***

What's this? The Reader, with the devil-may-care swagger of a man with nothing to lose (apropos, I suppose), questions the propriety of an epilogue?

Yes, some modern writers blanch at the use of preambles and epilogues. "If the text were written properly, neither is necessary," they whine. "To tack something on as a hasty afterthought is naught but sloppiness, the dereliction of concision."

Slender diaries of romantic conquests are the only experience these scribblers have of historical compendiums. (And I categorize these as "conquests" rather than "inexplicable examples of charity" out of graciousness.) An epilogue is not an afterthought, but a somber and concise reflection, the distilled essence of all that has preceded. Am I to trust the Reader with composing one? Did Bruckner permit his cleaning lady to sprinkle notes on his symphonies?

When that final trumpet sounds, "So that my notable deeds shall not perish with Time, I, Petronius Jablonski, transcribed a crystalline testament of my fantastic odyssey. Bereft of pretense, biased only by the inflexible contours of reality, aflame with the desire to guide the Reader's discovery of the exalted truths within, I now entrust these secrets to him," the Reader, once he catches his breath, will not complain of "hasty afterthoughts" any more than the first audience of Beethoven's Ninth complained of needless chorale parts.

Note well: the quote in the anterior paragraph was neither an actual part of the epilogue nor a crude approximation. It was merely a template used for purposes of exemplification. My epilogue, unprecedented in form and content, forged in the crucible of genius, cannot be contained or shaped by any mold.

***

Epilogue to the paragraph prior to the anterior two: The great Anton Bruckner did permit sundry morons to make changes to his symphonies, but this only reinforces my original point. A genius must shun contamination from inferior minds.

Essential Preparations for the Epilogue

Diplomacy dictates brevity. Observe the following. After finishing the triumphant Part XVIII, cosset yourself with a good night's rest. With the golden beams of the morning sun filling the room and the final movement of Beethoven's Fifth Symphony resounding throughout the house, you, attired in a tuxedo, are to slowly read my epilogue. Rise to your feet concurrent with the first sentence of the final paragraph and --

What have we here? Who might you be? I see. Your churlish brother is off practicing his marksmanship (or, more likely, taking the midnight train out of town) and has left my annals untended. My Dear, these pensive reflections are not intended for the eyes of such a comely, sweet lass. But may I say that regardless of the unpleasantries between your dissolute brother and I -- which, I assure you, will be resolved shortly -- there exists no quarrel between us. On the contrary, there is no reason whatsoever that --

Calm yourself. Your eloquent defense of your brother leads me to wonder if all the while I have been attending to the wrong pupil. With a few terse sentences you have shown more insight, more roughhewn potential than he with his gales of blather and nitpicking.

No, I do not deny that he attended to my annals with due solemnity, but, between us, no man can rise above an impoverished aptitude. Flicka the horse would prove more malleable to the training of a scholar than your blockheaded brother.

I apologize. You provide a striking example of Eletius' observation, "No beauty was as beautiful as her anger." Of course you love him, but he heeded a call demanding powers far beyond his modest ken. My criticism is but thinly veiled sorrow. A teacher's loss of a student can only be compared to a parent's loss of a child. Who shall comfort me?

A Declaration of My Intentions Regarding the Reader's Sister

O divine scintillation from the Reader's sister. With a cheerful animation to that goddess' shrine I come. Let the man who has won a comely damsel join my jubilant song. Let us all, with tumblers raised, praise --

By the gods. I took no advantage of her dear Reader, dear *brother*. Seduction is scarcely a zero-sum game. To oil the hinges of the day she may have enjoyed a fermented beverage or five, but I fail to see how --

Legal drinking age? What manner of oxymoron is that? My memory is telescopic, microscopic, and photographic and I cannot recall an interval of my life deprived of the divine lubricant (as though I would bow to the arbitrary decree of this despotic state). The Reader, *mon plus cher frère*, is urged to study the final pages of Part IX on the supremacy of free will. Animal magnetism, in conjunction with several fermented elixirs, may discombobulate this faculty, but they do not obliterate it. The Reader should remind himself that his sister, though I can scarcely believe it, is mortal.

It is understandable why he, *mijn geliefde broer*, given his deep sororal love, exhibits an irrational concern. But the seraphic wings he sprouts to look down upon her consensual, *animated* liaison presuppose an asymmetric standard: the hallmark of injustice and a stumbling block to her future happiness.

***

To Eros and Aphrodite I bend my knee. Let my song rise above the twinkling dome. To deities kind, indifferent, and flagitious, I proclaim my --

Either my ears deceive me or the Reader, *il mio fratello caro*, needs to get out more. His demarcation of "natural" from "unnatural" is quaint, but every whit as wrongheaded as all the others performed by those cowering behind this fig leaf. Rather than engage in the fool's errand of separating the two, I shall posit a demarcation as tenable as the rest: an act is natural if it does not violate the laws of nature. As the Reader's sister and I violated no laws of Newtonian or Relativistic physics, nothing unnatural occurred. Granted, this nudges more than a few actions to one side, but it is a welcome breath of sanity compared to the flatulent ravings of Natural Law theorists.

The only odd occurrence, but scarcely unnatural, involved an almost lethal encounter with the Reader's cherished foil ball. The behemoth nearly crushed us. *Mein faszinierender Bruder*, your sister told me all about the curio. It seems we are birds of a feather. Like Nabokov with his butterflies, Utz with his pottery, and Karpov with his stamps, we seek order amidst chaos by means of our beloved collections. Why, without my library of Pre-Socratic philosophers, nineteenth century chess books, and my assemblage of antique firearms, I swear I would lose my mind.

Patronizing? By no means. A pleasing diversion is a pleasing diversion. To each his own, *meu irmao sensivel*, to each his own.

***

Through the prism of bliss I behold life anew. The invisible tendril connecting us all, spun from a loom we cannot see, now shines like gold. Tears of joy dissolve all questions, and my heart whispers things my mouth cannot speak. In my comely maiden's arms I found --

Absolutely! That *is* a paradigmatic example of the First Petronius Sensation. I have underestimated you. Come, let us drink to bygones, dear Reader, εο αγαπημένος αδελφός μου, and watch the stream of Heraclitus disappear beneath the bridge.

"Hurrah for Jablonski!" the Reader, *мой велемудрый брат*, shouts ecstatically.

Indeed.

Appendix by Brian Bartul, Including a Glossary of Terms

I don't know why Petronius called me Buzzcut. I only had one haircut like that and it was for wrestling in tenth grade. He wrote his favorite quote from Wittgenstein in my notebook. "My world is limited by my language." Petronius took this literally. He hoped that by labeling previously unnamed thoughts and sensations he'd not only expand the horizons of our language, but of reality.

I'll start with the ones he forgot to add (you must have noticed there aren't nineteen). I'm not sure why he did that. I think he left the best ones out.

***

THE SECOND PETRONIUS SENSATION: In his *Exposition of the Manifold Horrors of Monogamy Volume VII,* Petronius included a theorem that can be used to determine when a monogamous relationship reaches the point of diminishing returns based on the frequency of the Second Petronius Sensation: thoughts about someone else during intimate encounters. "All poor souls scourged by the dreadful tyrant of monogamy seek this sweet repose, but our shame prohibits us from coining a word for it, just like everyone gorges on Schadenfreude but we have to look to another language to find an expression."

Unfortunately, my notes for the Second Sensation were drafted during a three night stand at a Cudahy tavern with a Bobby Darin CD in the jukebox. They're badly stained by whiskey and scattered between and around the essays "On the Greatness of Mack the Knife," "A Treatise on the Ontological Significance of Mack the Knife," and "Towards an Exegesis of Mack the Knife." The bartender begged me to get Petronius to stop playing "that damn song." I explained that he would interpret that as a violation of his first amendment rights, which would invariably result in his threatening to use his second amendment ones. The problem with the formulation of the theorem came from dissent on what the tipping point should be. Petronius said 1% but there was widespread dissent.

***

THE FIFTH PETRONIUS SENSATION: The Fifth Petronius Sensation is how "a man feels worse upon hearing of the suffering of animals than upon hearing of the suffering of humans. Our irrational guilt from this widespread phenomenon prevents us from even acknowledging it with an actual name." Examples aren't hard to come by. When you're watching the morning news, chomping through breakfast while listening to stories about a multiple shooting here, a famine over there, a civil war here, "and then there is a story about some hideous cruelty inflicted upon a dog and a man drops his fork and grinds his teeth in rage, secretly demanding the most medieval punishments." Few will openly acknowledge this sensation. Even when grieving for the loss of a pet, some people feel ashamed. Petronius thought such guilt was silly and misplaced. "The worst dog is better than all but a few humans."

***

THE SIXTH PETRONIUS SENSATION: The Sixth Petronius Sensation is "a volatile admixture of nausea and ecstasy." It was discovered as a result of his repeated encounters with the Fairy Gobbler. As many times as he'd swear he'd "never, ever cover myself in filth from that ghastly creature again," I'd see his Catalina parked outside Dick & Debbie's. "She offends me at every conceivable level: aesthetic, intellectual, and moral, yet the repugnance and remorse are positively intoxicating. Indeed, beyond a certain point, shame and revulsion become a heady pleasure."

He regarded this sensation as extremely dangerous and characterized by an enormous potential for destruction. When he was really loaded he used to joke about "marrying the detestable succubus to see if a man could bear the Sixth Sensation in so concentrated a form. Verily, it would kill him as certain as drinking a gallon of white lightning. Icarus beware, the Sixth Sensation is a deadly star that will send you to a fiery grave."

***

THE EIGHTH PETRONIUS SENSATION: The Eighth Petronius Sensation is "an enchantment with something great, during which the wondrous source of enchantment becomes the sole ray of sunshine piercing the gloomy clouds of a man's day-to-day life. (As best I can tell this is characterized by a state of mind rather than the object of enchantment, which can be fleeting (some, like Mack the Knife, lasting only hours). It was pretty easy to determine if Petronius was in the throes of his Eighth Sensation. When we went out drinking it was all he talked about. One week it was the "greatness of the Bushido honor culture." He read some book about it. Attempts to change the subject were futile. All roads led to the Bushido. Lefty "Righty"

Schlebrenski finally asked him for a demonstration of the proper method of hari kari. One weekend it was the "genius of Sextus Empiricus" (the founding father of ancient skepticism). Petronius became enchanted by the idea that you could "attain inner harmony by emptying your head of all beliefs rather than stuffing if full of nonsensical ones as most people are wont to do." This culminated in a contest where we tried to see who could doubt the most beliefs. He won.

"The man blessed with my Eighth Sensation has found his Holy Grail. For days, weeks, or months it suffuses his life with meaning. It is the rain nourishing the roots of his being."

"How is it any different from an obsession or perseveration?" I asked.

"Because it is not a pathologic condition, but a wondrous gift. To revel in the greatness of a thing is one of life's greatest pleasures. And these wicked pygmies, these psychologists and psychiatrists want to cast a curse upon it with pejorative labels. I swear they will not rest until we are all toiling in cubicles, neither happy nor sad, and certainly never distracted by the genius of Bach or Mikhail Tal. We must all crawl to them, begging for closure or catharsis or whichever sham concept they have invented this week. What pitiable darkness covers this age: a man may not, on pain of institutionalization or chemical lobotomy, even speak of enchantment."

***

THE TENTH PETRONIUS SENSATION: The Tenth Petronius Sensation is "pining for a better time while simultaneously recognizing that it was not a better time. Realizing that the Garden of Eden was a brier patch but longing for it nonetheless is a certain indicant of a noble spirit." Here's a classic example: Petronius always talked about "the inimitable grandeur of Rome." He also acknowledged how the absence of flush toilets, anesthesia, sedans, and the music composed from 1600-1960 would have made it "grim indeed." But he didn't permit these minor considerations to "sully his sweet pining. To long for a golden age a man must overlook the trifling detail that it was, in many respects, an age of bronze."

He was quick to criticize others for falling short of his noble Tenth Sensation, Sandy in particular. "She and her peers foolishly pine for the abominable 1960s by ignoring the horrors of Viet Nam and the destruction of American society by radical nincompoops. They instead focus on the tie-dyed dust kicked up by a culture writhing in its death throes"

"But suppose someone acknowledged the tumultuous nature of the sixties and still pined for it. Wouldn't that be an example of the Tenth Sensation?" I asked.

"How is that even possible? If a wise man were to pine for any period in the ghastly twentieth century in America, he would, beyond certainty, long for a manly decade like the 1920s, the late 1940s, the 1950s, and of course the first decade."

"But in theory one could experience the Tenth Sensation while pining for the 1960s?"

"No! My Tenth Sensation is an elevated state of mind, the bittersweet yearning of a noble spirit. It is not the flustered delusion of an agitated ne'er-do-well."

***

THE FIFTEENTH PETRONIUS SENSATION: The Fifteenth Petronius Sensation is a contemplative state achieved by Solomon and Marcus Aurelius with wildly different results. "Few souls can withstand it, much less name it. When a man reflects upon an earlier era, realizes that nothing remains, and then extrapolates the vaporous trajectory of his life and all that surrounds him, he is experiencing the Fifteenth Sensation." Petronius maintained that this isn't necessarily an unpleasant mindset. "Solomon lamented the vanity of life while the great Marcus Aurelius comforted himself with my Fifteenth Sensation on the battlefield." One can't fully experience the Fifteenth Sensation "if deluded by ravings of afterworlds, reincarnation, or maudlin drivel about surviving through his children."

***

THE SIXTEENTH PETRONIUS SENSATION: The Sixteenth Petronius Sensation is convulsive hilarity while experiencing the Fifteenth Petronius Sensation. "Most often, a man turns to puerile diversions to hide from the Fifteenth Sensation. The Sixteenth Sensation is the heroic response of the great man who recognizes that the vaporous trajectory of all things is the funniest joke ever told."

I don't get this particular joke, probably because I'm barred from the Fifteenth Sensation by my belief in an afterworld. I asked Petronius why such a thing, if true, wouldn't be tragic or sad.

"First of all, some things are not intrinsically funny, but how a man responds to them tells us volumes about his character. Second, the humorous element is derived from encountering the exact opposite of what one would expect to find. Behold a species that will someday not exist, lost in a universe which itself is destined to perish, yet countless of its members fret obsessively about the appearance of their abs."

"And this is funny to you?"

"Funnier than the inscription on the prophylactic dispenser. But one must reflect upon it a long time before hilarity seizes him."

***

THE EIGHTEENTH PETRONIUS SENSATION: The Eighteenth Petronius Sensation is "the truly tragic sensation. Oedipus would take comfort upon hearing of it. Sophocles, Euripides, and Aeschylus would gouge their eyes out with their styli upon beholding it. Job would shake his fists at the heavens using multisyllabic obscenities. A woeful synergy of rage, confusion, and dread, its roots have never grown in the garden of our language. Until recently, no man has had the fortitude to name it."

I can only explain this one with examples. I don't think it's one of his best discoveries, but nothing pissed him off quite like it. Sandy's mom was always asking him to put stuff together for her. She ordered furniture online that required assembly. One item, a huge dresser, must have had over a hundred parts. It was delivered in three separate boxes filled with boards and dozens of bags containing hinges and fasteners. The instructions had sixty-four steps.

"After hours of agonizing toil in that cramped bedroom I was finally finished. Just as I was preparing to test the drawers, I discovered a bag of screws and fasteners beneath the bed. It must have slid under when I tore the boxes open. The instructions were so vague, so ineptly written. Holding that bag in my hand, looking at the irreversibly completed dresser -- several of the steps involved glue -- a paralyzing chill ran through me: the first of nine stages."

"So what?" I told him. "It was still in one solid piece. You built a better mousetrap. Sandy's mom will never know."

"I thought so too," he said, stirring the ice in his drink, not looking up. "That is when the second stage begins: bargaining."

"Bargaining?"

"I had not tested any of the drawers yet. While Sandy's mother brought me another beer and lavished praise on the beauty of my creation, I bargained with the forces controlling this torture chamber of a world. I promised them anything if all six drawers functioned."

"And?" the bartender asked, spellbound.

Petronius poked at the ice cubes, splashing his shirt with whiskey. "It seems the screws and fasteners performed a role vital to the function of the top two drawers."

The bartender and I burst into laughter.

"And this is the ninth stage. Galling mockery from a man's inferiors."

I can't remember what stages three through eight are. He didn't like elaborating on his Eighteenth Sensation. It was too painful. Another example happened when he installed a car stereo for Beth (Sandy's sister). He was normally pretty good with those but in this instance he probably had his mind on other things. When he finished he discovered, to his "terror and dismay, a long green wire that had not been utilized correctly and played an integral role in the transmission of the signal."

***

Petronius really hated movies. "To his eternal credit, the visionary Gustav Mahler refused to compose any music for the Vitascope. He correctly deemed it beneath his genius and foresaw how no good would ever come from it." Petronius especially hated how they force you to listen to awful music as part of the soundtrack. On the other hand he hated it when they used great music because the movie was never worthy. That's why he expected you to listen to a variety of pieces while reading his book. "If a lousy movie can force you to listen to bad music, a great book can expect you to listen to great music."

If I hadn't intervened, Annals would have been almost incomprehensible due to his insistence on using his new punctuation additions. Just as he maintained there aren't enough names for all the important sensations a man feels, he believed our "inadequate, half-baked punctuation system restricts our ability to express our thoughts." These are just a few examples, from his essay "A Critique of the Underachieving Father of the Semicolon, Aldus Manutius (1449-1515)."

< > Indicates that the next passage must be read while listening to the piece of music listed inside the < >. For instance, if the Reader comes upon <Bruckner 8.3> at the end of the page, he must put the third movement of Bruckner's Eighth Symphony on his stereo before beginning the next passage.

{ } Indicates that the Reader needs to consume whichever type of beverage is listed inside the { }. So if he sees {CB} at the beginning of a chapter, he must have a Caffeinated Beverage before proceeding. {MC} would indicate a glass of Michael Collins, and so on.

_|_ Indicates that the Reader is to read the next passage while standing.

_//_ Indicates that the Reader is to read the next passage while pacing.

_--_ Indicates that the Reader is to read the next passage while jogging.

… … Was inspired by the modest … but indicates that the Reader is to pause in silent contemplation of what he has read for the period of time listed. *(At the end of Part II he wrote …1 month…).*

It wasn't the elements I objected to, but his insistence on complex conjunctions of them: {2vodka Martini} <Mahler 4.3> _|_ began one passage.

"If an awful movie can expect a man to hurl two hours of his life into a sewer, a masterpiece of literature can humbly request him to sip a vitalizing elixir while listening to great music."

"I think sipping martinis and listening to Mahler while standing is a great idea," I told him. "But the chance you take is alienating the average reader."

"No doubt they told Copernicus that his revolution would alienate the average stargazer."

"But your revolution is far more radical. Wait for a second edition. If the reader is offered a tantalizing glimpse of what you had in mind, he'll beg for it."

"Perhaps you are right. That way I will have one foot in the old world. The first edition will serve as a requiem for the deceased system of punctuation; the second edition will baptize the new one."

***

The rest are the sensations, theories, and inventions included in Petronius' book.

***

PETRONIUS' BLENDER: Petronius' Blender was crucial to many of his positions. With it, "the profoundest ideas of man can be mixed and pureed to produce original and superior recipes." In some instances it reconciled contradictory positions: "It lets the Stoic go tomcatting and drive a Fleetwood, it lets the Buddhist collect firearms and drink Martinis, and it lets a man dream of a libertarian emperor."

***

QUIETUDE: Quietude is "a state of mind tranquil and serene, yet confident and affirmative of life despite its precarious nature." It comes from a variety of philosophic traditions "mixed and pureed" in Petronius' Blender.

***

THE FIRST PETRONIUS SENSATION: The First Petronius Sensation is when you're "overwhelmed by the inexpressibility of things." It's the sudden and alarming recognition that even if you exhaustively described everything you "saw, smelled, heard, and thought, something frustratingly integral would remain untouched." This doesn't have to be the experience of something incredible. It's characterized by a desire to share an experience *and* the painful awareness that you can't. Petronius recognized that "to some degree all experiences are like this -- one simply does not notice or care most of the time." It's the "rare, mystical, and irksome times when you notice *and* care that constitute the First Petronius Sensation."

***

PETRONIUS' SHOVEL: Petronius' Shovel "penetrates the illusory surface and digs straight to the root of Reality to reveal the primordial strangeness of all things." When confronted by painfully strange circumstances, ask yourself, "Is this situation stranger than the existence of life itself? Is it stranger than the fact that *anything* exists?" The answer, invariably, will be No. But if it isn't stranger than the two most obvious things there are, how can it be strange? "Rather than giving it a pejorative but meaningless label and running about in a tizzy, it is simply a matter of becoming inured to it."

***

PETRONIUS' GENERAL POTATION THEORY: Petronius' General Potation Theory maintains that after a nap in the afternoon following a night of drinking one will feel better than if he hadn't been drinking the previous night. "Imbibing polishes the marble halls of a man's mind but he must wait until it dries before he can see the shine."

***

PETRONIUS' SPECIAL POTATION THEORY: Petronius' Special Potation Theory is an observation of the unique ability of alcohol to "alter a philosopher's outlook from dyed-in-the-wool misanthropy to near misanthropy."

***

THE THIRD PETRONIUS SENSATION: The Third Petronius Sensation is how "once a man begins a grave undertaking some of the urgency dissipates. He can savor the rapture of completeness: nothing more is necessary, or even possible, for the acquisition of his goal."

***

PETRONIUS' CRYSTALLINE AND IRREFUTABLE REFORMULATION OF THE ANTHROPIC PRINCIPLE: Petronius' Crystalline and Irrefutable Reformulation of The Anthropic Principle will "fill even the most hardened Skeptics with awe at the ingenious and philanthropic nature of the gods." In lieu of marveling at how our universe was fine-tuned for the evolution of intelligent life, substitute 'sensate beings capable of enjoying fellatio and cunnilingus.' "Verily, it will inspire all willfully ignorant and congenitally obtuse atheists to run outside and carve a graven image. O miracle most divine, what were your odds?"

***

THE FOURTH PETRONIUS SENSATION: The Fourth Petronius Sensation is "a wearying synergy of woe and agitation begot of the recognition that there is much to be done and one is not doing it." (It's important to notice that the Third and Fourth have a yin-yang relationship.)

***

PETRONIUS' THEORY OF THE CONTRARIAN PATH TO TRUTH: Petronius' Theory of the Contrarian Path to Truth loomed large in his thinking. "Being a contrarian is, *a priori*, virtuous. Most mortals are mongoloids. Holding an opinion contrary to a majority view *ipso facto* places one closer to the bosom of Truth."

***

PETRONIUS' WHEELBARROW: Petronius' Wheelbarrow separates the literal meaning of a phrase from its actual meaning. "Like a wheelbarrow, an expression should not be mistaken for what it transports." For instance, "A bird in the hand is worth two in the bush" acts as a wheelbarrow to carry a message; it doesn't pertain to the current price of birds.

***

PETRONIUS' LATTICE: Petronius' Lattice is his discovery of the metaphysical structure of reality, which "can only be safely traversed via a network of tangents. The philosopher cannot, on pain of becoming hopelessly enmeshed in a dense web of ontological goo, plunge headfirst." He "must meticulously navigate the catwalks of reality spider-like, stepping from one tangent to the next." This is a new philosophic method "far superior to the much-ballyhooed Socratic method. The meandering nature of reality renders all straightforward approaches futile." (It's also controversial. Our psychology professor asked Petronius if it was necessary to devote eleven pages of a fifteen-page paper on behaviorism to a blistering critique of Stravinsky. "Necessary? said Petronius. "Is it necessary to travel through South Milwaukee when driving from Cudahy to Kenosha? It can scarcely be avoided.")

***

THE SEVENTH PETRONIUS SENSATION: The Seventh Petronius Sensation is "Schadenfreude *before the fact*, the pleasure derived from the *expectation* of another's failure or misfortune. Note: the occurrence of failure or misfortune must be probable. Mere fantasies of them are in a separate category." (Petronius was particularly proud of this discovery.)

***

PETRONIUS' CRITERIA FOR TRADITION SELECTION AND REJECTION: Petronius' Criteria for Tradition Selection and Rejection conclusively resolves a legion of social and political issues. "Since both Reason and emotion can lead a man astray, the steadfast rudder of *tradition* is not to be shunned thoughtlessly. Ideas tested and perfected in the great laboratory of Time deserve precedence." "The questions of consummate importance are how to select from competing traditions and when Reason should override tradition." (In the absence of Petronius'

Criteria, there's little more than brute force to go by. Arguably, this is his greatest contribution.)

***

THE UNNUMBERED PETRONIUS SENSATION: The Unnumbered Petronius Sensation is the bliss of "getting away with something. Often, it's only experienced in flashes, moments of overconfidence when you're not worried about being apprehended. Its intensity is usually but not necessarily proportionate to the severity of the offense."

***

PETRONIUS' GARAGE: Petronius' Garage is his answer to Plato's Cave and all systems of enlightenment or salvation where "the aspirant invariably wonders, "'Do I really have it?' -- a certain indicant he has been duped." "To leave the cobwebs and oil stains of Petronius' Garage and enter the paradise of a sunny park" one needs to listen to Beethoven's Sixth Symphony after ingesting LSD. "If what he experiences is not 'enlightenment' then that word has no meaning and should be encased in lead and dropped into the sea." (I'm not a huge classic music fan, but I think this is a serious contribution to systems of enlightenment. Even Sandy said it's awesome.)

***

PETRONIUS' SECOND THEOREM: Petronius' Second Theorem is S/3. It enables one to determine the compatibility of other Beethoven symphonies with LSD. (For the layman, it's Beethoven's symphonies divisible by three.)

***

THE NINTH PETRONIUS SENSATION: The Ninth Petronius Sensation is a terrifying affliction where the "thick callus of familiarity that carefully covers our surroundings" is peeled away, "revealing the most mundane things as bizarre and unrecognizable." "The words we have to name things, which normally shield us from their primordial strangeness, lose all of their power."

***

PETRONIUS' THIRD THEOREM: One wouldn't normally think to ask "What is the sun?" because of Petronius' Third Theorem: "The frequency of a man's observation of X is proportionate to his disinclination to ask, "What is X?" or $x > f(x)$. "Such questions, however, become the norm during the frightful Ninth Sensation -- and no answers are forthcoming."

***

THE TENTH PETRONIUS SENSATION: The Tenth Petronius Sensation is "spellbinding aphasia at the eye-crossing stupidity of what one has just heard." "In its throes, a victim goes through four distinct stages: denial, anger, despair, and then back to anger."

***

THE ELEVENTH PETRONIUS SENSATION: The Eleventh Petronius Sensation is best described with an example. While driving on a long straightaway, Petronius slouched in his seat and looked up at the clouds. "A discombobulating sensation overtook me, insisting to my cowed senses that *we* stood still while the plane connected to the dark silhouettes moved beneath us. This was not merely an amusing hitchhiker picked up by my lonely intellect. *I felt it.* The earth spun beneath my car, suspended by invisible wires." This may have "interesting entailments."

***

THE TWELFTH PETRONIUS SENSATION: The Twelfth Petronius Sensation is "the experience of a *pleasure* that cannot be adequately described to another." This is owing to its uncommon nature.

***

PETRONIUS' THEORY THAT FOURTEEN IS UNLUCKY, NOT THIRTEEN: Petronius' Theory That Fourteen is Unlucky, Not Thirteen is based on the complete lack of evidence indicting thirteen and the mountain of calamities involving fourteen: the Black Death in the fourteenth century, WWI in 1914, Woodrow Wilson's Fourteen Points, the Cuban Missile Crisis taking place over a fourteen day span.

***

THE THIRTEENTH PETRONIUS SENSATION: The Thirteenth Petronius Sensation is when "the siesta of Reason indulges a man with the rapture of Now." "The present, formerly a watchtower from which I surveyed the grisly battlefield of the past while nebulous but threatening shapes amassed on the horizon of the future, became a meadow flanked by walls of gold, beyond which the terrain was of no concern, as though Reason had been cloistering me from my surroundings and informing me via outdated and arcane journals."

***

PETRONIUS TIME TYPE I: Petronius Time Type I is "an interval not objectively longer than the same period experienced by a third party engaged in something numbingly mundane but felt by me as lasting longer due to its extraordinary nature." For instance, if Mr. Jones is sitting in an algebra class and Mr. Smith is skydiving, an increment of five minutes will seem longer to Mr. Smith. (I told Petronius it would probably seem longer to poor Mr. Jones. "Then he is experiencing the agonies of Petronius Time Type VI, which I'm still developing," he snapped.)

***

PETRONIUS TIME TYPE II: Petronius Time Type II is "the taffy-like stretch that time undergoes whilst a man is under the influence of tetrahydrocannabinol."

***

THE SEVENTEENTH PETRONIUS SENSATION: The Seventeenth Petronius Sensation is reveling in the adoration of posterity. "Consider all who shall delight in my annals a thousand years hence. How will I enjoy the generations of ovations if not via the anticipation of them?"

***

THE NINETEENTH PETRONIUS SENSATION: The Nineteenth Petronius Sensation "refers to inauspicious situations where the threat of far greater inauspiciousness lurks like a sniper." (I had a nasty experience of this. Of all the mornings to cut myself shaving, the morning before a job interview was the worst, the most inauspicious. While driving to my interview, I kept checking the mirror to see if the wad of tissue had stopped the bleeding, which resulted in a fender-bender and an exponential increase in the inauspiciousness. Just when I thought the inauspiciousness couldn't possibly increase, the cop who arrived on the scene noticed the empty beer can Petronius had left on the floor in my backseat.)

***

PETRONIUS' BOX: Petronius' Box is the Fleetwood to the Pinto of Plato's Ring of Gyges. It enables one to freeze time and "violate moral norms with immeasurably greater ease and comfort than an invisible man."

Made in the USA
San Bernardino, CA
26 June 2017